PIONEER LADY

PIONEER LADY

Lester Fulford Kramer

Library of Congress Control Number:		2006906238
ISBN 10:	Hardcover	1-4257-2432-9
	Softcover	1-4257-2431-0
ISBN 13:	Hardcover	978-1-4257-2432-0
	Softcover	978-1-4257-2431-3

This is a work of fiction. Names, characters, places and incidents either are the product of the author's imagination or are used fictitiously, and any resemblance to any actual persons, living or dead, events, or locales is entirely coincidental.

This book was printed in the United States of America.

To order additional copies of this book, contact:
Xlibris Corporation
1-888-795-4274
www.Xlibris.com
Orders@Xlibris.com
33880

Dedicated to the memory
of the author and our father,
Lester Fulford Kramer,
and to his devoted son,
Valen Kendall Kramer,
who made sure his manuscripts
were preserved

FOREWORD

Our dad and grandfather, Lester Fulford Kramer was born on May 2, 1895 in Twin Falls, Idaho as Lester Fulford. His father and brother were killed in a snow avalanche when he was a babe in arms. When Les was six, his mother remarried. Her new husband, Alvin Kramer, was the sheriff of San Juan County, Colorado at the turn of the Twentieth Century. Les, adopted and adored by his stepfather, lived with his family on the ground floor of the jail in the high mining town of Silverton, nestled among the Needle and Red mountains of Colorado. His bedroom faced Mount Kendall for which his son, Valen Kendall Kramer was named.

Les graduated high school in Silverton and later was chosen to escort fellow army recruits to Denver for service in World War I. After the war he returned to Silverton. But his beloved stepfather soon died at the early age of 54 years, crushing the plans they had to run the Congress Silver Mine together. Les struck out for the West and made his way to California and then up through the Pacific Northwest. He had hoped to go on to Alaska but he fell in love, married and settled down in Washington state.

PIONEER LADY, was written by Les while later living and raising our family in Enumclaw, Washington in the 1940's. He spent many hours at the typewriter using the "hunt and peck method." Times were hard and an attempt made by Les to get this story and two other novels published were not successful. Copies of the loose manuscript of Pioneer Lady have circulated through the family for years.

Writing this story was a work of passion and research as were his other stories and poems. Our dad, as his writing reveals, showed the yearning he had to explore and revel in the beauty of the great outdoors . . . to fly with the wild geese. Among his papers Les' family found a letter written two weeks before he died, inquiring one last time if a publisher might be interested in publishing one of his stories. He never lived to have the reply.

My brother, Valen Kramer, and I talked about getting his books published for years. Finally, in the summer of 2003 I began scanning our dad's manuscripts into the computer because I thought this way would be the quickest. But scanning the papers was impossible, as the optical recognition capability didn't recognize the old typewriter's fs, rs, ls and other letters correctly. I finally gave up and began typing his stories directly into the computer. It was a long, slow process. When our daughter, Linda Bailey, surprised me with a disk of the entire typed manuscript of Vallecito, the second of his books, I was elated and encouraged and told my brother, Valen, that we were finally going to get the books typed, proof-read and published! One and a half months later our brother died suddenly and the project was shelved with a heavy heart.

Now, in 2006, it's with a fulfillment of not only our father's dream but of his son, Valen's, as well, that we see these books published, not only for his children, grandchildren and great-grandchildren, but for anyone interested in the early days of the West and the great outdoors. The other books are Vallecito, (which means Little Valley), Son of "Tuscon" Moorfield and Honey Boy, his last. We also hope to publish a book of his poems and short stories in the future. These books were conceived and written in the late nineteen thirties and nineteen forties and we hope you, the readers, will enjoy them as much as his family.

Rita Kramer Yeasting,
the daughter of Lester Fulford Kramer

PIONEER LADY, by Les Kramer (1895-1973)

Seen through the eyes of older brother, Eddie, Stella Thorne is the reluctant pioneer lady. The story begins in 1845 when Stella is a lovely young woman of 16. She is the daughter of Culver Thorne, a prosperous farmer and landowner who gets the bug to move his family to the Oregon country. Doctor Marcus Whitman is the subject of an argument in Green's General Store, where Eddie & Stella go to pick up dishes for their mother's birthday present. Stella's ardent admirer, Joel Hallor, the perfect Southern gentleman, is talking against Dr. Whitman when Jeff Moorfield, a stranger in town, enters the store. An accident with the dishes puts the blame on Moorfield, and Hallor's interference gets Stella and Jeff's first meeting off on the wrong foot and makes Jeff a bitter enemy of Joel's.

Eddie and Stella finish school before they head West. As the family outfits their wagon in Independence, Missouri, the captain of their caravan becomes ill and dies and Jeff Moorfield, who is also heading West, is persuaded by Mr. Thorne to guide their caravan. Joel Hallor invites himself along and is a constant thorn in Jeff's side. Filled with humor, pathos, and danger, the long, hard journey westward on the Oregon Trail takes many twists and turns, while Joel and Jeff vie with one another for the affections of Stella Thorne.

THE OREGON TRAIL ROUTE

from Missouri to Oregon

The Oregon Trail wound 2,000 miles westward through the territories of the United States—crossing rivers, prairies, deserts and mountains from Independence, Missouri to the Pacific Northwest. It was the main route to the West in the 1880's. Thousands of pioneers have walked this trail, wearing out many pair of shoes and sometimes having to go barefoot. They braved hardships, hunger, disease and sometimes death to seek land and opportunity.

The discovery of gold in California in 1849 attracted many more pioneers who turned off at Fort Hall to follow the California Trail to seek their fortune.

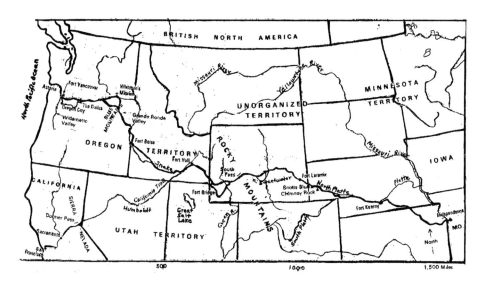

The journey to Oregon from Independence, Missouri took around four to six months driving covered wagons pulled by oxen. Men on horseback traveling without caravans could make it in a much shorter time. Now, 157 years from the time when gold was discovered at Sutter's Mill in California, the landscape has completely changed and a similar trip would take just two to three days by automobile and only a few hours flight by airplane.

Beginning Setting: Illinois farm country
September 2, 1845

CAST OF MAJOR CHARACTERS

THE THORNE FAMILY:

EDWARD THORNE—18 years old when story begins, called "Eddie," who tells the story of their journey on the Oregon Trail.

STELLA THORNE—Eddie's lovely 16 year old sister

CULVER THORNE—father and prosperous farmer who has caught the Oregon Fever

GRACE THORNE—the wife of Culver and beloved 37-year-old spunky mother of five

MARJORIE, AND MABEL—two younger Thorne daughters

SUSIE—the youngest of the Thorne daughters

OTHER MAJOR CHARACTERS AS THEY APPEAR:

JEFF MOORFIELD—the stranger in town who later acquiesces to guide the Thorne Family caravan

JOEL HALLOR—handsome Southern Gentleman from Virginia

BUSH GREEN—owner of the General Store in Illinois

DR. MARCUS WHITMAN—missionary to the Cayuse Indians

DR. PRESCOTT—the Illinois doctor

ABNER PIERCE—the man who bought the Thorne farm

MR. SCHOOLCRAFT—signed on with Thorne party in Independence

ELEANOR SCHOOLCRAFT—the pretty widow of Mr. Schoolcraft

CUTTER JONES—the profane and cruel captain of one of the other Caravans traveling the Oregon Trail

BEAUT SAVAGE—one of the men in Jones' caravan

BLESSING BREWSTER—the 15 year old boy In Jones' Caravan

JEB BROCKER—one of Cutter Jones' henchmen

JIM BRIDGER—a great American frontiersman who built Fort Bridger in SW Wyoming in 1843 as a way station for Oregon Trail immigrants

MR. & MRS. PETE WAMSUTTER, MR. & MRS. LARRY MARTIN, AND MR. & MRS. SINGLETERRY—some of the families in Moorfield's caravan

MOTHER NARCY—Mrs. Marcus Whitman

MARY ANN BRIDGER, the daughter of Jim & Mrs. Bridger and HELEN WEEK—both little girls lived at theWhitman Mission

PETER SKENE OGDEN—Hudson's Bay Company agent

BANDY HACKETT, GILLIS SHORES, HANK & BILL FREEDMAN—rowdy but good men and friends of Moorfield

MAJOR JOHN FREMONT—explorer, soldier & political leader; sometimes called "*The Pathfinder*." He explored much of the region between the Rocky Mountains and the Pacific Ocean.

JOHN SCANLON—U.S. Marshall

This story is a work of fiction. However, Dr. Marcus Whitman and Mrs. Whitman, Jim Bridger, Major John Fremont, Mary Ann Bridger and Helen Week are all people who lived during the time frame of this story. All other characters are fictional and any resemblance to people living or dead is purely coincidental.

CHAPTER 1

I was Culver Thorne's boy, Edward, eighteen years of age. My sister Stella, sixteen, eldest of four girls, had come with me to Bush Green's store to get a set of china for mother's thirty-seventh birthday. We landed in the middle of a hot argument about Dr. Marcus Whitman.

Dr. Whitman was a missionary to the Cayuse Indians in the far Oregon country. Took his wife and moved out there in 1837. In the winter of 1842-43 he made a trip back to civilization and set our part of the country on fire with first-hand accounts of the Far West. Father and I fell under the spell but the rest of the family were of a different opinion.

Joel Hallor, a handsome distant relative from Virginia, had the floor, but when he saw us he stopped and bowed and scraped for Stella's benefit, even though he had left our house only two hours ahead of us.

"Ah! Miss Stella! Ah trust yo' jou'ney in was without mishap."

Stella smiled and said, "Very pleasant, thank you, Joel." She turned to Bush Green. "Could I see the china, please? We've waited a long time and I want to fix it into a beautiful present for mother."

Bush led her over to an aisle between the counters and came back to his usual place near the money box. She began digging into the pieces, counting, admiring and making sure they were all there.

At that moment a stranger entered, but Bush, in an argumentative mood, didn't seem to care whether he sold anything or not. I could see he was hot under the collar.

"Marcus Whitman is a fanatical fool, a dremuh and a liah," Joel said, giving the disagreement a new kick and playing for Stella's approval. He never made a move that wasn't intended to impress one or more of the opposite sex. "You say he isn't, Ah say he is."

The stranger stiffened and looked hard at Joel. He had been riding hard from somewhere that afternoon of September 2, 1845. Dust covered his flat-brimmed hat and clung in layers to his clothes. A week-old beard was loaded with it. But shining through all the dust was a pair of dark blue eyes, unwavering and stern. On his hip he wore a gun in an old brown holster.

"You don't know what yuh're talkin' about," Bush snapped back. "Might be a dreamer but he ain't no fool or a liar. Fool's your opinion; why call him a liar?"

The stranger was walking in their direction.

"If that country was like he says, the English would have it sewed up tight. Ah know the English. Ah've been to London."

"Yeh?" Bush Green started to answer and then it happened. It looked to me like the stranger threw out a foot and tripped my sister when she was bringing the small box of china to a counter nearer the door, not bothering to call me.

Anyway, she fell and the stranger almost fell on top of her. Cups, Saucers, plates went in all directions. Most of them broke as they landed. It made me shudder. I knew how Stella had her heart set on that present for mother. She had talked of it for months. Bought with money she had saved.

"Shucks, ma'am, I'm right sorry," the stranger said sorrowfully as he helped her to her feet.

Stella shrugged his arm loose and looked him up and down. A reddish glow spread over her face, and increased the natural pinkness in her cheeks. Poor fellow. I felt sorry for him as she weighed his dustiness and plain clothes along with what he had done. "Your apology is ridiculous—" she began saying.

"Heah, Miss Tho'ne, let me settle with him," Joel said, hastening to her side. "Now, suh, what have you got to say fo' yo' self?"

The stranger's eyes teetered on Joel for a second, swung around to Stella and back to Joel. "Guess my business started with her. Where do you put in on it?" And his tone was decidedly different than the one he used when he helped Stella to her feet.

"Yo' business is with me," Joel shouted. "Ah champion huh cause. I'm to be a membuh of huh family."

"Aw, shut up, Joel," I said, "let it go. No use making a mountain out of a mole hill. We can get something else for a present."

"Shut up, yo'self," Joel roared. "Ah'll handle this."

The stranger's eyes flicked to me and back to Stella, searching her face. "The lady doesn't deny it, Windy. Calm down, I apologized. She wouldn't listen." He glanced at Bush Green. "How much for the mess?"

"'Bout forty dollars," Bush said. "Cain't git no more less'n six months."

The stranger pulled two gold pieces from his wallet and laid them on the counter. Carefully putting his wallet back in his pocket he picked a cracker from a barrel and began crushing it in his hands. "If that isn't enough, say so," he said.

"Plenty," Bush answered.

"What about Miss Tho'ne's humiliation?" Joel snarled. "You all act like it's something to be proud of."

He gave Joel a cold look. "You said Marcus Whitman was a fanatical fool and a liar." He kept on pulverizing the cracker into dust. "You know him? Guess you don't or you wouldn't run off at the mouth that way."

"Suh, Ah wa'n you—"

"I know Whitman," the stranger interrupted. He poured the powdered cracker into one hand and held it up as though weighing it. With a sudden puff he blew it full in Joel's face. "Be waiting out in front a while. Enough ruckus in here," he said and calmly walked toward the door. On the way, he gave Stella a danger-hunting glance and kicked an unbroken cup across the room where it broke into a hundred pieces.

Joel let out a bellow of rage, digging at his eyes. Stella rushed to him and began dabbing at them with her handkerchief.

"Are you hurt, Joel? Did it blind you? Can't you see?"

"He kin see all right, Stellie, when the cracker dust wets up," Bush said. "Old trick. Seen it comin'. Stranger's been around. Must know Whitman."

"I don't care who he knows or where he's been, it was a cowardly thing to do," she stormed. "If you saw it coming, and didn't warn Joel, I'll tell my father and he'll stop trading here."

"Suit yourself," Bush answered calmly. "Thinkin' of goin' to Oregon myself when I sell out."

"Ah'll kill 'im," Joel was groaning. "Ah hope he waits—Ah'll kill 'im fo' that."

"What with?" Bush asked sarcastically. "Didn't yuh see the gun on his hip? Tough bird tuh tangle with." Bush looked at me. "Maybe you'll help me pick up the pieces, Eddie? People'll be comin' in pretty soon."

"Hurry up, Joel, and go after him," I said. "Looked like you could whip him easy." I winked at Bush. "When you get close, grab his gun and then hit him."

Picking up the pieces while Bush went over to clean up the cup across the room I saw several large buckshot on the floor where the stranger had stepped out of Stella's way. The shot bin was right above the spot. I put them in my pocket and looked around to see if anyone had noticed. Stella was still helping Joel and Bush was busy. She would think that a man had deliberately tripped her with her arm full of dishes. Kind of tickled me. I sneaked over to the door and took a look. The stranger was nowhere in sight.

"You can come out now, Joel. He's gone," I called back.

"Know what was good fo' him," Joel snarled. "Wish he'd waited. If ah evuh meet him again ah'll fix him plenty—the low-down dog."

Stella and I rode home in the family carriage while Joel followed on horseback. He was peevish and mad at the world. Stella was still wrathy, too.

"Didn't know you were promised to Handsome Hallor, Sis. How come you didn't tell us?"

She gave her head a rebellious flirt. "I'm not. He had no right to say it, but I wish he'd given that coward a lesson in manners."

Being two years older I felt in a position to advise her. "He wasn't a coward, Sis. I'd never pick him for one."

"He tripped me, blew crackers dust in Joel's eyes and then ran away—what do you call that?"

"Maybe it was an accident, maybe he was in a hurry. Maybe running away was out of respect for you. Sorry about the dishes, but mother will understand."

"He tripped me and broke our dishes," she said and couldn't hold back the tears any longer. "That terrible Oregon country again!" she sobbed. "Why does it have to keep jumping up? Bush Green's thinking of going, he said. Wish Dr. Whitman had stayed home. I almost hate him and all his friends."

"Maybe so, Stell, but Joel committed a bigger crime than the stranger. He didn't have any business talking like that in public."

"He did too. If he feels that way about Whitman he can say it if he wants to."

"No argument, Sis," I said, clucking to the horses, thinking what he had said would be his future relation to our family. Usually we had a fight on fewer grounds, but suddenly I felt sad and mournful. Always felt that way at the idea of some mere man marrying my lovely, spirited sister. Didn't seem right and never would. Thoughts of Hallor being the one made me sick. When we drove home and told the family what had happened, the other sisters put up a howl while mother comforted Stella.

"Of course I'm sorry, dear, but your intentions were the best present I could have. Rude of him to do it and I'm glad it didn't lead to trouble for Joel—not any more than what happened."

Father patted Stella on the shoulder. "Buck up, honey. You'll get over it. Too bad. Order some more." He turned to Hallor. "Didn't know you felt that way about Whitman, Joel. Always thought he was a fine man."

Joel squirmed and was about to answer but father motioned for me to meet him at the barn. There he had me tell it all over again and laughed heartily.

"Hurt Joel worse than if he'd knocked him down. Had it coming. Wish I'd seen it."

"You didn't hear it all," I said. "When the stranger asked Hallor where he put in on the deal, Hallor said he was going to be a member of the family someday."

Father jerked his head around and looked at me. "He meant—Stella? Don't suppose it's gone that far, do you? What did she say?"

"Denied it on the way home. Said he didn't have a right to say it. She could have said more but she didn't."

"Lord help us! He'd drive me crazy in six months. Wait until he mentions the subject to me—I'll tell him. What did the stranger look like?"

"Tired, weary, and dusty clothes. Got me beat about four years, maybe more. Hair was kind of long and hadn't shaved for a week or two. Eyes pretty hard and blue when he looked at Joel. Tall like Joel but Joel stands about two hundred. Stranger looked twenty pounds lighter. Joel was making a play for Stella's benefit, but maybe he didn't do any good for himself. Stella's no fool.

"Maybe not," father groaned. "Can't always tell. Keep quiet about it. She's stubborn. If we tried to change her mind it might go the other way. You say the fellow hauled off and kicked the last cup across the room? Got spunk. Don't like the idea of him trippin' her, though."

"It was an accident, Father. He slipped on these." I took the buckshot from my pocket. "Found 'em when I was picking up the pieces. Spilled out of the shot bin."

"Good!" father said. "Feel better about it. What did Stella say?"

"Didn't tell her yet. Wanted to see what you thought."

He pondered a while. "She's so danged pretty it might not hurt her to think that a horse tramp deliberately tripped her. Let's keep it to ourselves. She'll never marry Hallor if I can help it."

"Amen," I added.

Father was owner of Thorne's Meadows, six hundred acres of rich rolling land in Illinois, fully equipped with horses and cattle and everything needed on a prosperous farm.

Those horses and oxen. I knew them all by name. So did Stella. Marjorie, Mabel and Susie. Each of us had ponies and tore around like wild Indians when there was a vacation and breathing time from the insufferable studies our parents insisted on.

Father was related to the Thornes of Virginia. He came to Illinois with money and made more money after he got there, but never seemed at ease or at home.

People said Stella was stuck up, and I'll admit she had some pretty lofty ideas when we argued about pioneering. For her, west of the Mississippi did not exist.

We listened politely the night Dr. Whitman came. Everything was great in the picture he painted. The plains to cross, the mountain ranges. The forests in Oregon, the rivers, unlimited acres, unlimited game, and fish bigger than a young boy's dream.

Huddled by the fireplace, listening to them talk and watching the coals flare up as a chunk rolled and settled to start burning again, watching the smoke drift up the chimney. While my sisters popped corn and roasted chestnuts for all present, I didn't blame him—I was with him in spirit right from the start. Then when Dr. Whitman opened up on the theme that the Oregon Country must have settlers of all kinds to win it for the United States, father grew very quiet and thoughtful—the same as when he saw a horse that he wanted and didn't need, and wondered how he could buy it without mother taking him to task.

I glanced at mother. She was thoughtfully studying the effect on father. She might have been wishing that Doctor Whitman would suddenly become deaf and dumb.

"Hardships?" Doctor Whitman asked as his keen eyes held father's. "Yes, there are hardships to be endured, worse on some than others, depending on guiding and good preparation. But when wasn't a country like that worth a few hardships? It naturally belongs to the United States. We need the Columbia River for navigation and power. Same day there will be a vast civilization built up around it. Irrigation projects supplying thousands of acres that beg for a drop of water to make them come to life. In future years some one will find a way to lift water from the deep gorges and valleys of the Columbia and put it to work in a thousand ways. And the mighty forests near the coast. You have to see to believe. Mile after mile of trees between two hundred and three hundred feet high. Some twenty-five to thirty feet and more in circumference."

CHAPTER 2

We children went East to school for another year and Joel made sure to visit us during vacation time. More of an eyesore than ever to father and me. But he seemed to please mother and Stella.

During this time father made money but pined and moped for Oregon. Said very little about it. Mother cooked and did her best to make the home more enjoyable, with a look in her eyes that made me think she was focused on a threatening avalanche.

One night father came home rip-roaring drunk.

"Come on in, Jeff!" he yelled from the front doorstep. Friend of mine's allish welcome. The damned females can't run me f'rever."

Jeff said something in a low voice that we couldn't understand. By that time I was out of bed and urging father to calm down. But Joel, still visiting, ran out to see who the other man was. There was a scuffle and we heard a horse clattering away in the dark.

Joel came in dusting his hands. Ah made him hit for town," he said boastfully.

Father, resisting mother's pleading to stay put and be good, staggered out and heard Joel say it. "Las' frien' uh mine yuh'll chase off! Wait'll I git my rifle!" he said and headed for the gun rack.

Joel looked about him in sudden fear and indecision.

Stella came to him and said, "You did right, Joel. Father coming home that way was bad enough without bringing some drunken crony along."

"Thank you, Miss Stella. Ah thought it was mah duty."

When I came back from helping mother pacify father, I said, "Don't know what your idea was, Joel. Father will hold it against you to his dying day."

It was yo' mother and sistuhs Ah was thinking of."

"We'll do the thinking and deciding," I said. You stuck your nose in where it didn't belong."

"Yo' sistuh praised me fo' it," he said with an air of being hurt.

"Yes, but she isn't Father. Drunk or sober that might have been some one he wanted to stay here. Makes a difference."

"If you'll excuse me, suh, Ah think Ah'll go back to bed." I was feeding the stock next morning when father came out. He was blear-eyed and reeked with stale odors of whiskey. The first affair like that he had indulged in since I was a little boy.

"I'll feed the cattle," he said brusquely.

"Ride over to Bush Green's. If Jeff Moorfield's still around tell him I want to go East with him. Better eat breakfast first. Your mother's in the kitchen."

"Didn't know you planned on going East, "I said. "When . . ."

Don't stand there with your mouth open!" he ordered impatiently. Get a move on!"

I hurried to mother and said. "Got to have breakfast in jig time. Have to go see Bush Green."

"What for?"

"Message to a man named Jeff Moorfield. Father wants to make a trip East with him."

She dished up some mush, laid a slice of ham on to fry and broke a couple of eggs. "Who's Jeff Moorfield?" she asked as she spread several hotcakes on the griddle. "Your father muttered a lot about him and Oregon after he got to sleep."

"I'll ask Bush. Must be the Jeff who came home with him."

"Let me know what you find out," she said grimly, reminding me of a man looking to the priming of his gun before going into battle.

In fifteen minutes I was galloping the ten miles to Bush's place.

"Moorfield left last night after he took your father home," Bush said. "What damn fool jumped him when he was doin' the best he could? Was it you?"

"That muttonhead of a Hallor," I answered. "Told him what I thought about it. Who's this Moorfield fellow?"

Bush eyed me for what seemed half a minute. "Gittin' into politics, son. Better ask your dad. Your mother'll be my enemy for life. Don't want tuh make your dad one, too. He'll tell yuh what he wants yuh tuh know."

"Well, where's he going in such an all-fired hurry? Why should dad be wanting to go with him?" I persisted.

"Same answer on your dad. Moorfield's takin' a letter to Senator Benton from Marcus Whitman about the Oregon country."

"Thanks," I said peevishly. "Some light on it anyway."

"Look worse before it looks better, mebbe," Bush said. "If I wanted tuh go out there as bad as your dad does, all hell itself wouldn't stop me."

"You don't know my mother then, or my sister Stella. Father thinks a lot of his family."

"Was raised with Culver Thorne. Know him. Maybe you don't."

"Is it that bad, Bush?"

"Looks tough for peace and comfort, Eddie. Better keep your mouth shut an' let nature take its course. Don't get whip-sawed between your parents when trouble starts."

"That's a tough job in my family," I groaned. "Guess I better be heading back. Thanks, Bush."

"Don't thank me," he said gloomily. "Just an innocent bird off to one side. They met here but it wasn't any of my plannin'."

I took my time riding home. I wanted to think. Bush's refusal to tell anything about Moorfield bothered me. But it did no good. Couldn't recall anyone by that name. On arrival I found father out in the barn looking things over.

"Tell your mother all you found out if she wants to know," he said when I told him' that Moorfield had gone hours before I got there. "How long's Hallor planning to stay this time?"

"Don't know. Haven't bothered to ask."

"Don't want him to marry Stella. She could do a lot better. Mean as to a man, not money. Your mother is dying of curiosity." Better go and get something to eat."

Gloom settled on all of us after I talked with mother. A nervous feeling like when a storm is brewing. Father was short-tempered and plainly building up to something. It happened two weeks later, an hour after supper. He called us all into the large living room. "Going to Oregon next spring. Want to go with me?" he said, with the same flat black look he had worn for days.

"Culver!" mother gasped. "You never said a word about this to me in private. What on earth has come over you?"

"You know as well as I do, Grace. No use in a senseless argument. You ran away from the subject ever since Whitman was here. Who's the head of this family, anyway?"

"You are, but I think the rest of' us should have some consideration," mother replied with spirit. "You don't mean you would sell out and move to that terrible country?"

"Lock, stock and barrel. Things've been going from bad to worse here. His glance rested on Joel for an instant. We've been making money," mother disputed.

"Money isn't everything. Wasn't your objection right after Whitman's visit. Disputed territory then, think you said. Part of United States now. England signed it away early this year. Didn't hear anything from you after you read about it in the paper."

Silence. A cold, deadly one.

"What about the children's education?" mother finally asked.

"We'll organize schools out there. If Eddie doesn't know enough about civil engineering now, he never will. Doesn't take a lifetime to learn it. Knows enough for a new country." Again his glance toward Hallor. "Stella hasn't learned much in the last two years that I can see." Stella flushed a blood-red and looked puzzled over father's exact meaning.

Father rose. "That's all. Quite a spell to get ready in. Make the best of it." He started to leave the room and then turned to Hallor. "Almost forgot to mention your part of it, Joel. If you want to go along, it'll be to drive one of our wagons. Made a remark once that you expected to be a member of this family. Don't forget this, if you fool around and marry Stella without my permission, I'll fill you full of lead!"

"Ah guess Ah got my oduhs," Hallor said with a small laugh. "He didn't say no, and he didn't say yes."

None of us said a word. Suddenly mother yielded to scalding tears. Stella rushed over to comfort with tears rolling down her own cheeks. Marjorie and Mabel followed suit but Susie, the youngest, sat as though lost in thought. Finally she exclaimed, "That's it! Father was like a king in a storybook! I think I like him that way, too."

There were only two people in our family with courage to stand up and talk to father in this hard, brittle mood: Stella and Susie. But Susie was too busy with her school work and planning on how she could fit herself to a caravan and at the same time leave everything behind that she felt necessary to life. Not by the slightest word or action did she object to father's ultimatum.

The week following his declaration was filled with whispered conferences. When the three youngest girls were in school, mother and Stella carried on by themselves. I wasn't included, but Hallor was always roosting around, aiding and abetting whenever he could do so without appearing too disloyal. At the end of the week I was given an opportunity to take sides.

"Eddie," Stella said, "You've been laying low like a scared grouse. What do you think of it?"

"Oregon doesn't sound bad to me. Haven't any choice. Might as well make the best of it."

"Well, mother and I have a choice and we intend to be heard," Stella said heatedly. "Will you find father and ask him to come and hear us?"

"Not me," I replied. "I was raised by Culver Thorne. Know him. Maybe you don't." Bush's words came in handy.

"You're afraid," she said bitingly. "No help to us. You never were."

"Maybe so. Might be fear when a fellow doesn't care to be whip-sawed between the two best parents he ever had."

Mother wasn't saying a word, nervously picking at a frayed hem.

"Do you mean to say you aren't going to object as a matter of principle? When our beautiful home, education and everything hangs on father's notion that he would like Oregon better than here? Joel says—" Stella caught herself and stopped.

"'What'd he say?" I snapped. "Better keep his big mouth out of this. Tell me! What'd he say?"

"I won't tell you now," Stella flared. "You might make trouble. He's going home soon, anyway. The quicker the better," I growled. "Got trouble enough without him around, helping you two fight father."

"Don't be so rude, Eddie!" mother complained. "Sorry we called you. We'll find a way to put our side before him. Don't have a fight with Joel before he leaves!"

"I'll try not to, Mother," I said, and left them.

That afternoon father and I were looking over the horses when I saw Stella coming. The sun glistened on her hair, parted in the center, drawn back and braided, with the braid folded back to her head in an artful manner, leaving a short doubled coil on her neck. What she couldn't do with that gift of wavy brown hair wasn't worth mentioning. Everything else that she did reflected the same care. Her manner of walking, her posture while standing, and her cool, musical voice won people to her favor. Her complexion was ivory-like about her eyes, with a delicate peach hue in her cheeks. Slightly irregular teeth, that fitted her mouth to perfection, gave you the impression that here was the standard by which teeth should be judged.

Her clear, fearless blue eyes balanced her red lips and small stubborn chin. She was five feet, five inches tall, slender and wasp-waisted. The day was warm, and she wore a freshly ironed muslin dress which she held at the proper height as she picked her way over clods and rough ground.

Stopping about twenty steps distant she waved a small white handkerchief. There was the usual look of admiration in her father's eyes.

"What's up?" he growled. "Why the white flag?"

"A truce, kind sir. I want to talk."

"Advance and start."

I made as though to walk away, but he said, "Don't be in a hurry."

"Mother and I would like to have reasons for moving to Oregon; we wish you would tell us one or two good ones," she said. "Two thousand miles to a savage wilderness worries us."

"That isn't all that worries you. Gave you a good one the other night. Few more won't hurt. You and Eddie have been spending too much money in eastern schools and not getting full value. Both a jolt."

"Surely those aren't the only reasons, Father. They're mighty flimsy. A person would be insane to treat his family like that for those reasons."

I would have sworn that most of her words were first said by by Hallor.

"No? Here are some more. We're needed out there. Big tracts of land. Coming country. Our land here is getting worn out. Slow times ahead. Values dropping. War coming over the slave question."

"Oh," Stella said thoughtfully. "Seems to me this fine home and risks of crossing the plains would offset all that. Mother's health, too. Perhaps mine."

"Your mother's one of the healthiest people I know. So are you. Just grown soft with too much coddling." He seemed to growl that out with particular relish.

"I think that's open to argument, Father, but who is this Moorfield man who brought you home the other night? You seemed to change right after that?"

Father glared at her, like one time years before when I talked back to him and he booted me about ten feet. Stella met his gaze without flinching. She was angry and disappointed.

"Young fellow, twenty-three or four. His parents died on the plains. Fur traders took him to Oregon. He was with Lieutenant Fremont two or three years. On the way East to see Senator Benton. Conversation's about wound up, far as I'm concerned."

Never thought father could be so hard with his favorite daughter. She had displeased him some way. The same idea must have struck her.

"Just one thing more, Father. If I promise never to marry Joel, would it make a difference?" she asked.

"Not a bit. Took care of that the other night." He turned to me. "Eddie, walk back to the house with Stella and bring the Stock Book. That bay horse is still a puzzle."

Which was a curt dismissal. Father never forgot anything about his horses.

After we were a safe distance from him Stella said, "Do you suppose this Jeff Moorfield and the man who blew cracker dust in Joel's eyes could be the same?"

"No chance for this family to be blessed from the same source twice," I said.

Quick as a flash she slapped me hard on the cheek and then ran most of the way to the house. When I got there, she and mother were crying their hearts out. I found the book and hurried back to father.

"You against me, too?" he asked when I came up. "Haven't said much."

"So far as possible, I'm backing you, sir."

"The hell you are!" he exclaimed. His eyes were red as if dust had blown in them. "How about Susie?"

"Same way, I think. Heard her tying into mother and Stella the other day. Said 'Mother, you always taught me to obey Father. You two make me tired with your sniveling.'"

Father slapped his knee. "Well, I'll be damned. Two of you, and I never knew it. That makes me feel like a man again. Want you to help me with the sale next month, son. We'll keep the ten best horses, four cows that will be fresh, and thirty head of oxen. Figuring on three wagons. Moorfield might happen along, and maybe I can talk him into driving one and acting as guide. Next Spring's the time to go. Indians tamed down with smallpox and cholera. Plenty of buffalo.

The plains indians will be tougher later, according to Moorfield. Sure like him. Hope he comes our way."

"How about Crusader?" I asked, with a sudden pang of fear clutching at my heart. He was our prize stallion, pure white, bought as a colt for a thousand dollars, and raised practically by hand. Little over five years old. Great-hearted with withers of velvet. Stamina, speed and endurance never yet tested. Arrogant as a saucy kitten and just as gentle and lovable for those who knew him. Darley Arabian strain, direct descendant of the great Messenger, imported about 1788.

"Couldn't leave him," father said without a moment's hesitation. "Rather shoot 'im than let Hallor's folks have him, like I promised if we ever wanted to sell."

"Glad of that," I said, much relieved.

One day, about a month after Hallor had gone home, Stella received a letter from his parents, asking her to spend the next two years with them while we were getting started in Oregon. Also to remind father about Crusader. She read it aloud at suppertime.

Without a moment's hesitation father said, "Go if you want to. Better leave right away. Crusader stays with us."

"Oh, Father!" she exclaimed joyously. "That's too good to be true." She ran over and gave him a big hug and a kiss.

He smiled, the first time since he froze up, patted her on the back and said, "Always try to be reasonable with my family."

In two days I was driving her to Kaskaskia, leaving behind a sad and mournful family. They had parted as though it were the last time on this earth. When we were within a mile of town, she stopped me.

"Eddie, I can't go any farther. Take me back home. It's Oregon for me, too, I guess."

I hugged and kissed her and never was so happy in my life.

Father was near the gate when we drove up. He opened it for us, saying, "Forget something?"

Stella jumped out of the rig and threw her arms around him with a little wail, "I changed my mind, Father."

"That's fine, honey," he said, patting and hugging her like she had been gone a year, as several big tears ran down his weather-beaten cheeks. He climbed in with us and we drove to the house.

The meeting at the house turned into a festival. That night our parents occupied the same room; the first time since father had come home drunk and sounded his cry of "Oregon."

Unwillingly or not, the family fell to with a vim and began shaping things up to leave, debating on what could or could not be taken. Mother had her bad moments but held up well. Time slipped by and father gave notice that the place was for sale the first of March.

The kind of money it took to buy our place was scarce. After much dickering around we sacrificed it to a man named Abner Pierce for eight thousand dollars down and a thousand dollars a year for five years. He was a pretty fair-looking man, but we hadn't seen his family.

At the last moment, before the papers were signed, mother insisted that, in consideration of the mortgage we had to take, the place could not be sold until the mortgage was paid in full. And also that we could come back any time before the first of June to reclaim the place by returning Pierce's money without interest.

I went to bed thrilled with the thought of going to Oregon. It was a long time before I went to sleep, only to be wakened by Stella yelling in my ear.

"Eddie, wake up! Eddie! Eddie! Mother's dying. Father says get Doctor Prescott quick, while we work on her. She's unconscious."

After a mad ride in the cold, barely dressed, I had the doctor there in two hours. Mother had revived and was sitting up in bed.

"Well. What's this, Mrs. Thorne? He felt her pulse. "Liver and worry. Pulse strong. Must be nerves. Had an appetite lately?"

"Very little, Doctor. Haven't felt well for several weeks."

He poured some pills into a cup. "Take these, one every four hours. We'll see how things are in the morning. Get some sleep now and stop worrying. Good night."

Father followed him outside and I followed father.

"Guess this cooks the Oregon trip, doesn't it, Alvin?"

"Culver, you ask the damndest questions at times. Don't know now. Tell better in the morning."

"These doctors surely keep a man hanging by the ears," father said when the doctor had gone. "He'll say not to go and maybe I'd do the same thing if I were in his shoes. Doctors have a big responsibility, making up people's minds." He was talking to cover the deepest disappointment he had ever suffered, composing himself to look cheerful when he went back into the house.

Some deep force within mother came to her desperate aid. She wanted to please father and she didn't want to be sick" contrary to plans laid at the foundation of his being. I think we saw some kind or a miracle that night.

When Doctor Prescott came next morning, he looked at her and gave a professional grunt. "Came here expecting to issue an ultimatum against your trip, but now, in all fairness, I can't do it. Whatever you had was only temporary and you'll be fit as a fiddle in a few more days."

Mother watched father's eyes and saw the double look of relief there, that she would be well and his precious trip could be carried through.

Before Doctor Prescott left us, he smiled and said, "Heard the trail west either kills or cures; if you have a chronic case of liver complaint the diet and fresh air of the plains might help you. Much of that region has been contaminated by victims of cholera. Camp on as clean ground as you can find, drink the best water you can find and be careful of malaria. Do you still want to go?"

"Yes," she replied without flinching. "I prefer to go." The bravest lie a woman ever told to please the man she married.

"Well, then God bless you all. Your urge to migrate is deeper than my reason goes. Wish you good luck and happiness. May not see you again, so I'll tell you good-bye now."

The bitter days of leaving. The haunting hallowed memories of my childhood that came back to me when I was about to say farewell to the place which made them possible—the friendly earth and the house which always had been home. The favorite tree in the orchard where I sat in a leafy bower and gorged with cherries. The brook where I sneaked off to fish and the clump of brush where I hid when I didn't want to be bothered. Or the cellar I robbed periodically to satisfy a devilish instinct to be doing something mean. Or where the roof of the barn projected out, in the floor of which was a hole where I waited for hours to drop an overripe peach on my favorite sister.

And then the final moment of departure, when mother came down the steps for the last time with a shawl on her head, and father handed her up to the seat. The younger girls finding places to look out from the rear end of the wagon, each with little bags packed with all the earthly belongings they were permitted to take. Crying and waving and calling, "Good-bye, lovely old house."

A final remark of Susie's was, "I wouldn't mind it so much if I could take my room and all my things along. Seems like we just can't take anything we want. Hope I find a papoose out there I can have for a pet."

They left in the first wagon. Hired men and I were to bring the other two wagons and the extra stock.

Abner Pierce with his slatternly wife and runny-nosed children, wet feet and filthy clothing, were waiting at the gate to drive in when I drove out with the last wagon. That was the agreement; he was to stay off the place until we were entirely quit of it. I thought what a shame it was for our fine farm to fall into hands like that. But his money was as good as any when one had the Oregon fever.

Mother had never seen Pierce's family. The only times she had seen him he presented a rather respectable appearance, but that day he looked like a tramp. Some of it might have been the way I looked at him under the circumstances.

At the last moment I went to where the girls had their toys and playthings laid out in a neat pile, hopping and praying that some power might intervene and say, "Well, girls, load up your keepsakes now." But they didn't have the nerve to speak of it to father—not even the undaunted Susie. Tears came to my eyes. I carried most of them out and loaded them on top of the plows, extra harness and rope that we had in my wagon. With everything else, I couldn't bear to think of the girls' treasures falling to that herd of vandals.

Finally I snapped the bull whip and drove out the gate, jerking my thumb to Pierce to indicate the place was his to murder. That was one of the worst moments I had in braving the trail to Oregon. It sapped my resolve to think of mother leaving the home where she had found deepest content, with not even a little enthusiasm for going to a new country. Between pity for her and resentment and pity for myself the heart had gone out of me.

The road though fairly level was unrelenting mud. The sky threatened rain and more mud. Thoughts came to me of, what if the oxen should get sick and die, way out there miles from anywhere? What if the family got the cholera and some of them died? Or malaria? We were brave now but what about Indians when they attacked and we were alone on the plains? Or they stole our oxen? Or the oxen would get terribly sore feet as often happened.

I didn't even have the satisfaction of knowing that Hallor wouldn't be along, for Stella had received a letter from him saying he would join us before we reached Independence. "To help you people on your great journey."

But we had turned our heads west. There was no alternative but to keep on driving the something over two thousand miles ahead. Nobody knew the exact distance. I held to two thousand as the figure and for the first few days kept subtracting our guess at the miles driven.

About dark I overtook the family camped in a grove near a creek. They had a rousing fire going and mother had the stew pot on waiting for us. The smell of coffee and being with the family again cheered me. Mother kissed me and patted me on the back. But our moody father! He was actually in high spirits.

He slapped me on the back and said, "Son, we're started. The first day down; only three months and twenty-nine days to go. Wait till we get in buffalo country."

When I showed the younger girls their nonsensical trifles (and made them realize I was one brother in a million) their delight was pathetic.

Father came over and smiled at them. "You girls had better enjoy those things while you can. We finish loading up with supplies at Independence."

As soon as supper was over and the stock taken care of the girls sang songs about the campfire. The others sat and basked in the heat. The sky had cleared and the stars came out bright and cheering. We dried our boots and beat the mud from them. It was cheerful and seemed to knit the family closer together. When I finally settled in my feather bed, the feeling of gloom had left me and I felt contented.

Tired as I was, I couldn't go to sleep right away, but pulled the canvas back and alternately watched the stars and the dying embers of the fire. This was a new epoch in our lives and vague yearnings stirred in my blood. I even exulted at the thought of buffalo ahead and many nights like this on the road.

A delicious breakfast of ham and eggs next morning helped the feeling. I touched mother on the arm and said, "This isn't so bad is it, mother?"

"You know, Eddie, I kind of like a little bit of this. Guess there's some gypsy in me, too."

CHAPTER 3

It had been a hard winter. Grazing was slow in developing. The oxen and other stock weren't getting enough to eat, and we had to buy hay. Finding a solitary farmer we approached him. He looked at us in a way that he must have thought was the essence of shrewdness and said, "Where you goin', nebber?"

"Heading for the Far West," father replied.

He rolled his eyes back in his head and cackled, "Gawd! Ye must be crazy as loons." He looked at mother and the girls and meditated. "They'll all look fine scalped by Injuns, ur starving" in some gawdforsaken hole."

Father was five feet, ten inches tall and solidly built, weighing about a hundred and seventy-five pounds. His fist shot up to the farmer's chin and laid him flat. "Drive on. I wouldn't buy hay from a muttonhead like him if the oxen never ate."

"Culver!" mother scolded. "What's got into you? He was merely speaking his mind."

"Taught the ugly fool a lesson," father snarled. "Might have better sense next time."

That afternoon about sundown we bought some good hay for the stock and camped in another grove just before dark after a splendid, sunny day. We had made fifteen miles.

The grass became better as we approached St. Louis and we also came into one of the main emigrant channels leading from the East. Strings of wagons became more frequent.

Ferrying the Mississippi at St. Louis, south of the Missouri, I was looking at the far shore when Stella seized my arm, saying frantically, "Eddie, that barge down stream is overloaded; they're going to capsize!"

Shrieks of men and women, as they clutched each other and thought of their children, were heartrending.

"They might have left homes like ours, filled with hope and spirit," she sobbed as they were swept away to their doom in the dark, swirling waters.

It saddened us all but Stella always hit the depths at sight of people suffering. And worst when she couldn't do anything to help them.

Once in St. Louis, we put up at a hotel while father scoured the city. He came back fagged and unhappy. "Figured plenty on Moorfield," he confided in me. "Wanted to see him pretty bad. He went through here a month ago. Place is a madhouse. I bought three saddles and four rifles. We'll skin out in the morning."

With exception of a day now and then the road was not dusty. We enjoyed the comparatively easy traveling and picked our way to avoid the deeper ruts and worse mud holes.

Ten miles out of Independence we met a long wagon headed back in the direction from which we had come. Father halted us to have a talk with the man and his wife, sole occupants.

"Not giving up are you?" father yelled to him.

"Afraid so," he said. "We don't know anybody to travel with and I've changed my mind. My wife wants to go on but I can't be as hard on her as some of the others are. Independence cooked my goose. Women crying, wanting to go home. Men fighting. Streets filled with drunks. Everybody packs a gun and uses it on half an excuse." He looked us over. "Is all this your outfit, sir?"

"Yes," father answered. "It's Oregon or bust for us."

"Not thinking of going it alone all the way, are you?"

No. At Independence we'll have to join up with others and make a caravan. Too risky otherwise. My name is Culver Thorne."

The man extended his hand. "Mine is Schoolcraft. Glad to meet you, sir. 'Culver Thorne!' I've heard that name recently. Wait a minute until I talk to my wife."

He went to his wagon and returned, saying, "There was a young man at Independence looking around among the emigrants a week ago inquiring for a man named Culver Thorne. Wife heard him asking at one of the other wagons. Said he guessed you gave it up and weren't coming West after all."

"Was he tall and handsome and spoke with a southern accent?" Stella interrupted.

"No, ma'am," Schoolcraft replied. "He was tall and good-looking but the rest of it doesn't fit."

"Moorfield!" father boomed excitedly. "Where did he go? He was looking for me."

"Don't know, sir. I'll ask my wife, maybe she knows. Women listen to stuff better'n men."

Mrs. Schoolcraft was a tall young woman about twenty-one, with a form like a statue, the old Greek kind, plump bosom, well filled hips, put together with a pleasing seductive charm to the eye. Her eyes were pretty and roving, set beneath a high forehead. Her hair was a reddish-brown, piled heavy on her head, bright and gleaming in the sun. I particularly noticed her hair for it seemed that it recently had been washed, the way it sparkled, contrasting with Stella and mother whose hair, in the rush of camping, wood smoke and frying meat, had become dull and lusterless. She was easily the most beautiful woman, excepting Stella, we saw on the trail. Right then, she almost dazzled me. She acknowledged our introduction with a graceful smile, displaying even white teeth, set like tiny pillars in firm pink gums. Good deal like Stella's blessing in that respect.

"That's about all I heard," she replied to father's questions on Moorfield. "Gathered from the way he talked that he might be in Independence a few days longer. The party he was talking to said something about the Mexican War. Mentioned Fremont. They both seemed to know him. Think he said he was looking for Fremont, too. Captain Fremont, I believe he said."

"That settles it. Eddie, you take one of our saddle horses and hit the grit for Independence. See if you can find him," father commanded. "Want to talk to him again."

"Yes, sir. Who'll drive my team?"

"Stella can sit in the wagon and pull a lead rope. Late now. We'll make a camp at the first likely spot."

We thanked the Schoolcrafts and were walking away when they called to us and wanted to talk some more.

"If you'll let us trail along with you, we'll go back to Independence and think it over," Schoolcraft said hesitantly.

"That's agreeable to us," father replied thoughtfully. "Have to group up at Independence anyway. But we are to be in no way responsible for your change of mind, remember. Everybody to his own brand of poison."

Schoolcraft did not seem glad to be on the trail west again. It appeared that his wife was doing the urging.

Saddling a horse, I was soon on the way to Independence. Made it well before dark and managed to find something to eat in a smoky little restaurant next to a saloon. Since I didn't know my man by sight, it was like hunting buckshot in a sack of wheat expecting to find him in the crowds of emigrants, traders, squalid Indians and others who thronged the streets.

Blacksmith shops, saddle shops and wagon makers were open and going at top speed, as well as the stores selling provisions and farm implements. Everything seemed to be in business the clock around. Reminded me of an ant hill.

It was the stopping point for emigrants who had come up the Missouri and any other overland travel. The one bright busy spot in a vast lonely expanse, save for buffalo, Indians, antelopes and wolves.

I inquired in saloons, restaurants and any other place which seemed to offer a possibility of finding a man named Moorfield. A little after midnight I sat down in a corner of a saloon to rest and think things over. Driving an ox team all day, riding ten miles on top of it and walking endlessly through heaving, jostling crowds had me tuckered out. Giving in to the urge, I slept like a dead man until four o'clock in the morning when a bartender shook me saying, "Sober up outside! This ain't no hotel. No place fur bums."

"Beg your forgiveness," I replied. "I'm neither a drunk nor a bum."

"My mistake," he said, looking me over. No argument. Go on back tuh sleep if yuh wantuh."

"No, thanks. Looking for a young man named Jeff Moorfield. Was everywhere last night but couldn't find him."

"Too bad ever'body can't find ever'body," the bartender said sympathetically. "Try the rest'rents. If he's a bach'ler, he gits tired of his own cookin'; if he lives, he eats; ever'body goes there before he heads out an' starts batchin' again."

Thanking him for his advice I wandered around some more, hoping to find Moorfield and afraid I'd find Hallor.

It was about six o'clock when, with a start, I saw the man who had blown the cracker dust in Hallor's face. He met an army officer and went into a restaurant. I followed and took a seat near them.

"Well, how are you anyway?" I heard the officer ask. "You're a long way from the Oregon country."

"Been back East," the other man replied.

"How about signing up for the Mexican War now? We need scouts. Army'll do well by a young man like you who knows Indians."

"Can't do it," my man objected. "Looking for Fremont. His father-in-law wants some more information on the Oregon country. Friend of Whitman. Promised to help on land grants out there now that the British gave it up."

"General Kearny had Major Fremont arrested for insubordination. Just heard the news a short time ago. Fremont's on his way to Washington, D.C. under military escort."

"How come?" the other bridled. "Fremont's a good man. Like him. Old Kearny's a damn fool."

"Can't sit here and listen to such talk," the officer said reprovingly. "General Kearny is my superior officer."

"If you don't like it, you can lump it," my man said briefly. "I'm not in the Army yet, and if Fremont's under arrest, I know danged well I won't be. Politics somewhere."

"No politics about it," the officer snapped. "Commodore Stockton appointed Fremont Governor of California. General Kearny outranked Stockton and wouldn't ratify the appointment. Fremont guessed on Stockton's authority and guessed wrong."

"I say Kearny was lousy jealous and playin' dirty," the other maintained. "But if Fremont's on his way back to Washington, he'll see Senator Benton and save me hunting anymore. Hope he makes that old pelican back water at court martial."

"Sir!" the officer said, rising. "I refuse to eat with anyone who speaks of my superior officer in such a manner. I stand for General Kearny."

"Go to hell then! I stand for my friends and Fremont's one of 'em!"

The officer glared at the revolver the other wore at his side. The officer wore one.

"Good notion to challenge you," he declared.

"Mean you'd like to be able to," the other said, getting to his feet. "You're just mouth and parade ground."

I was the only other one in the place by that time. Never saw a house empty so fast before.

"Who's that fellow watching us?" the officer asked.

"May be another friend of mine," my man replied, keeping his eyes on the officer. "But I don't need help."

The officer glanced at me and then back to the other.

"Beneath my dignity. Let it pass this time," he said.

"Too damned bad about your dignity, you windy bastard," the other said. "Army's cursed with whickerbills like you."

The officer gave him a bitter glance and strutted from the room.

"Hello, Thorne," my man said, looking at me for the first time. "Don't you know enough to clear out for a shooting scrape? Might get shot."

By that time the diners began filing in and a large man came over to us. "You Jeff Moorfield?" he asked bluffly.

"Who the hell wants to know?" the other shot back tensely.

"Take it easy you young fighting cock. My name's Cander. Asked someone your name. Heard the scrap and want you to work for me."

"Bad practice askin' people their names west of the Mississippi. What's your deal?"

"Want you to guide our outfit to Oregon. Hundred dollars a month and food."

"Family train?"

"Yes."

"No. Wouldn't for a thousand dollars a month."

The big man held out his hand and said, "Glad I met you anyway, young feller. No harm in asking."

Moorfield smiled and they shook hands.

"Let's eat, if they don't throw me out for the scrap," he said, motioning to his table.

"So you're Jeff Moorfield? Been looking for you," I said. "How did you know my name so fast?"

"Saw your sister through the window that night I took your father home. Asked Bush Green about the family. You by yourself?"

"No. Family's ten miles east. Rode ahead to see if I could find you. Father sent me. Wants to see you pretty bad. Didn't you kind of make a deal with him about Oregon?"

"Hell, no!" he said quickly. "Family train again. Goin' to drive me crazy. When your dad and I talked, I didn't know who he was. Did he say I did?"

"No. Was just fishing. But he wants to see you."

"Want to see him, too. Fine man." He laughed self-consciously. "Bet I'm poison to your sister over that china deal."

"You couldn't help it," I said. "There was some buck shot spilled on the floor."

"Does she know that?"

"Yes," I lied.

"Make any difference in how she felt?"

"Might have," I lied again. "Hard to tell. She doesn't like the idea of Oregon." Didn't want to kill him dead with the way she actually felt and still I didn't want to encourage him, knowing what he would run into when Stella learned who he was.

"How's everyone standing the trip? How many wagons you bringing?"

"Fine," I replied. "Three wagons. Hired man is driving one, father one, and I'm on the third one."

"Who's driving in your place now? The big fellow who was going to lick me?"

"Stella's driving. Hallor didn't show up yet. Was to meet us in St. Louis. Why didn't you lay him out that night you brought father home? Wasn't any of his business who stayed at our place."

"Rushed out like a mad bull and knocked the wind out of me first clatter," Moorfield said. "Then bounced me around on the grass plenty. Finally found my horse and got away. Kind of handy, isn't he?"

"Don't know," I said sarcastically. "Never saw him in action. Too careful what he does."

The subject changed to the West and Oregon.

"Show you a good place to camp when we finish eating. Meet you there this evening. Got a little fooolin' around to do. Maybe you'd better lope back and drive that wagon for your sister."

When we were parting he said, "Don't say anything about this fracas to your family."

"Not if you insist," I said. "See you this evening. So long."

"So long," he replied, as if far away in his thoughts.

CHAPTER 4

The Thorne family, with the Schoolcrafts following, was making good time when I met them, much to Stella's relief. "Funny how the Schoolcrafts changed their minds so quickly," I said to Father.

"The bug bit again when they saw us, I guess," father replied, walking away from the others. "Find Moorfield?"

"Yes. Coming to see us tonight. Showed me a good place to camp. Same man who raised cain that day in Bush Green's store."

"Knew that already," father said impatiently. "How did he act? How'd he talk? Say anything to indicate what he intended doing?"

I related all that happened. When I told him how Jeff answered Cander his face fell.

"Doggone it! Had hopes he'd guide us but sounds like a family train's poison to him. Well, let's move on so the family can see what Independence looks like," he said, in his short, disappointed manner. "That young fellow's got a lot of grit. Hope we can make him change his mind, some way. See anything of Hallor?"

"No. Didn't even hear him in the distance."

"Some luck at that," he said gloomily. "Mean more trouble if Moorfield did decide to guide us."

"Eddie," Stella said in a low tone when I went back to my wagon where she was waiting, "did you see anything of Joel?"

"No."

"Did you find that Moorfield father is looking for?"

"Yes. Same man who was at Bush Green's that day."

"Ugh!" she said, making a face. "Was sure he would be."

"You don't seem to like the idea, I take it."

"You and father make me sick! You get roped in with every blowhard you hear."

"Suppose you'd like to have your squawky Virginia dude on our hands and a thousand slaves at your beck and call? You'd like to play the lady—a pioneer lady—wouldn't you?"

"Well," she said thoughtfully, "it wouldn't be a bad combination. We'll need a thousand slaves before we get to Oregon, or die on the way."

"Don't let mother hear you say that," I said crossly.

"You're not mother. I can say what I like to you. You haven't any tender feelings. Won't even ride on your filthy old wagon."

She got down and ran to the lead wagon.

"Poor little steel spring," I thought as I watched her go, "I'm sorry. Your clothes are soiled. Your scalp itches from grime and dirt and you hate the whole idea. If you had loved your family just a little less, you wouldn't be here—same as mother. Only mother is following the man she loves while all you have is worry."

I was like that with Stella. The only time I could quarrel with her was when she was right before me. Let her get ten feet away and I wanted to hug her and tell her I was sorry. But I made a mighty resolution right then—a large one for me. I determined that if Hallor did show up on the scene I would treat him as kindly as I could for Stella's sake, even though I had to pray for strength to do it.

We drove through Independence. The dust was a foot deep in the main street and rose in clouds as we wormed our way along, past bawdy houses and saloons, cursing, ribald teamsters and trappers. Indians wandered about like dusty brown imitations in white men's clothing. They looked as if their last hope in life had gone. Black hair hung to their shoulders in ropy grease-loaded abandon. Dogs barked. Oxen grunted and heaved, horses neighed. Men filed in and out of trading houses. The smell of hides and offal filled the air, along with visible piles of filth besides houses. Men were careless of the presence of women in the passing wagons. Over it all loomed a feeling of fierce, tragic competition between many individuals—buying what they needed in the face of the unyielding pressure of time.

Independence! The place was well named in more ways than one. It boiled and bubbled. Like the first froth on a wine barrel with nothing to skim and purify it. Yet it was like a lusty, bawling animal fighting a chain with every hope of breaking all restraint. Or a riptide that reached for you and tried again and again.

Once through the town I took the lead and guided them over acres of ground made filthy by former camps of emigrants until I came to a grove and gave the signal to stop.

Mother and the girls stepped down at once to look around.

"What a heavenly place to camp in after that mess!" Stella declared. "How did you find it, Eddie?"

"Moorfield showed me this morning."

"Well, he at least did us one good turn," she admitted. "Turf to camp on and heavenly water to wash in, even if it is muddy. I'll never have the courage to leave here."

Jeff rode out to see father that evening. Mother and the girls acted as though they acknowledged him solely to be polite. All except Susie who gave him long admiring looks.

There was another one who paid strict attention to his being present—the handsome Eleanor Schoolcraft.

Jeff, in the setting that later I learned he lived and breathed and loved, was decidedly pleasing to the eye. With his trousers tucked in the top of his boots and shirt open at the collar, the ever-present gun at his belt, and his hat slightly to one side, reminded me of a captain standing on a bridge looking for a world to explore and conquer. His lean, dark, deeply tanned face and searching blue eyes did not dispel the illusion. Nor did his cool even manner. Stella said later that she thought he looked like a pirate. "A prairie schooner pirate."

"Jeff," father said, when there was a tactful opening, "I want you to guide us to Oregon. Pay you well."

Moorfield squirmed with dislike of refusing father this request, for it was evident there was a mutual admiration and respect. I never saw father take to a stranger so quickly and so unreservedly as he did to Jeff.

"I'll help you buy what you need, Mr. Thorne, and tell you all I can about the Trail, but I can't promise that. Guiding a family train would kill me. You'll have to join with a larger outfit, anyway, and you won't need me once you get started. If I could draw water out of the desert when I wanted to, or make a smooth road by wishing, I wouldn't hesitate a minute. I've heard babies crying while their mothers died, and men waited to dig graves. Big men, scared because they couldn't bring the dead back to life. Too much for me. Some fools think the Trail is easy, and Indians don't try to steal you blind. I know better. I'm a coward, I guess. Can't face it. For every wagon that gets through there's a grave and a wrecked family back on the trail. Families start out only half ready and others leave them to starve . . ."

He looked up and saw mother and Stella listening.

". . . but with a fine outfit like yours you don't have to worry so much. With the maps and descriptions of markers I'll make for you, you could guide a caravan there yourself. I'll mark every waterhole, and where game is plentiful. You'll be in buffalo country pretty soon; the finest meat in the world. Miles and miles of beautiful grass and wild flowers. When you pass some of the barren spots and get in the foothills of the Rockies you'll think you're in heaven. When you meander through Grand Ronde, this side of the Blue Mountains you'll know it. Pick out a good bunch to travel with and stay together. That's the way to do it."

"When you hit the Willamette Valley you'll want to get down on your knees and kiss the ground; it looks that good to a man who loves it. I've seen men with beards like a dusty mattress hug and kiss their wives and dance around like idiots when they pull through and head up the Willamette."

"I'll be along sometime after you get there. If you haven't found a good enough spot I'll show you places that'll make your mucky flats in Illinois look sick as a kid on green apples. After you know Oregon you wouldn't snap your finger at a million states like Illinois if you could own 'em all."

I looked at mother and could see she wasn't convinced. Stella's face bore a look of disgust.

He didn't stay long after that but promised to return next morning.

In a few minutes mother called father to her. The Schoolcrafts were at their wagon, and the girls were busy washing clothes, the first chance in two weeks. Though I was within earshot, and had a pair of excellent ears, mother seemed not to care whether I heard or not.

"Culver, I don't like the looks of that Schoolcraft woman. Do we have to take them with us?"

"Why, I don't see anything wrong with the Schoolcrafts," father replied impatiently. "This is no time to be picayunish, Grace. Seems like a good specimen of a woman to me. She's the one who decided to go to Oregon. Have to admire her nerve."

"Eddie, come over here," father called to me. "Mother objects to taking the Schoolcrafts along—Mrs. Schoolcraft, to be exact. Do you see anything objectionable about her?"

"Gosh, no!" I said. "With that body and that face, she's the kind I'd pick to head off into the wilds with."

Father laughed boyishly. Mother looked anything but pleased with my answer.

"That's just the trouble. She's a threat to every unattached man in camp. You men are blind as bats. She talked Oregon harder than ever after Moorfield showed up again, even if she is married."

"He's old enough to look out for himself. Don't believe he even saw her," father declared.

"Don't ever think it. She saw him and he saw her. I was watching. She started to come over while you were talking but changed her mind."

"In this country a man's innocent until proven guilty. Goes for women, too. Can't condemn her this way. How do you vote, Eddie?"

"Wow!" I exclaimed. "I vote *for* her if it's up to me."

"So do I," father said. "Two to one, Grace. You lose."

"Maybe I'm just too smart," mother said grimly and joined the girls.

"Women pick at the damndest things when they get nervous and bothered," father grumbled. "That Schoolcraft woman would be a fine specimen in any man's country. I'd be in big business acting on a suggestion like that."

He snorted and started to walk away when he turned to me again. "Moorfield wasn't very encouraging, was he? Notice how mother and Stella looked?"

"Yes. They didn't even hear the last chapter."

"Son, you never change a woman's mind. It just has to wear off, or wear out."

"Mother changed hers about coming out here."

"Wrong. Merely yielded. Her mind won't change until we get a better place in Oregon, if she likes the climate and it isn't too lonesome. Hope she doesn't keep on brooding."

I couldn't agree on that but soon learned better.

The sun was up and everything was spinning busily about the camp when Jeff came to take father and me to the best places to buy supplies.

"Both of you leaving us here alone?" mother objected.

Father paused in his hurry. "Maybe you'd better stay, Eddie. Jeff and I can tend to everything."

"Suits me," I agreed. "I've seen Independence. Smelt it, breathed it, and still tasting it. Hope to wash it off me, if I have any luck and some soap."

"We'll bring back a jag," Jeff said, smiling.

Schoolcraft pulled out and joined them with his wagon.

Seeing that mother had something she wanted to talk about I made it as easy for her as possible. Thought it might be the pleasant subject of Mrs. Schoolcraft.

Stella and the girls were washing their hair and wouldn't return until the bright sunshine had done its work.

But mother hesitated to mention what was wrong until I spread out the harness and began looking it over. She came over and sat down near me, saying, "Been thinking of the home place today, Eddie."

"Well, in a short time we'll be there, Mother, on good old Oregon soil, wondering why we didn't come sooner, wishing we had a million years to live."

"You're quoting Jeff Moorfield. I'm thinking of our farm in Illinois."

Before I could reply she began crying. Not the light, easy letting down when your mind is only half made up, but the deep heavy kind that keeps on making up your mind, that reaches clear down to the ankles for a sob.

"Eddie, I can't stand any more. I'm whipped. I've got to go back or die. Thought I could but I can't. I've been a good mother and a good wife; I never deserved anything like this. Hell isn't my home and the devil isn't God."

"Mother!" I protested, "You can't feel that bad about it."

"Oh, can't I?" she groaned. "You don't know how awful I feel. Nobody does. Nobody but a woman like me can."

She stopped talking and did a good job of it while I tried to think of what to say or do.

"I've grown to almost hate your father. Doesn't matter about you so much; you like it and want more of it. But think of my darling little girls growing up in the awful years ahead of us." Tears flowed without restraint. "Think of your beautiful sister, Stella, with stringy hair and ragged nails, putting up with this day after day, when she could have had all the advantages. We were doing well at home and I'm going back. Want you to tell your father. Then he and I can fight it out. You can take Crusader and make it by the first of June to reclaim the place. That's final."

For once in my life I didn't have anything to hang to and I was in over my head, cramped and drowning.

"Mother, calm down and listen. We simply have to go to Oregon. Where is the gameness all of us children are so proud of? You're looking backward too much."

I paused, groping for words and remembered some reasons.

"Mother, we can't go back. There's something I never intended to tell you—the old place isn't as you remember it now. I saw what was moving in—all of Abner Pierce's family—a slatternly wife and eight of the filthiest children you could imagine. That beautiful home of yours must be a muck pile by this time. Bet they've carved their initials everywhere in the house. Dirt in the corners. That kind of a family would keep a pig in the kitchen. You never could make it seem the same again—."

She started to interrupt me but I kept going while I had the floor.

"There's something else. That proviso you and father put in the deal with Pierce, giving us until the first of June to reclaim it, would never hold water. We took his money and he took possession. Nothing was said in the paper about the deal being null and void and that he would have to get off the place, or accept our money. Do you think he'd move off? How would you like to live there with a family like that?"

A deep, doubtful pause. She was silent so long I began to worry. A woman can stand only so much, I thought then.

"Eddie, you sure about that? You're just talking to fool me."

"Mother, I know a few things about real estate. Do you think I'd deliberately lie to you?"

I affirmed my statements to be true only by inference, things equaling the same thing equaling the other. There's a difference. Didn't really know exactly. Was merely of that opinion.

"I'm going to lie down for a while. My head's about to split open."

"Think it over, Mother," I urged gently. "Sleep on it and if you still want to take the chance of going back I'll go the limit. Only it'll be the same as murdering father at this stage of the game."

Peeking at her a little later I found her asleep and cautioned the girls to be quiet. After about four hours she called me to her. Her face was set in grave firm lines, pathetic with marks where tears had dried on the ground-in dust of the road.

"I may decide to go on. Don't mention what I said. Guess I was nervous and tired. Feel better now after a good sleep. Take some milk over to the Schoolcrafts. Don't think she cooks what they should eat. Probably her idea not to bring a cow along."

My leather-like conscience didn't hurt a bit. I might have saved the day but there wasn't a soul I dared tell about it.

About an hour before sundown I sighted father and went to meet him. The oxen were lumbering along in the general direction of camp. He was singing a ribald song, drunk as a lord. Every so often he would whoop and yell, "Gloriish country!"

"Father, hold up a minute!" I yelled, stopping the oxen. "You can't go home this way. You're drunk."

"Whoosh drunk?" he frowned. "Can't go t'Oregon drunk. Get off'n my wagon."

"Father, come alive! You're making a fool of yourself!"

"Ah," he jeered. "Purity. Too nice. Half skunk an' half rabbit. Gonna give yuh a lickin', yuh long-eared pup."

He climbed off the wagon. I had to hold him to keep him from falling. When his feet were on the ground he made wild swings at me, ripping out some terrible oaths. I stayed out of his way until he grew tired, after which he fell in a stupor.

A horseman was streaking out from town. It looked like Moorfield. I waited, feeling pure and righteous.

Jeff rode up and looked at father. "Gee whiz, how did he get that way?" he asked miserably.

"Maybe you can tell me?" I replied coldly.

He leveled a pair of hard eyes on me and said, "You think I got him drunk?"

I shrugged my shoulders. "You were with him once before."

"Christ almighty!" he flared. "What kind of a layout is this? Grab his legs and we'll load him up."

"Don't bother," I said. "I can manage from here."

He took father under the shoulders and legs and lifted him up by himself. I didn't realize he was so powerful. Did it easily. "Now," he said, "get up in that wagon and drive home or I'll knock your damned block off at the roots."

Having just talked mother out of her notion to go back to Illinois, I hated to take father to camp, but Jeff followed on horseback.

When we arrived I got down and started to the back of the wagon. But Jeff wasn't wasting any time. He lifted father out and laid him on the sod under a tree.

Mother was standing to one side making up her mind what to do and say.

But not sister Stella. She came, sniffed a couple of times, then looked Jeff up and down, not saying a word.

Jeff turned squarely toward her and looked her up and down. Without a word he mounted his horse and rode toward Independence.

"What'll we do with him, Mother?" Stella asked, as though father were a tramp.

"Throw a blanket over him and let him be. Go start supper. The rest of you girls get busy, too. I'll tend to him." Her voice was edgy and cold.

"Mother, listen,—" I began.

"Rather not talk now. I'll say plenty, later."

We ate supper silently. I went to bed after tending to the cattle and picketing the horses on new pasture. The coming quarrel made me miserable all over.

Sometime after dark father revived enough to know he was in trouble. We could hear him gagging and groaning. After that he got to his feet and began staggering around in the dark until he fell down.

"Lord, I'm dying," I heard him say weakly. "Wonder where my family is."

He began retching again. Sounded bad to me. I got up and went to him.

"Who's there?" he asked.

"It's Eddie, Father."

"Where am I, Son? Get your mother. I'm cashin' in."

"You're in camp, Father," I said, lighting a lantern.

Then I looked in horror. The violent action had ruptured a blood vessel. He was bleeding internally while the terrible vomiting kept on.

"Mother!" I yelled frantically. "Get out here and help me! Father's dying!"

She came and gave an agonized scream. "Get a doctor! Hurry! Oh, Culver, I didn't realize it was so bad. Even wished you more of it."

"Take hours to bring a doctor here, Mother! He might have been drunk but he's been poisoned, too. Don't you know some home remedy? Come alive! Do your wailing later. Think hard. What do we do?"

Mother, with a great effort, got herself under control. "Needs something to take up that poison and stop the bleeding," she said, running to the wagon. By this time the younger girls were standing around wailing, wringing their hands.

She returned with some flour saying, "Stella, bring water. Eddie, lift the things off the medicine chest. Take out that powdered alum. Puckers your insides. May work."

We brought what she needed and she mixed what she thought was best. "Now we'll have to force it down him," she said grimly.

It was a big job. We held our breath and prayed for results. It gradually eased him and stopped the bleeding. The stomach spasms grew less violent. For several hours we stood by him, sleepless and hardly daring to breathe, until two horses came tearing along in the moonlight, bringing Jeff and a man with a small black bag. They pulled to a rearing stop when they saw our light.

"Here he is, Doc. He's the other one. Maybe we got here in time."

The doctor felt father's pulse and then turned to us. "What have you done for him?"

"Flour and alum and water," mother said fearfully. "Forced it down him."

"Worked, I guess. Heard of it. Thank your lucky stars, madam. Might have been dead by now. Cupric poisoning. Bad cases tonight. Come on, Moorfield. Got to get back."

"Where's Schoolcraft?" I asked Jeff. "His wife's worried."

"Dead. An hour ago. Didn't find him in time. I'll take her to town with me. Two more dying."

"I'll go with you," I said.

"Stay here!" he snapped. "Don't need any help."

Father, having an excellent constitution, improved steadily and began to want food about noon the next day. "Where's Jeff?" he asked as soon as he was better.

"We haven't the slightest idea," mother replied. "And don't care. I've seen enough of him and his helpfulness."

"Don't blame Jeff. He had a list we figured out and was rounding up a lot of things we needed. Schoolcraft and I met Gleason and Berkley, a couple of friends I haven't seen for ten years. We went in a place and waited a long time for several drinks. Don't remember much after that. Must have been awful stuff to get me this way. Never again. Where's Schoolcraft? Bet his wife raised thunder with him."

We were silent.

"What's wrong?" he asked suspiciously.

"Schoolcraft is dead, Father," I said. "So are Gleason and Berkley. You were drinking what they call 'forty-red.' "The doctor said it must have been whiskey distilled in badly corroded copper coils, made by a fool."

Father's face was a mixture of shock and suffering. The family moved around in a solemn hush. Death had come awfully close in an unexpected manner.

But Moorfield had not returned to see us.

While I was saddling one of the horses to find him and apologize, two horsemen approached at a gallop. It was Moorfield and—my eyes bulged at the family's misfortune—Hallor!

They dashed up and ploughed to a stop. No sooner had Jeff's horse slowed down than he was off in a flash and caught the other horse, holding it respectfully while Hallor eased himself down.

"Thank you," he grunted to Jeff. "Hello," he called sweetly to us. "Ah just arrived by the rivuh. Bettuh traveling."

"Joel!" Stella cried and ran to shake hands with him. "Was afraid you wouldn't get here, or weren't coming at all."

"A Halluh nevuh goes back on his wo'd, Miss Stella. Least of all a Halluh to a Tho'ne."

He carefully pawed the earth and paid his respects to mother. The girls, other than Stella, weren't much impressed and Susie looked positively disappointed.

"Mr. Hallor," she said critically, "didn't you bring any slaves? I heard Stella tell Eddie we'd need a thousand before we got to Oregon."

"Susie, be careful not to quote people," I warned. "Just let the matter drop."

"Well, he's a slave owner, isn't he? He isn't ashamed of them, is he? I don't see—"

"Susie!" father called loudly, "that's enough!"

Susie, the terrible, shut up.

But Jeff's treatment of Hallor made me almost as sick as father had been. It puzzled me.

I went over to where he was talking with father. "Jeff, I'm sorry about our attitude the other night. Hope you'll accept my apology for the whole family."

There was forgiveness in his eye as he said, "Think nothing of it, Eddie. Bothered me at the time but I got over it. Telling your father I'm glad he pulled through. Looked plenty bad when Schoolcraft died."

"Which reminds me," I said, "what about Mrs. Schoolcraft, now she's lost her husband?"

Jeff's eyes flashed a momentary hardness. "They started out for Oregon, didn't they? And planned to string along with you folks? What does *she* want to do?"

"Don't believe she's said anything," father answered. Better have her come over, Eddie, while we're on the subject. Has to be faced sometime anyway."

I strolled through the grove to where the Schoolcrafts had pitched camp and found her forlornly gazing off into the distance. If I had expected to find her with frowsy hair and her clothes untidy I was pleasantly surprised. Not that individual. Even though sad and wan, her lovely hair had had perfect care. My heart sped up its beat. "What a package of gunpowder! What a widow!" I thought.

"Mrs. Schoolcraft," I began hesitantly, "do you feel equal to coming over and having a talk with us? Father sent me."

"A talk?" she asked doubtfully. "Any idea what about—Eddie?"

A lot of people called me Eddie right off the griddle but it seldom affected me like *her* "Eddie" did. I dumped my whole brain in her lap.

"About going to Oregon. You joined with us before your—misfortune, and he wants to know if you intend to go on. If you do, say so when they ask you."

"Your father is very kind," she replied, getting to her feet and hastily patting her hair.

I led the way, kicking imaginary dragons out of her path and wondering what kind of a viper mother would think me if she knew I had urged the beautiful widow to stand for Oregon. Mother had been very kind to her in her bereavement but things went in a groove with mother.

Mrs. Schoolcraft had excellent manners, and her bearing in greeting the family and Jeff, and in acknowledging my introduction of Hallor to her, left nothing to be criticized. She also smiled sweetly at me when I fixed a place for her to sit down.

Hallor bowed and pranced with pleasure at meeting her.

"Mrs. Schoolcraft," father said when Hallor's brightness dimmed enough for us to talk without going blind, "we asked you to come over and tell us what you intend to do, now that your situation has unfortunately changed. Speak your mind in any case."

"Well," she said hesitantly in a low voice, looking away as though confused. "I should return, I suppose, but I want to go on. It might be too much for me, driving oxen, but I could try. Have some money and could hire a driver—if I knew where to find one."

Father appeared pleased with her answer. "Would you really continue with us if we could find you a driver?"

"Yes," she said slowly, her eyes cast to the ground, enabling a pair of long lashes to plead for her. "There must be a place out there for me, surely."

My active eyes caught mother's sphinx-like face, and Stella's, in a fixed look of great and labored reserve.

"How about it, Jeff?" father asked bluntly. "Here's a lady in distress. Could you drive her outfit? My hired man quit and went home."

Jeff looked at father quickly, fleetingly, measuringly. "Sir, I spoke my mind about a family train—"

"Come now, Moo'field," Hallor said patronizingly. "Mustn't think of refusing. Yo' all will ansuh to me again if you don't."

I saw something strike and mull out in a ball of fire in Jeff's face for an instant.

"The only way I'll go is to pick a string of wagons and be the captain," he said quickly. "Seen too many lunkheads blundering along on the far end of the trail. In that case I'd drive a team—might as well be Mrs. Schoolcraft's."

"Good!" father declared happily. "Spoken like a man. All settled. We'll pick our caravan. Jeff will drive Mrs. Schoolcraft's outfit and Joel has promised to take over our third wagon, if he can learn to gee and haw at the right time. What do you think of it, Joel? Agreeable with you?"

"Puhfectly, suh. Moo'field's rathuh young to be a captain, but he can try. Whenevuh he's in doubt he may consult us."

At that I turned and bit a limb off the nearest tree, badly as we needed shade. This Moorfield-Hallor setup was going to drive me to drink—father's latest brand or anything. That brazen criticism settled on me like a spreading smell of something rotten.

"Thank you, Mr. Hallor," Jeff said, humbly. "Appreciate your offer to try me. Makes me feel good to know where to go—when I'm in doubt. Now, we'd better finish with the list of what we need in Independence, before everything's bought up."

"Yes," father agreed, picking at the grass and not looking up. "Better check Mrs. Schoolcraft's wagon first thing, then ours, and we'll get at it. No time to lose."

"You kind people must know how relieved this makes me feel," Mrs. Schoolcraft said. "Couldn't ever thank you enough, all of you, and especially you, Mr. Moorfield, for changing your mind. I hope you find no cause to regret it."

"I, too, Jeff," I said to myself.

He went with Mrs. Schoolcraft. Hallor and Stella took a short stroll. Mother came to where father and I were exulting over Jeff's decision.

"What do you think of it, Grace? Good job well done, eh?"

"Humph," mother exhaled with poison. "From here on anything can happen."

We got everything ready for a start but father was sick. We called the doctor who diagnosed his condition. "Extreme toxicity and infection of the inner lining of the stomach. I have no cure. If you don't get well in a few weeks, you'll have to go East."

CHAPTER 5

The days dragged on while we waited in great uncertainty for father's health to indicate what we should do. One caravan after another headed for the prized Oregon country and we could do nothing but wait in the best grace possible. All the time afraid that even Jeff would desert us, though he gave no indication of it. Mother tried to allay our fears by saying he wouldn't miss driving the widow's wagon for a million miles.

It was nearly the first of June before father could attempt traveling and we decided to make the start. Jeff had been killing time in Independence.

"Might be a good idea," he said when I told him. "Pretty late, though, for anyone to be headed that way."

We waited another week until a belated caravan of fifty prairie schooners drifted in to Independence for supplies on their way West. Jeff reported it one evening and we set out early next morning to size them up and see if they came up to his requirements. "Didn't look like much," he said when he brought word.

As we approached, the captain, a giant of a man with a tobacco-stained beard, and very profane, was conducting the trial of a fifteen-year-old boy. The women and children had been ordered back to their wagons. We stood and listened.

"Then yuh admit yore guilt, yuh damned little bastard. Yuh stole grub from Sinker's wagon, didn't yuh?" he cross-examined with cruel, wolfish eyes.

"Did not," the boy defended himself. "Might of later, 'cause I want to get to Oregon. Could work and pay my way."

There was no whining for mercy.

"Hang the dirty little liar," the captain ordered. "Pull up two wagons, raise the tongues an' drop the rope through the peak; hang 'im an' we'll git on our way. We gotta make a example of this."

I glanced at Jeff. His eyes were casting a peculiar hazy light.

"What in hell's goin' on here?" he asked in a harsh, cutting voice.

The bearded captain turned and insolently looked him over. "Who the hell be you, stranger? I'm capting of this here caravan."

"None of your damned business who I am. Don't care who you are. All you fellows don't cotton to hangin' a kid, do you?"

"Not by a damn sight," one of the group replied. "They's a bunch of us feels the same way. We'd rather hang the capting. We taken your dirt, Cutter Jones, ever sence we started."

"By God, I say hang the little thief," another yelled.

"All in favor of lettin' the kid work his way step over here by me," the first man spoke again, whose name I later learned was Beaut Savage.

Twenty men quickly stepped to his side while the others remained with the captain.

"Major'ty rules," the captain declared. "Git the rope."

"Get your guns, men, if you mean business," Jeff said to Savage's group. "We'll even this thing up mighty fast. The first man that lays a rope on the kid gets drilled between the eyes."

"Mighty big talk," the captain sneered. "Yuh ain't much more'n a kid yoreself. Yuh're a dividin' my outfit and splittin" us up in our rightchus duty. Go back to yore mama, yuh young bluffer."

"Try me and see if I'm bluffin'," Jeff said raspingly. "Lay a rope on the kid and find out. Wouldn't mind killing you or any son-of-a-bitch like you."

And he was the man who kowtowed to Hallor. You couldn't imagine that raspy, edgy voice knuckling to anyone.

"Hand me a rope," Jones said, taking a step toward the boy.

Then he looked at Jeff again. "If we was out further, I'd do it, but we be still in Missoury. This young snipe might make trouble an' hold us up. But, by Savage, yuh ain't a goin' tuh Oregon with me. An' the rest of yuh that stood by him ain't goin' either. Yuh kin find yore own way, an' damn yuh, I hope yuh rots on the way."

"Ruther rot an' have my fam'ly rot with me than go with yuh, yuh old pelican," Beaut Savage replied. "Ef we has to travel with the likes o' you, tuh hell with it! What yuh say, boys?"

"Damn right!" most of the twenty answered.

"You fellows don't need to worry," Jeff said. "We held up here waiting for Mr. Thorne to get over a sick spell. I know every inch of the trail to Oregon. Let old Pouchy Eyes take his bunch and high-tail it alone."

"Whoopee!" Beaut Savage yelled. "We got a new capting, boys. Whar's yore outfit, mister?"

"Four wagons all heeled and ready to go," Jeff replied, pointing toward where we were camped. "Buy what you need. Be ready tomorrow morning at six."

"That's us, Capting. We'll be thar. Ain't got much but we'll make 'er do."

"Come over here, kid," Jeff called. "What's your name?"

"Blessing Brewster," the boy replied. "Bless, for short."

"What a name!" Jeff said. "Where are your parents?"

"Died a week ago in Independence. Sold the outfit for medicine and a decent burial."

"You don't look like a thief. Did you swipe some of his grub?"

"Should say not! Gosh, they almost hung me, anyway." He shivered when he said it.

"Can you drive four oxen?"

"Sure. Drive eight. Swing the leaders an' bend the middle."

"Guess we'd better take him along, Mr. Thorne. Come in handy. Better feed him, first thing."

"Yes, I think so," father replied, pleased as all get out with Jeff. "Come on, Blessing, and we'll see you to a good breakfast. After that you can wash your clothes and spend the rest of the day getting ready. Got anything to wear on cold nights?"

"No. Lost my bundle and couldn't find it. Guess it was swiped."

"After you eat, we'll take you to town and see what we can find. Coming with us, Jeff?"

"Think I'll have these wagons roll a quarter of a mile south of you while I look 'em over," Jeff said, barely above a whisper. "Might be short on grub in spots. If some are flat broke I still have a little money. We need 'em as much as they need us. Makin' a late start."

Without a moment's hesitation, father declared, "I'll back your judgment two thousand dollars worth, Jeff. Just let me know, and don't spend any of your own money."

"Thank you, sir." He yelled, "Swing around here, you fellows. Line up and we'll move out."

Old Jones yelled, "Give 'em a lickin' afore they leaves. They cain't git away withouten a scrap—the damned good-for-nothin's. Shore wish Brocker'd come."

Women screamed and children started crying.

Jones was only a few steps from us. Jeff covered the ground in a hurry. "Play that tune again, Jones, with a different fiddle, or go for that gun you're packin'."

Jones glared at him but didn't make a move. All his men stopped and waited. Wide-eyed women peeked from the wagons.

"I kin hop a gun purty fast myself, seein' as how yuh wants it that a way."

"Suits me," Jeff said coolly. "Start reaching'."

They held for about a minute. Father's face went white with thoughts of all that could happen. But he was game. Didn't say a word. Can't describe how I was feeling. No place to hide. No place to run to. Nothing to say that would help.

Jones weakened. "Wal," he said, "hit's a long ways tuh Oregon. Mebbe we'll meet somewhar. Hold off ontil later, men. Yore all yaller or yuh'd had 'em licked by now. Be diff'rent if Brocker'd come along 'bout now."

Twenty schooners pulled free of Jones' layout and lined up. Jeff's eyes gleamed with satisfaction as we swung along with them.

"Would you really have shot him, Jeff? I asked.

"Just bluffing," he said carelessly. He spurred ahead and caught up with Beaut Savage who was leading the string.

I took the boy to camp and he ate like a wolf as mother spread food out before him. She looked after him until Hallor breezed back from a flower-picking jaunt with Stella and the girls.

He eyed the poor kid with open disdain. "Wheh did he come from?" he asked in his bad-bug-finding manner.

"Jeff rescued him and he's going with us to drive an ox team," I answered.

"Oh, the othuh Tho'ne team," he said pertly. "Ah'll have to thank Moo'field fo' that."

"Don't know," I said wearily. "Up to Jeff; he's the captain."

"Oh—Moo'field," he said with an impatient frown. "He'll see it mah way. That's the wagon, yondeh, boy."

"I'm takin' orders from Jeff Moorfield or Mr. Thorne," Blessing said edgily. "Who're you?"

"You all will find out, boy, in due time."

"Yes," I said. "Bless, you will find out—in due time." And winked at him.

"What's yo' name, boy?" Hallor asked, slightly nasal, with his color a trifle up.

The kid had spirit and my wink must have stimulated him. "Brewstuh, suh. Blessing Brewstuh," he mimicked with a smile.

"That's enough of that, young man," mother said crossly. "You'd better go rest until it's decided what you'll do."

"Yes, ma'am," the boy replied, throwing a look of disgust at Hallor, of such intensity that I knew I'd have an undercover ally if I needed him.

Father had gone to the other layouts' wagons and later in the day came back with Jeff.

"Ah reckon the boy will do well at driving the othuh wagon, leaving me free to assist in othuh ways and at the daily council, suh," Hallor said to father when they arrived, ignoring Jeff's status as captain.

"You undertook to drive the third wagon to Oregon as one of the reasons for coming, Hallor," father snapped at him. "I expect exactly that. There won't be any daily council."

"Then what was Moo'field's idea, suh, in fetching the boy along? He should be made to wo'k. What do you say, Moo'field?"

Stella was standing near, listening and worrying about Hallor and the way he was taking chances with father.

Jeff deliberately looked at her and then turned to father. "Might not be a bad idea, Mr. Thorne. Brewster could drive your third wagon and Mr. Hallor could drive Mrs. Schoolcraft's. Her wagon's lighter and easier to handle. Wouldn't be so hard on Mr. Hallor while his muscles are toughening up. Leave me free to ride and scout. That is, if it's all right with Mr. Hallor."

"Good idea," father growled, bending over to examine his boot. "Joel, you drive Mrs. Schoolcraft's wagon. Now, shut up!"

Father was still fiddling with his boot and I could see he was having a hard time to keep from laughing. He and Jeff didn't need to plot mischief in advance; it hatched in mid-air.

The look Stella gave Jeff could have been jelled, cut in chunks, and killed every rattlesnake we ever met on the desert. Mother's would have brought up the rear and killed all the horned toads and lizards.

That was the end of that skirmish, but later in the day I caught Stella alone and whispered, "They're a gwine tuh fa'm yo' man out tew the widduh, Ah heah, Sistuh Stella. Halluh done agreed."

Her cheeks flushed blood red and her eyes gleamed with rebellion. She drew herself up archly, above her trim waist. "You villain. I think this was planned."

"I did think, Stella, Halluh was a sure thing for a name," I threw at her, "but there'll be doubt cast upon it now as the beautiful widow's eyelashes begin to lash. Thought I heard 'em swishing today."

With a look of deep disgust she left me only half through. But, spying Susie and Blessing in an earnest conversation, I ambled to a place where I could listen.

"Are you really fifteen?" Susie asked, looking critically at him. "You don't look it. Maybe you've had a hard time of it. Was your mother kind to you? I'm almost thirteen."

"I'm fifteen, all right," Blessing answered studiously. "My dad said I needed buffalo meat to make me grow. We sure had a good outfit but I guess it wasn't meant to be. Who's this Hallor?"

"Oh, him. Don't let him scare you, except he's mother and Stella's pet. If you want to stand in with them be careful how you treat him, though. Father doesn't like him and neither does Eddie. He's going to marry Stella when father says when. Stella's mad because he's going to drive Mrs. Schoolcraft's wagon. She thinks father and Jeff and Eddie arranged it that way on purpose. Jeff acts like he's afraid of Hallor."

"Gosh, is your sister gonna marry Hallor with a man like Jeff around? Bet Jeff never was afraid of anything."

"Goodness, don't ever let Stella hear you say that. She thinks he's awful—perfectly awful. Words can't describe it. And Jeff doesn't think any more of her. Of course, Stella's my sister, but I like Jeff awfully well. Hope, if he marries any of us girls, it's me. Isn't that terrible?"

"Yes," Blessing agreed, "but I guess it can't be helped. People just feel a certain way and that's all there is to it. I wouldn't ever get married; I'm goin' to roam alone."

"Don't you like women, really?"

"Oh, they're all right, but gee, they're a lot of trouble."

"Blessing Brewster, I don't like that. You can just talk to yourself if you feel that way."

Father called for me then.

"Eddie, you'd better take Hallor and show him how to hitch up the oxen. Don't be too rough on him. He's lying over there in the shade, resting."

Finding him sound asleep, I took fiendish delight in waking him. Got down by his ear and yelled, "Indians! Run for your life!" He leaped to his feet like a deer and ran a hundred yards before he saw that he had been fooled.

Father laughed until the tears ran down his cheeks. So did the younger sisters and I, but mother thought it cruel.

"Don't you ever do that again," mother scolded. "Remember the boy who called wolf when he didn't mean it, and the shepherds—"

"Mother, please don't compare Joel with a shepherd," Stella interrupted, trying to keep from laughing with us.

"No, Mother. Leave him where he belongs. He's Mrs. Schoolcraft's ox herder now," I said, nodding to Stella in agreement.

Hallor came up just as Stella slapped me with the dishrag she was using.

"My, what a puhfect aim yo' have, Miss Stella, and Ah am shuah it was deserved," he said in his bland endearing way.

"Never mind criticizing my brother," she flared, giving him a withering look and walking away.

"What's the mattuh with yo' sistuh?" he asked me.

"She was mad because Eddie said you were Mrs. Schoolcraft's ox herder, now," Susie spoke up, showing that expert listening ran in the family. "I don't think she likes it."

It was a day well spent. Stella and Hallor sat by the fire and quarreled until father yelled, "Shut up and get to bed!"

Jeff routed us out at 4:30 a.m. and reminded us to be ready at 6:00 a.m.

"How did Hallor do with the oxen?" he asked me.

"Maybe he'll learn in time. Be all right on level ground. Seems to like his contract."

Stella heard me say that and gave me a mixed look of dirt and weeds.

Jeff, seeing her, smiled and said, "Who wouldn't? The lucky dog!"

When we pulled over to the caravan, Jeff called all the drivers together for instructions.

"We'll go up the Little Blue until we reach the Platte River, then we'll go along the south bank of it for a long ways. The main trail follows the Missouri to the north bank of the Platte but the Mormons were traveling it when cholera broke out. Hundreds died. Take your drinking water from the main stream; it's safer. Don't dig holes in the bank and drink seepage; drink the muddy water; has less alkali in it. If you don't know what alkali means now, you will later.

Be as easy on your food as you can. When we begin killing buffalo, you'll have more dried stuff to use with it. Don't gorge yourself on too much fresh meat. Causes diarrhea. Every night inspect your wagons and make repairs before you break down. Mr. Thorne's wagons will lead today, tomorrow they'll drop back. We'll rotate every day. If you're hot-headed and the trail bothers you, don't pick fights. The other man's up against the same thing. Now, back to your wagons and fly at it!"

"My! Who does he think he is?" Hallor asked me. "Talks like he was the whole show. Ah jumped him in Independence and he was meek as a lamb. Ah'll do it again befo' long."

I could see trouble looming in that direction.

The long delay at Independence, plus my advice concerning the old home place, had mother tempered for anything, just so she could be on the move away from there. And, as the whole family gauged their feelings more or less by hers, they were in high spirits. Father was like a child with a new toy. He had had his way with Jeff and was headed for Oregon.

With a short delay at noon for lunch, and a rest for the teams, we drove steadily until sundown and made about twenty miles. A good day's travel as we were to realize later.

After supper the girls, full of pent-up energy from riding so long, began singing without being coaxed. Mother and father beamed with pride as their beautiful voices blended in harmony and carried out over the prairie. Then Stella sang a solo and I never heard her sing better. The setting of the evening with darkness ready to fall, the wagons spread out around us, and scents from numerous flowers drifting in, as their perfume increased at dusk, was one to remember.

Jeff had been busy in other places but when he heard the singing he came to our wagon, as did practically everyone else. When Stella began singing the solo, I could see that it gripped him from the boots up. He looked as if he might have been entertaining visions of going to far lands, crusading for love and glory.

When she finished and the applause quieted, Jeff said to me, in a husky voice, "Ask her to sing "*The Last Rose of Summer.*"

"Sis," I called, "Jeff wants you to sing "*The Last Rose of Summer.*"

"Damn you!" he gritted, "What did you mention my name for?"

Before I could answer, Hallor began sounding off. "Oh no, Miss Stella. Please sing "Ah'm Shedding Feathuhs."

Stella glanced at me, included Jeff, and began on Hallor's choice.

At the conclusion of Hallor's choice, Stella immediately began "*The Last Rose of Summer*" but Jeff had risen to his feet and was walking away. He didn't stop to listen.

From then on his polite treatment of Hallor increased so much so that one day mother said to me, "Eddie, why is Jeff so ridiculously polite to Joel when it isn't his nature? Anyone can see that."

I sighed. "Mother, that's one question I can't answer. It springs from some source beyond my depth, either in heaven or the hot place—I hope the latter."

"You're a bad boy. You're continually trying to stir up trouble for Joel."

"Now why do you say that, Mother? Don't I treat him politely? Have you seen me do anything wrong to him?"

"No, I haven't *seen* anything but I know where a lot of things start. Do you think it's being fair to Stella?"

"Mother," I said, "do you think she's being fair to a fine lot of brother and sisters to hope to wish a dolt like that on us as a legal relative?"

"That's unkind, Eddie: I'll hear no more of it. You and your father are like two dogs—you never forget where you buried a bone. I'm disappointed in you. I like Joel, and intend to defend him."

"Fine," I agreed. "I'll help you. Tell me what to do next."

"Couldn't trust you. I've seen samples of your helpfulness. But you might speak to Moorfield and ask him to tone it down. It's too obvious to all except Joel."

"Now there, Mother, you've laid your finger on the whole trouble. That egg doesn't realize he'll never hatch. He thinks life is coming to him through the shell, and that it's solid gold and a privilege to feed him that way. Wouldn't speak to Jeff about it for anything. It bothers me, but I can stand it if Joel—and Jeff—can."

"But Jeff is rude, while Joel is the utmost in politeness."

"And Jeff is going to get us to Oregon while Joel will be a lot of useless baggage. He's a troublemaker."

"Get out of my sight. Go talk with your father; you think alike."

Stella never spoke directly to Jeff is she could help it, and, thank goodness, I was on hand to hear her this time. It was on Friday evening shortly after we had stopped. Going to the river to get a small pail of water, she met Jeff. He stepped aside to let her pass him making no attempt to take the pail.

"Day after tomorrow is Sunday. Are you going to have us stop for the day?" she asked him, coldly.

"Certainly," he shot back at her. "The oxen and Mr. Hallor both need a rest." And he kept on going.

"Fine weather we're havin', ain't it, ma'am?" I couldn't help saying when she passed me and I reached for the bucket she carried.

"You shut up, Eddie Thorne, and don't you tell that on me. Who does he think he is?"

"Sounds like a page out of Joel Hallor's book," I said angrily. "Heard him sounding off before. He'd better stop it."

"Well, this Moorfield isn't Napoleon Bonaparte. I think Joel is right."

"Maybe Joel thinks he could run a caravan like this and keep everyone going? Imagine that if you can stomach it!"

"Depends on one's viewpoint," she said calmly.

CHAPTER 6

After a week's travel over the sweet prairie sod, Sunday came again. We camped on the Little Blue and those so inclined had prayer meeting and sang hymns, in which our family took a large part. Other members of the caravan played cards and repaired harness, or tried to fish in the muddy water. And they all washed clothes.

"I guess the Lord will forgive us for using Sunday for washday," mother said, "since He put such a tremendous spirit of travel in the men of this caravan, godly and ungodly alike, in very liberal portions." Saying this, she seized the washboard and led the girls to work.

Jeff and I took fresh horses out of our string and scouted miles ahead. We were on high ground and were just topping a ridge when Jeff yelled back to me, "There they are."

I looked hard and saw ten head of buffalo on a side hill scarcely three miles away.

"Gee, is that all?" I exclaimed in disappointment. "Expected to see a big herd."

"Stragglers," Jeff replied. "Always find some. Main herd may be twenty miles away. Must not be many wolves and Indians around here. Good sign."

"Jeff," I said, "speaking of Indians, shouldn't we be with a larger caravan? Seems to me more would be safer."

"Yes," Jeff said, reluctantly. "Didn't have any choice. Your father was sick too long. Indians are hell to figure out."

"What kinds do you expect to meet?"

"Sioux, Crows, Banatees, Cayuses, for sure. Maybe some Utes."

"Which are the worst of all?"

"Any big band of 'em is bad on the war path. Guess Utes are worst. Big brutes. Some of their wives kill themselves to get away from the onery pups."

"Poor things," I sighed. "Must be an awful life they lead."

"Poor things!" Jeff snorted. "You know what they do if the bucks bring back too many squaws they take from some other tribe? If the bucks'll stand for it, and the wives don't need 'em for slaves, they hack 'em down."

"Hack 'em down?"

"Kill 'em. Bucks just sit around and look on. Life doesn't mean anything to an Indian—other fellow's life. Shoshones not so bad. Or Nez Perces. Stand pretty well with them. But I sure hate Cayuses and Banatees."

I felt better when Jeff decided to return. His opinion of a small outfit worried me more than ever. "The many moods of camp life partly took my mind off the future. "Your night to stand guard, Hallor," Jeff said, several evenings later.

With the whole family in earshot, Hallor said, "Ah refuse, Moo'field."

"All right, Mr. Hallor," Jeff agreed. "I'll get Burdick. Hasn't had his turn yet."

Burdick's was the next wagon and he was listening. "Don't mind standin' guard, Capting, but I'll be danged if I'll take that coyote's place."

Hallor reddened at the wattles and puffed up. "Did Ah unde'stand yo' to call me a name, suh?"

"Guess yore hearin' is good, lad," Burdick replied. He was a husky man about forty years old.

"Then Ah demand an apology, else Ah'll be of a mind to challenge you."

"What with?" Burdick sneered. "Guns? Fists? Knives?"

"Ah favuhs fists."

Jeff didn't object by word or sign. They walked away from the caravan and surrounded by men only, squared off. Burdick rushed Hallor, Hallor struck him with a heavy upward blow on the chin and Burdick fell, unconscious. The fight was over.

Jeff said nothing as he walked back with me to our wagons.

"The idea!" mother sputtered. "Letting those two fight like a couple of animals! Why didn't you, as captain, stop it, Mr. Moorfield?"

It was plain to see that Jeff had come to talk with father about something, but instead he calmly regarded mother. "Wasn't feeling up to it, ma'am. Captain of this outfit can give orders but it's up to others to see they're carried out."

He turned to where his tent was pitched and went to bed.

Jeff had dodged the issue with Hallor again. I went to bed with a heavy mood weighing me down. Sleeping in the same tent, I determined to question him.

"Hey, Jeff, you asleep?"

No answer. I spent the next hour thinking and cursing to myself. Maybe my opinion of him was too high. He might be a spineless worm unless he could shoot people like he threatened Cutter Jones, captain of the group that wanted to hang Blessing. Was certain he wasn't asleep.

At the end of the hour, a delegation of drivers strode up to Hallor's tent. Pulling the tent down, they yanked him out of bed.

"Hallor," I heard Beaut Savage say, "we needs a guard out on the picket line, pronto, and we wants a damned good job done. Git at it." He aimed a kick at Hallor's rump which made good connection. Another one struck him on the jaw and at the same time one of them held his feet and let him fall flat. Then they grabbed the tent, tossed him in it, and threw him about twenty feet out on the prairie.

It was bright moonlight. Jeff stealthily raised the tent on his side and looked out. Then he began laughing, great loud haws—haws that carried over the whole caravan.

"What are you laughing at, Jeff?" I asked sadly, feeling how he was still failing my former opinion of him.

"Must have been dreaming," he said.

Hallor came in at dawn somewhat marked up and sullen-faced. Jeff, just getting up, looked at him in feigned surprise.

"Where have you been, Mr. Hallor?"

"Standing guard," Hallor snarled. The "guard" sounded like "god."

"Then I must thank you, kindly. Was certain your conscience would lead you to do the right thing. Thank you again. Thank you, sir." He more than laid it on.

The widow was already up, with water warming over a fire, and solicitously began helping Hallor with his cuts and bruises.

"Ah'll get even with Moo'field for this, Ah shush will."

I walked over to him. "Moorfield didn't have a thing to do with it. He was asleep."

"Get out!" he gritted. "Ah kin whup you with one hand behind me." He drew back a fist.

Jeff, seeing this, took a few steps in our direction and then, spying Stella peeking out from her tent, stopped.

"That might be true," I agreed, "but I'll bet you, Hallor, fifty dollars that Moorfield could tie you in a knot if he wanted to." And then I left him.

"Heard that, Eddie," Jeff said. "You must be a regular spendthrift. My! Isn't he big and strong? Sure will make your sister a fine husband—if someone doesn't beat her to him. Miss Stella ought to have been up and had the fire going. Doesn't it say something in the Bible about the virgins trimming their lamps?" A roar of laughter ripped from father's tent.

"Please ask your father to be careful," Jeff said again, loud enough for Stella to hear. "He might get Mr. Hallor mad at me and then where would I be?"

"Bruised and beaten by the trail, I guess," was my reply.

"Yes, bruised and beaten," he repeatedly sadly, "with no one to bind up my wounds."

We pulled away from the Little Blue and struck the Platte in a short time. The road was terrible in many places, where the oxen pulled their hearts out and it looked like wagon after wagon would roll down the slope or never pull to the top of it. Men got out with shovels and dug a rut on the upper side to insure the train's passing over a treacherous spot without mishap, not once but many times. It was usually that way when passing from one river system to another. The valley of the Platte looked good to us when we descended to the south bank of it.

Jeff had ridden ahead and was waiting near a clump of trees. I was thinking of its possibilities for a camp site, though it was only two o'clock in the afternoon, when he halted us.

"Pitch camp," he called. "Herd of buffalo around the bend. Fresh meat for supper."

Buffalo! The word made weariness vanish. Everybody helped and camp was made in a hurry.

Father owned the only horses with the exception of three that Jeff had brought along, two saddle horses and a pack horse. But there were only five saddles including his.

He talked a few moments with father and then said, "I want four men to come with me to round up a couple of buffalo and bring back meat. We'll be near 'em from here to south Pass, so don't quarrel over the chance."

Father, Beaut Savage, Hallor and I went with him.

"Kill only two," Jeff suggested. "Last winter was a hard one. Buffalo been held back on account of feed. See thousands in the next few days and right along after that. Don't slaughter 'em. Leave some for Indians and the settlers coming next year. They'll all be hungry. Fun soon wears off. Let's go."

We rode into view and galloped down for the kill. Some plunged into the Platte and headed for the other side. Others dashed upstream. But the main part of the herd was slow to start, held up by cows who had new born calves, and stubborn slow-witted bulls.

We quickly circled and killed two, a young bull with his hump well rounded and a young cow that didn't have a calf trailing her. Hallor seemed to go mad with the lust to kill. He reloaded and fired at a worthless old bull, striking the lower jaw and shattering it. Quickly reloading he fired at another one and would have kept on but his gun jammed.

Jeff had not joined us other than to circle the first one. When Hallor started his ruthless slaying, I saw him look toward the rise where the balance of the caravan had come to watch us, wildly cheering. The second one Hallor shot was dying, but father and I had to run the old bull down and kill him.

Other men drove a team of oxen over and hauled back a fine load of meat from the first two killed, leaving Hallor's victims lie where they had fallen.

"What do you think of Hallor now, Father?" I asked on the way back.

"Made a fine display, didn't he?" father replied disgustedly. "Would've killed the whole herd at one shot if he could. Better not mention it at camp. Save trouble with his boosters."

The grove had been picked clean of wood by former campers, but piles of buffalo chips, the dried, flat dung of years before, made a fair fire. With whoops and hurrahs the caravan sliced the rich red meat and cooked supper. The huge steaks broiled and sizzled in pans that had long waited for them. Hands were burned by careless snatching.

Though Jeff had supervised our drinking water with great care, he said nothing at the gorging of huge piles of fresh meat by people who wouldn't leave it alone as long as they could eat. Hallor was one of them.

"Why don't you caution them again, Jeff?" I asked. "Looks to me like they're overeating. Didn't you say something about bad effects?"

Told 'em once," he replied with a frown. "No use talking too much. They'll learn. Even the kid'll know better in a day or two. Good place to camp if we have to."

Raising his voice he said, "Did you have a good time today, Mr. Hallor?"

"Ah sho did," Hallor answered coldly. "Why?"

"Just wondered. Nothing like a good hunt to make a man forget his troubles."

"Ah'm going to kill a la'ge numbuh of buffalo befo' we leave them. Ah don't intend to be dictated to. That is one of the reasons why Ah came. You don't own 'em."

"Guess not," Jeff replied agreeably. "Have a good time while they last. Be something to remember on the other side of the mountains."

"Ah intend to—that will be something fo' you to remembuh, Moo'field."

"Yes, certainly, sir. Sorry I spoke of it," Jeff replied, eyeing him in a peculiar manner before walking away.

We lost a day and progress was slow for the next two.

On the morning of the third day from there, Jeff drew me aside and whispered, "Large party of Sioux ahead. Your wagon's in front today. Keep your eye open for a signal from me. When you get it, circle up. If you don't see me and the Indians show up, circle anyway. Don't let 'em get too close before cutting loose. They don't mean to be friends. Telling you so the others won't be worried. Might pass over."

Guess it didn't make any difference how much I worried. We drove until nearly noon before I saw Jeff on a rise, half a mile ahead, waving his arms and galloping toward us.

"Circle up," I yelled. "Sign of Indians. Jeff told me to tell you."

"Ah don't see any Indians," Hallor objected. "Besides who's afraid? Ah'm not. Don't intend to be."

Everybody else was obeying the order but Hallor was stubbornly showing that he was beyond the law in that he despised the source of the order.

Jeff was riding at breakneck speed.

"Hallor," I said, "help now and question later."

"Ah'll see what Moo'field has to say. Looks silly to me."

When Jeff arrived he saw that Hallor was delaying things.

"What's the matter, Hallor? Why haven't you got your wagon chained to the others?"

"From the info'mation received, Ah haven't made up mah mind."

Jeff looked at father, included Stella and swept on to mother and Mrs. Schoolcraft.

"Hallor, I hate to do this but we have to act together on the trail to keep alive. Work him over boys," he called to Beaut Savage and others near by.

They stepped up and slammed Hallor around between them until he yelled for mercy.

"Take keer o' yore wagon, pronto," Beaut Savage said. "And after this, when the order comes tuh circle up, you be the fust one."

The Indians came, whooping like demons. Tall, lean savages on a small grade of horses, leaning down on the off side. Arrows, and bullets from a few rifles, plunked into us. Some of the bullets spattered on heavy wheel rims. Arrows ripped through the canvas tops. Screaming of the wounded and frightened filled the air.

We fired heavily with telling effect. They rode away, leaving us with one family man and a child dead, and three dead oxen. Also ran off three of our best horses.

Five savages lay on the prairie, deserted in their comrades' hurry to get out of range.

"Hallor, go see if they're all dead," Jeff commanded.

He went without a word of protest. "Two still alive, he reported on his return.

"Go back and kill 'em if you want to. Good hunting," Jeff said sarcastically.

"Ah refuse. It's not mah duty," he replied and sulkily walked away.

We buried those of our company who had suffered misfortune. The oxen of that one team were turned with the herd and the family doubled up with another one for want of a driver. The poor widow and weeping children, with the parents of the child who had been killed, cut us deeply. We left the dying Indians on the prairie with their dead comrades and hurried on when it was safe to string out.

The company was short-tempered after that with their nerves tight, expectant of more trouble. Jeff was the only one who didn't seem worried. Jeff and Hallor. Hallor burned with resentment at Jeff. Only fear of the other drivers seemed to keep him from violent action. If Jeff noticed it he gave no indication.

The next day we passed three wagons from a former party, lying mute and forlorn where they had been abandoned. We buried some bones bleaching near them. The evil days had come upon us. It looked as if we never would regain our good cheer and happy spirit. The hundreds of miles ahead seemed filled with misfortune and doubt.

Jeff and I had walked from camp that evening and were talking about the trail ahead when a party of teamsters came up to us, led by Beaut Savage.

"Jeff," Beaut said, "we hates tuh say it but we're a gittin' danged tired of thet mouthy Hallor lordin' it around an' makin' threats what he could do tuh yuh in a fist fight withouten anyone tuh help yuh. Makes us sick. We wants yuh tuh fight him an' lick him, if yuh kin. We ain't got no right tuh ask it, yuh done well by us, but it jest makes us miser'ble."

Looking about him at the various faces, Jeff held out his shapely hands and glanced down at them. "You fellows go back and mind your own business or pick another captain. Satisfied to act as guide. When I can, I pick my own time to fight. None of your damned business as long as it's my business."

Beaut glanced at him reproachfully and turned to his companions. "come on, felluhs. Guess we're barkin' up against the wrong tree. He ain't in a fightin' mood tuh night."

Without another word they began walking away.

"Wait a minute," Jeff called. "Bring Hallor here. Want to talk to him."

Hallor came willingly enough, so willingly that I began to fear if I had underestimated his ability. It would be a calamity if he defeated Jeff.

"Understand you want to fight me, Mr. Hallor, is that right?" Jeff asked him.

"That would give me great pleasuh," my beautiful would-be-brother-in-law replied.

"But I don't get your idea," Jeff wheedled. "You seen to wish me harm without cause. What reason you got for despising me? Haven't I treated you right since we had an understanding in Independence? When you made me take you to the Thornes?"

"Ah nevuh had any reason to like you. Ah do not rega'd you as a propuh man to lead this assembly. You and Mr. Thorne disreg'ded mah suggestion fo' a daily council and yo' mannuh of being captain is too high and mighty. Ah'm not alone in that contention."

"Who else?" Jeff inquired.

"Miss Stella Tho'ne thinks as Ah do on the subject."

"She's only a girl, ignorant of danger. Wouldn't let her influence you in a matter of life and death for this whole caravan, would you?" Jeff turned respectfully to father. "Mr. Hallor seems to be one who sets out on a trail and then lets female influence make up his mind. Delicate subject and I'll keep my mouth shut if you object, considering Miss Thorne's your daughter."

"Go right ahead, Jeff," father replied. "I'll trust your judgment."

In turning to look at father I saw that Stella was disobeying mother's general orders about fights and had sneaked up to listen.

"Thank you, sir," Jeff replied. "I'll fight you, Mr. Hallor, for two reasons. One is that you have challenged me. I'll fight you with guns. Go get yours."

Hallor smiled disdainfully. "That is as Ah expected. Ah have no pistol, and if ah did you must know that you can use one bettuh and that ah would be no match fo' you. Ah desiah to settle it physically, man to man. You can't bluff me."

"Then you must feel that you're a better fighter, sir. If we fight, it will change everything. I've seen you in action. Even saw you kick Blessing the other day. I prefer not to fight. I'll concede the point."

Hallor looked at Jeff patronizingly and said, "Ah am also obliged to demand yo' apology to Miss Tho'ne fo' yo' slighting reference to huh youth and intelligence."

Jeff thought for a moment. He didn't seem in the least abashed or ashamed for his stand.

"On what grounds?"

"On the grounds that she is my fiancée and to be mah wife, someday."

"Whew! Jeff exclaimed. "That's some contract. How did you want to fight, Hallor?"

"Man to man, any way you prefuh," Hallor said cockily.

"All right," Jeff agreed. "You keep me off you and defend yourself; I do the same. Is that it?"

"Physical combat was mah intention. Ah might even choke you to death."

"Give me a chew of long green, Beaut. I'm kind of nervous; might run away," Jeff said.

Beaut handed him a plug of tobacco and he bit off a piece. "Let's go, Hallor. Add my scalp to your belt."

Hallor seemed ready and glad to, thoroughly confident.

Jeff walked around and around Hallor then made as though to stand up to him, but instead he ducked Hallor's wallop and then tripped him. As Hallor fell, Jeff ran up and kicked him gently on the rump. The crowd roared.

When Hallor got to his feet and made a lunge for Jeff, Jeff dodged and ran behind Beaut Savage, peeked out and said "Boo!" Then he ran out and tripped Hallor again, repeating the kick on the rump, gently, barely a shove with his toe. The crowd of men almost died laughing. Poor Stella! Her face was red as a beet. Hallor got to his feet again and stood waiting for Jeff to attack. Jeff ran up to him as though to strike with his fist, ducked Hallor's fist, which fell on empty air, sprang behind him and leaped on his back.

"Get up, horsy. Ah gotta git tuh O'egon," he said and waved to the crowd. "Bum hoss but Ah guess he'll do."

That almost paralyzed Beaut Savage. The tears ran down his face he laughed so hard.

Then Jeff let his long legs drop and trip Hallor, rolling over and over in the dirt with him. Finally Jeff rolled free and lay on his back watching Hallor get to his feet.

Hallor, seeing Jeff down, mouthed a wild cry and ran to jump on him, leaving no doubt of his intentions. Just as Hallor leaped over to land on him, Jeff ejected a long thin stream of tobacco juice that caught him full in the face. Jeff rolled out of the way while Hallor hit the ground so hard it made him grunt.

Hallor got to his feet, completely out of his head with rage. He lunged at Jeff but Jeff wasn't there. Instead he bent low in back of Hallor and grabbed a foot, holding it in the air and running with him, so he wouldn't fall but was forced to hop on one foot to keep from falling. Tiring of that Jeff gave the foot a heave and sent Hallor sprawling.

Hallor was a maniac by that time. He ran for Jeff but Jeff dodged and hopped on his back again, this time crooking an arm under Hallor's chin and using the other arm to press it back against his throat. His legs were around Hallor's waist.

A look of terror swept over Hallor's face for an instant as he realized what Jeff could do to him then.

"Aw, I guess I won't choke him," Jeff drawled. "think I'll give him the Oregon Trail baptism; he needs purifyin'."

Saying that, he glanced at Stella, pulled the tobacco quid from his mouth and smeared it all over Hallor's face. Dropping his feet to the ground, he gave Hallor a big shove and said, "Go wash your face, Buffalo Pete, so you can see to leave more dead animals on the prairie and kick little fifteen-year-old orphans around."

As Hallor staggered in the direction of the Platte, Stella stepped up to Jeff. "I never saw a more ungentlemanly thing in my life, Jeff Moorfield," she said, and slapped him hard on the cheek.

Jeff rubbed his face a moment and then turned the other side to her.

She hauled off and slapped him on that side.

At the second slap, he seized her and kissed her. Then held her at arm's length. "Thank you, Miss Stella. Just wanted to see how a lady did things. Now maybe you'd better go help Buffalo Pete with his face—maybe you'd better trim your lamp before—"

She glared at him a moment, catching his meaning, then ran and helped Hallor down to the water where he could wash the tobacco off his face.

Jeff turned guiltily to father. "You said you'd trust my judgment, Mr. Thorne."

Beaut Savage and the others crowded around.

"Boy, yuh shore did it up brown," Beaut said. "Did me more good than anything I seed in a long time. Reg'lar circus."

Others were loud in their praise, but Jeff was gazing sadly toward where Stella was going with Hallor. "Guess I made two enemies for life now, but it couldn't be helped."

Suddenly he put his hand to his mouth and ran for a clump of brush. I went over to him in a few minutes and found him lying on the ground white and pale.

"You did fine, Jeff," I praised him. "Did us all a favor. What's the matter?"

"Swallowed some of that danged stuff Beaut calls tobacco. Made me sick."

When I returned to our wagons the news of the battle had preceded me and another one was just beginning.

"The idea of Moorfield doing that to Joel, and kissing Stella," mother said. "It's unspeakable. Can't understand you these days, Culver. You should have interfered. What were you thinking of, letting him treat Stella as though she were a common wench of the streets?"

"If Stella hadn't been there, she wouldn't have been mixed up in it. Might not have been a fight. Hallor got what he was looking for. Came off lucky. Was like an ox trying to fight a panther. The big fool. If Hallor says a word to me about it, I'll swing on him myself. Imagining he wanted to be captain! Couldn't even lead in a nursery. Sick of the day I ever agree to let him come."

"You and Moorfield planned it to happen. You two knew Moorfield could make a fool of him. You get him out here in the wilderness and take advantage of him. I feel sorry for Joel."

"Think we planned it?" Father's anger was rising by the moment. "I was afraid for Jeff. Didn't know how it was going to turn out, but was banking on him and I wasn't disappointed. Knuckled to you and Stella long enough. She'll never marry Hallor as long as I live. Rather it'd be anybody else."

"Moorfield, I suppose," mother replied hotly. "You seem to think he's the only one who matters."

"Haven't that much imagination," father retorted.

"Well, I'm for Joel and I'd just as soon Moorfield didn't come near us again. This vulgar thing he did to Joel and Stella has sickened me of him."

Father went white with anger and abruptly walked away, ending that session. I wished Hallor was dead and buried.

Jeff must have heard of mother's declaration for he stayed away from our part of the caravan. When father or I wanted him, we had to hunt elsewhere. Burdick must have heard and told him, and of course it was too delicate a subject for father to go into.

But my two parents were at odds over it and not cordial to each other. Stella was sulky and estranged from the rest of us. The whole atmosphere in our part of the caravan was tense. Susie, the unafraid, summed it up one morning with, "I don't see why that cussed Buffalo Pete had to cause so much trouble. We used to have a good time—once in a while."

Mother slapped her, saying, "Where did you learn to say such things?" 'Cussed' amounted to almost a swearword in our family. Also "Buffalo Pete" was like putting your hand in hot water, with mother.

"Well, that's what they all call him," Susie said, crying. "If he isn't cussed, what is he?"

A few days after that, when we had started up the South Platte, the bruise caused by Hallor's kick became too sore for Bless to sit and drive. I noticed that he had been walking alongside the oxen all day long and seemed to be in pain.

He wouldn't tell me until it became so bad he couldn't keep it up, then I called father and we examined him. We had to talk with Jeff.

Jeff shook his head when he looked at poor little Blessing's injury. "Pretty bad. Bone must be bruised. Have to rig him up in a bed. That where Hallor kicked you, Bless?"

Bless nodded his head silently.

Jeff looked at father and father looked back miserably.

"We'll have to shift things around a little. Hallor will have to drive your third wagon and I'll drive Mrs. Schoolcraft's. Don't know what else to do unless we drop one wagon. Should be scouting, but maybe we can make it to Jim Bridger's. Might pick up a driver there if Blessing isn't well by then. Where's Hallor?"

"Gone after some water for the widow," I replied.

When he came up the trail we were waiting for him.

"Hallor," Jeff said, "Blessing isn't able to drive. You'll have to take Mr. Thorne's third wagon and I'll drive Mrs. Schoolcraft's. Make the change at once."

Hallor slowly started to set his buckets down, suddenly dropped them and at the same instant leaped on Jeff, the one thing Jeff had been avoiding.

With his left arm encircling Jeff's neck in a powerful grip, he struck Jeff in the face with his right fist. Jeff squirmed and twisted, trying to free himself, but the merciless hammering kept on for six heavy blows. Jeff's nose was smashed flat, his eyes were swelling, his cheeks laid open and blood spurted.

I wanted to interfere but knew I didn't dare as long as Jeff was conscious. Hadn't realized Hallor was so powerful. Hatred seemed to increase his strength. No man of ordinary ability could have held Jeff, I knew that.

Jeff finally broke Hallor's grip enough to turn. Hallor let go, stepped back and then struck Jeff a hard blow on the chin. Jeff fell to his knees, and tried to wipe the blood from his eyes.

The whole camp was gathering around and with them came father, the man I was praying would come.

"Stop it, Joel!" he roared. "That man is captain of this caravan!"

But Hallor hesitated only a second and leaped on Jeff who was trying to get up. They rolled over and over on the ground, then broke and both got to their feet. The rolling seemed to have cleared Jeff up a little.

"I'll be damned if I break my fists on you," I heard him mutter through smashed lips.

He dodged Hallor's next swing.

"Beaut!" Jeff commanded. "Keep 'em back until I get through; I'm goin' to kill 'im."

Beaut Savage whipped out his gun. "Back, ever'body! It'll be damned good riddance."

"Then Ah'll kill you mahself," Hallor sneered. "Ah'm fighting mah style now. How do yo' all like it?"

"Stop it, boys! Father commanded. "This is no place to kill each other."

"Stop, hell!" Jeff answered, kind of blurred.

He didn't dodge Hallor's next rush. He stepped right into him, blocking the blows with his arms, never attempting to use his fists.

Hallor tried to dodge, but too late. Jeff's right hand found his throat and with his left defended his own face and body the best he could, taking some of Hallor's blows.

Hallor flung himself around, trying to shake off that terrible clutch, while Jeff's eyes glittered out from between swollen slits. And his face was a terrible sight, battered beyond recognition.

With bulging eyes and a look of terror, Hallor gave a final terrific effort and then began to sag to his knees.

"Culver, stop him!" mother screamed. "He's murdering him!"

"Father, do something!" Stella begged. "Don't let it go on!"

"Jeff's captain of this outfit," father snarled back at them. "Can't do a damned thing."

Women were screaming. Children were crying. Only the grim-faced men were quiet.

Suddenly Jeff let go his hold, seized Hallor by the hair of the head and seat of the pants. Lifting him high in the air he threw him about ten feet. Hallor landed in a lump and lay still.

With a wild Indian whoop, Jeff whipped out his belt knife and began creeping up on him like an animal after its prey. At last he sprang on him, knife gleaming. I tried to shut my eyes but couldn't tear them away from the horrible sight.

He raised the knife high above his head and brought it down. Just before the knife plunged into Hallor's throat, Jeff seized a lock of his victim's hair and sliced it off.

He got to his feet. Walking over to Stella, he tossed the hair down in front of her, saying, "If that white Cayuse crosses my trail again this trip, I will kill him. If you own him, take care of him."

Jeff began walking away, rubbing his cramped hand and working it to limber it up. He stopped and looked at Hallor. "He'll come to pretty soon. Take his things out of Mrs. Schoolcraft's wagon and move it up in the lead."

We found some water and began washing the blood off Jeff. His nose was smashed flat at the bridge.

"Pretty bad, Jeff," father said, with a look of horror. "Wish we had a doctor. Doggone, I sure do."

Beaut came up to us. "Christ, Jeff! Yore face's all beat tuh hell. We got tuh fix that nose or yuh cain't ever git yore wind right ag'in."

"You know how, Beaut?" father asked hopefully.

"Shore. Hurts like hell. Had a squaw work on me once. Ain't I a beauty?"

Beaut's nose was straight and even.

"Don't believe me, huh? Fetch me a gal with long slim fingers an' I'll show yuh."

"Go get Stella!" father ordered me.

"No, Mr. Thorne. Don't. Don't make her suffer," Jeff begged. "She hates me enough now."

"Go get her! Tell her to leave that worthless hunk alone and hurry up."

I hurried to Stella. "Father wants you," I said.

"What for?"

"Beaut's going to work on Jeff's nose and needs some long slim fingers."

She looked at me searchingly and said, "His nose is smashed terribly, isn't it? I'll help if I can."

Jeff squirmed in misery when he heard us coming. His eyes were swollen shut by that time. "Don't pick on her, Mr. Thorne," he objected again.

Beaut pulled Jeff over on his back. "Sit on his waist, Eddie, whiles I hold his head so he cain't move."

"Don't need to hold me. I can stand it," Jeff said.

"Thorne, cut some cottingwood twigs 'bout the size of this purty gal's little finger whiles I watch things. Girl, you take your little finger an' reach up there an' press them bones out, gentle like. Your palm up. Feel yore way along. Wipe them tears outa yore eyes so's yuh kin see. Guess I better trim that fingernail down close."

After trimming the nails on her right hand to the quick, Beaut broke off a small stick and put it in Jeff's mouth. "You kin bite on that an' breathe at the same time, Jeff. Now, girl, git at it!'

Stella gingerly pushed her finger into Jeff's left nostril.

"Further up!" Beaut commanded. "Till yuh feels bone, then git under it and push up."

"For goodness' sake!" she moaned, tenderly feeling the smashed part. "*That* must be broken bone."

"Easy like, girl. Keep goin'." He turned to the audience that was collecting. "The rest of you birds clear out. This ain't no circus."

"Ah! Now I see how it goes," Stella said. "But the small part of my finger isn't long enough."

"Keep going'. The front part'll push back up."

"It'll hurt him too much."

"Cain't help it. Got to be done."

Sweat rolled off poor Jeff's forehead. Not a groan came from him. But he bit on the stick and breathed hard.

Stella nerved herself. "I'm clear up to where there isn't any more broken bone, I think."

"Fine. Now press up at the end of yore finger as yuh pulls it out, slow an' easy."

Beaut grabbed a twig from father's hand, measured it on Stella's other finger, rounded off the ends and gave it to Stella. "Push it up there, bark an' all. That's balm in the bark. Stops poison. Stock eats it an' gits fat. Nothin' like cottingwood bark."

She quickly shoved in the round plug to support the broken bone.

"Now, hurry up an' git the other'n."

Which was a repetition of the first operation.

"Go wash yore hands, now, girl. Yuh did purty good," Beaut said when the other twig was in place. "Week, mebbe, we kin take 'em out. Buffaler steak on his eyes tuh night an' he kin see in the mornin'."

Before she got up from kneeling beside him, Stella cast a long searching glance at the horrible-looking Jeff. Taking a small white handkerchief from her blouse, she leaned over and wiped the blood from the corners of his mouth. Then smoothed the hair back from his hot forehead. As she did so, tears, of which she was unconscious, dropped gently down on Jeff's face. With a light pat on his forehead, she said, barely loud enough to hear, "I'm glad you didn't kill him." Getting quickly to her feet she hurried away.

Jeff's hands flew to his face. Digging at one of his eyes, he pried it open and watcher her until she was out of sight.

"God!" he breathed. "Keep water off my face for a while!"

CHAPTER 7

After buffalo steak was applied and left on Jeff's eyes all night, he still couldn't quite see when morning came.

"Camp here another day," he ordered. "Fix harnesses. Look at reaches. It'll help us when we can go." He talked like he had a bad cold in his head.

"Damn it, Jeff, you kin ride even if yuh cain't see. Some of the wimmen kin drive on this kinda ground. Caravan's all right," Beaut Savage protested. "No use wastin' a whole day. If we hits tough goin' we kind stop."

"No," Jeff said and that's where the argument ended.

He sat in the sun most of the day and let it bake down on him. By afternoon his wounds had turned a brownish black. Bleeding had stopped entirely and he was a worse-looking sight than ever.

Towards evening his eyes had begun to open, when he tried hard. We sat near him, talking to keep him company, well in front of the camp where it wasn't so noisy. I saw a rider approaching from the west.

"Who's that coming?" I said. "None of our men been out that way, have they Beaut?"

"Nope. Looks familiar though," Beaut replied.

When the rider came closer, Beaut said, "Thet's Jeb Brocker, one of Jones' cutthroats. Wonder what he wants. Wasn't thar thet day they wanted tuh hang the kid, Bless Brewster."

"Get some rags and bind up my hands in a hurry!" Jeff ordered.

Stella wasn't far away. I motioned to her. "Let's have some rags, quick, Sis."

She hurried and brought some and was helping us bind up Jeff's hands when Brocker rode up. None knew what Jeff had in mind. "Lay it on about the fight," he had said.

"Howdy," Brocker said, trying to make a show of friendship. "Ain't got a extry reach fur a wagon, hev yuh? Hope they ain't no hard feelin's. Whar's yer capting?"

"Over thar," Beaut said. "Had a hell of a fist fight. Got the tar whaled outen him."

"My hands!" Jeff moaned. "My poor hands!"

Brocker went over and took a long look of pleasure. "God A'mighty! Look at his face! Hands cain't be no worse, kin they?"

Beaut shook his head sorrowfully. "Busted all tuh hell. Won't never throw a gun fur a long time. Mebbe never ag'in."

Brocker looked around with hungry eyes. "Well, yuh gonna let me hev thet reach I asked fur?"

"Don't know. Ain't the capting, myself. Ask him."

Brocker went over to where Jeff was lying and said, "Hey, kin we borry a reach from yuh?"

"My hands! My poor hands!" Jeff muttered.

Shrugging his shoulders, Brocker came back to Beaut. "He don't know anythin'. Shore a hell of a outfit. Why don't yuh take over yoreself?"

"Naw, I cain't do that, Brocker. Just cain't. Go over thar a ways an' wait whiles I jar him loose. The rest of 'em ain't 'lected me capting, yet."

Brocker walked away and looked our camp over with busy eyes. Beaut went up to Jeff and yelled, "Hey, Moorfield, wake up! A man wants tuh borry a reach." He appeared to listen and then said, "Talk louder. Cain't hear yuh." Then he got down near Jeff to listen. In a few seconds he got up in disgust. "Hell!" he called to Brocker. "Yuh kin hev a reach fur yore wagon anyway. We got a extry one. Even go with yuh tuh help yuh git it thar. Eddie, you git one an' hurry up about it. Bring my hoss an' one of the capting's pack hosses. Tell my fam'ly I'll be back tomorrow."

Leaving Beaut to entertain Brocker, and keep him from nosing around, I did as he said. When I came back they were talking like two cronies and Jeff was still groaning. He'd switched to talking about his face and must have meant part of it. But I noticed he wasn't interfering with the conversation.

When Beaut was leaving, he said, so Brocker could hear, 'If he ain't no better by mornin' load him in a wagon an' come on. Mebbe you simple buzzards'll learn a thing or two without a capting. Meet yuh on the road. Got tuh help Brocker git this reach tuh his camp so's they kin git fixed up. Tell muh wife."

"What's up, Jeff?" I said, when they were well on their way.

"Jones crossed the Platte two days ago. Knows the trail as well as I do. Either has cholera or aiming at us. Beaut'll find out. Been thinking a lot about it. We'll travel slow tomorrow. Tell your father. What you got on my hands?"

"One of Stell's petticoats. Couldn't find anything else in a hurry. Who'll drive Hallor's wagon? And yours?"

"What's the matter with Hallor? He didn't get hurt any."

"Hands 're all swollen up."

"I'll drive my wagon," he said slowly. "and Hallor'll drive his. Or else I'll shoot him. No drivers to spare. Next time he'll know better. Let me alone, now. Getting' sleepy for a change."

I was walking away when he stopped me. "Here. Better take these back to your sister," handing me the rags that bound his hands.

Jeff led with the widow's wagon next morning and if it pained him any, no one could tell. The Trail was dusty. By noon we were covered with it, as usual. Jeff's face was indescribable. In the sun of the day before, the raw spots had dried in almost one large ugly patch. Now, covered with dust which couldn't be washed off, he looked like a man's body wearing a head from a Grecian fable. Part of the time he walked. When the going was easy he sat on the wagon with Mrs. Schoolcraft.

Stella rode with Hallor on our third wagon and drove for him when the oxen needed pulling into line. She felt sorry for him. From my few glimpses back at them Hallor seemed to be talking without letup. Part of the time they were arguing about something. And once, when Jeff had given the lead line to Mrs. Schoolcraft, and was standing looking at the wagons as they passed him, as he often did to see how they were holding up, Stella hastily gave the oxen line to Hallor. If Jeff saw Hallor's disobedience of his orders, he said nothing about it.

Shortly after noon we saw Beaut coming back. Jeff halted us in a good spot and waited, calling father and me to be present for what Beaut had to report.

"Better camp hyar till we talks it over, Jeff," Beaut said when he dismounted.

"Find out something?" Jeff asked.

"Plenty. We better talk private like. Jest you an' me."

"No," Jeff said, when father and I made as though to walk away for politeness' sake. "Let the Thornes hear it."

"Wal," Beaut began, "Cutter Jones knows we loaded up plenty stuff in Independence, thanks tuh you folks. Figgers he's goin' tuh run short, mebbe, on the fur end. Got us blocked whar we got tuh fight or cross the Platte, mile or two behind 'im, or divvy up some grub. If yuh're still alive when we gits thar, Jeb Brocker's goin' tuh find a way tuh kill yuh, so's this outfit won't have no guide. That ain't all. Some of the young bucks knows they's single women in this crowd an' they craves female company. Cutter figgers Thorne's got plenty money with 'im. Guess thet's my story. Got some friends in the bunch what told me, far's they knowed." He was silent a moment. "Jeb Brocker got a eyeful of Thorne's oldest gal, when he war here for the reach they didn't need. Spotted yore Crusader stallion, too."

"Hear him say anything, Beaut?" Jeff asked. "Talk's cheap in a game like that."

"Plenty likker, Jeff. Heerd him say she'd be his floosie afore they got tuh Oregon. "Long with a good hoss."

"Just drunk talk," Jeff passed it off.

Which angered me. No one could talk about my sister that way. "I'll settle with him for that, personally," I said.

Beaut looked at me in scorn. "Thet's jest what Jeb Brocker'd like best—after he puts Jeff down, when Jeff shows his hands ain't been hurt."

"What do you say, Mr. Thorne? Cross, divvy up, buy him off, or fight?" Jeff asked father.

"Well," father answered slowly, "I never was much on going out of my way to hunt trouble. You're captain, Jeff. What do you say?"

"We'll belly up to 'em and see what they do about it," Jeff replied.

"They's jest one little doubt thar, Jeff. We ain't none of us seen yuh shoot. Brocker was drunk in Independence the mornin' we took Bless Brewster away from 'em. Moughta been different. Looked fur trouble afore now."

"Brocker better'n Jones?" Jeff asked.

"'Bout a standoff. Yuh bluffed Jones once. Yuh kin do it ag'in, but Brocker don't bluff."

"Then it's between Brocker and me? Who you backin', Beaut?"

"I wants tuh back yuh, Jeff, but it looks scary as hell."

"How far ahead are they?"

"We'll go on five miles and camp. Meet 'em tomorrow morning. If we get the run put on us now, it's a long way to Oregon." With that he went back and started his oxen. The rest of us followed, we didn't know where. I felt panicky.

Just as we were about to leave at sunrise next morning, Stella happened to pass Jeff. "How is your nose?" she asked him.

"Not bad," he mumbled. "Hurts a little. Feels like the bones are knitting."

She stepped closer and looked. "Swelling's going down. You'll be a great sight by the time you can shave again," she said, laughingly.

Jeff might as well have been wearing a mask. He couldn't smile and his eyes gave the appearance of glaring. "Never was much to look at," he said in a harsh voice.

Stella couldn't help stiffening a little at his unexpected harshness. "Seems to me, if you're going to fight so much, you ought to learn how to use your hands and not trust to brute strength," she said with a critical look.

"Maybe I will sometime," Jeff said.

Just then Beaut Savage, with a group of the other drivers, came up and Stella left. I stayed to listen.

"We decided we don't want no fight, Jeff. Even if we has to divvy up. Think it's better. When Cutter Jones an' Brocker find out we fooled 'em about yuh yestiddy, they'll be plenty hostile."

"Where does that leave the Thornes? And me?" Jeff asked him.

"We'll git along some way, Jeff, if we takes it easy. We got friends in the other bunch. Mebbe we kin work out a deal."

Jeff's eyes moved from face to face, slowly, scornfully. "We picked a fine bunch to go to Oregon with," he said. "Back to your wagons! Let's git movin'!"

"Looks bad," father said when I told him, "glad the women don't know what's up. Brocker sounds worse'n Jones."

"It's all bad," I said. "After all, what do we know about Moorfield? Didn't seem bothered by what Brocker said about Stella."

"Noticed that, too. If he fails us we're lost, with this bunch of coyotes," father said, looking pale and worried. "Too small an outfit to go anywhere or do anything by ourselves. Even if we could pull away now. Be careful what you say around our wagons."

Jeff had a few more words with Beaut and then we started. Without a halt we pulled up to Jones' camp, where the river swung in close to a steep bank and there wasn't room to go around. When they saw us coming, they made room for us to pull up in a string alongside of them. And there Jeff stopped the lead schooner, just as I prayed he would keep going and there might not be any trouble,

"Hi, Jones!" Jeff called as best he could. "Here we are."

"Hi, thar!" Jones yelled back. "Glad ye're j'inin' up with us." Brocker was standing near him.

A small noise of protest ran along our caravan. Jeff got down and began walking over to Jones and Brocker. Beaut did the same. Father and I were moving to join them when mother yelled, "Culver Thorne, what does this mean? This caravan was doing all right by itself!"

"Give 'em fits, Mrs. Thorne!" a woman by the name of Wamsutter screamed. "We won't j'in with that mess of starvin' hoptoads. The damn fool men're crazy if they think we will."

"We ain't either hoptoads!" a woman of Jones' camp screamed back at her, running over to pull her off the wagon.

But she didn't need to pull. Women from both sides came to help. In a half a minute it sounded like the day of reckoning.

Mother and Stella sat spellbound at the battle mother had started. I ran back to them just as mother said, "Come on, Stella! Our side's getting licked in a righteous cause."

Father was right behind me. "Get back on that wagon!' he yelled. "You women lost your minds?"

"No, but you men have!" mother screamed at him, with her chin thrust out and still heading for trouble."

"Grab Stella!" he said to me and at the same instant he seized mother. We put them back in the wagon by sheer force of masculine strength. By that time the husbands of all the wives were trying to do the same and finally succeeded.

Father and I hurried back to where Jeff was standing by himself watching everything. Since he looked like the first crack of doom, anyway, I couldn't tell what he was thinking.

Brocker came over to us. Beaut Savage went up to Jones and began talking.

"Looks like yuh ain't got much control of yer mob, Capting." He laughed in a sneering way as he said "Capting."

"Looks like it," Jeff agreed.

"Guess, mebbe, yuh ain't much of a capting," Brocker said.

"Guess not," Jeff said mournfully.

"Notice thet good-lookin' floosie didn't git messed up none."

"That's my sister," I blurted. "You can't talk about her that way."

"Oh, cain't I? We'll see about thet."

"You started in to pick a fight with me, didn't you, Brocker?" Jeff asked him.

"How'd yuh know my name was Brocker?"

"Saw you at my camp the other day," Jeff replied, shifting a few steps over, away from the wagons. "What does 'floosie' mean in your language? Been wantin' to ask."

"Gun fight!" one of Jones' rowdies yelled. "Brocker an' the mud-faced hyena over a floosie. Hooray for Brocker!"

Father grabbed me by the arm and we hurried back out of the way. The whole layout grew still. Brocker was enjoying his importance and waiting for things to quiet before he answered.

"You didn't answer me, Brocker," Jeff said, in his dubbed-off way, on account of the splints in his nose.

"Floosie means whore in my language, Mud Face," he yelled loudly. "If it makes yuh mad, go fur that gun yuh're wearin'."

Jeff's gun gave a whanging roar while Brocker's was still swinging up. Brocker slumped to the ground with a loose, slack-jawed look, blood staining the left side of his shirt. At the same instant, Jeff wheeled and covered the bunch of rowdies.

He walked up to them. "Who yapped his head off over here? Step out!"

Not one moved.

"Mr. Thorne! Lift their guns while I keep 'em covered! Eddie, go and see how Beaut is coming along!'

All of a sudden I thought of Jones and looked around for Beaut. Jones was lying flat, while Beaut sat on him with the muzzle of his revolver in Jones' mouth. The sense of relief that came over me was vast and fervent. Jones' men, all those in favor of him were caught by surprise at the quick fall of their leaders and our drivers were quick to cover them.

"Knocked him down, Jeff. Say the word an' I'll blow his brains out," Beaut bellowed.

"Let him have it, Beaut!" Blessing yelled from his bed in the widow's wagon. "Better late than never."

"Tie 'im up. We won't kill 'im till morning," Jeff said.

Jeff was complete master of the situation. He went to where a number of Jones' married men were in a group. "Any you fellows want to palaver on how you stand."

"Beaut Savage kin vouch for me," one of them said.

"Me, too," came from several others.

"Mr. Thorne," Jeff said, "tell Beaut to come here You stand guard over Jones till we get through."

"Any good men in this bunch, Beaut?" Jeff asked him when he came.

"Ten of 'em," Beaut said. "They wasn't in favor of hangin' the kid but they was loyal tuh Jones. Be jest as loyal to you if yuh give 'em a chance."

"Step out!" Jeff ordered. 'Call their names, Beaut! Pull your wagons into our string and get ready to travel. Rest of you will have to stay back of us. Figure on keeping Jones for a while. You can follow. You won't get lost."

One of those not chosen said, "Give us Jones. We don't want tuh go with yuh."

Jeff shook his head, "Beaut, soon as your ten families get ready, yell out. Throw Jones in one of the wagons."

Shortly after we were on the move, Jones' caravan started. We camped on the Platte about an hour before sundown.

"Pitch a tent out there for Jones," Jeff ordered. "Hallor, you guard him tonight."

Joel looked at Jeff and said, "Ah'm daid on mah feet—"

Jeff whipped out his gun and shot in the dirt about six inches in front of Joel's right foot. "You son-of-a-bitch, come alive!"

I went with Jeff to Mrs. Schoolcraft's wagon.

"Why do you think Hallor objected to changing wagons that time, Eddie?" Jeff asked me. "Isn't he supposed to be in love with your sister?"

"Got me there, Jeff. Might love my sister but he doesn't think much of some of the rest of us. Might be the reason."

"Might be," he grunted but didn't seem satisfied.

The widow quickly had her camp in shipshape order and she was as neat as a pin. I liked her better every time I saw her. A few nights before, I had come in from standing guard to get some extra help on account of the oxen bellowing and shifting around. She was brushing her hair. It was a warm night and she was ready for bed with a loose shawl draped over her shoulders. Her hair glistened in the soft moonlight. I marveled at the picture she made as the shawl slipped with the motion of her arms and exposed her milk-white breast. She hadn't heard me approach until I said, "Fine evening, isn't it, Mrs. Schoolcraft?" "Goodness, but you scared me," she said, clutching the shawl about her.

I envied Jeff his job. A man would lose a lot of sleep though, staying awake to watch.

"Howdy, Eleanor!" Jeff greeted her. "Got any supper on for a hungry wolf?"

Her eyes lighted with pleasure as she said, "It'll be ready in a few minutes."

I noticed that she showed a few marks of the battle mother started.

When we were eating supper, mother glanced over to where Hallor was guarding Jones. "Poor Joel. Moorfield's pretty mean to him. Seems to me his conscience would bother him after killing a man like he did today. Just because the man was smart enough to see the kind of a woman he wanted at first glance. Of course, he must have been a low-downer but he didn't deserve to be killed that way."

I threw a quick glance at father. His eyelid dropped just a trifle, meaning, "*let me handle it.*"

"What woman was that, Grace?"

"The widow. It's all over camp. All the other women know. Where have you been all day?" Mother favored him with an indulgent look. "You'll learn after a while that you can't fool me, Culver, on people like that."

Father almost strangled on the coffee he was drinking. "You're pretty sharp, honey. Got to admit it."

Mother straightened up a little. "Well, I called the turn when Moorfield led us into that mess, didn't I? Only I didn't think things would happen so fast. Funny. This caravan life must change a person. I felt just glorious today and wanted to pull hair out in great wads."

Father laughed loud and long. It did my heart good to hear him, remembering how worried he had been.

"You ladies were seeing eye-to-eye with Jeff and didn't know it. He wanted to fight, right from the start," he said when he quieted down.

"Well, we saved him the trouble," mother declared, with a half grin. "I started it and my amazons finished it."

"Wish Jeff would come to our camp once in a while," Susie said wistfully. "He looks horrible right now, but I like him awfully well."

"Jeff heard that your mother didn't want him to come around us any more. Be a long time before he does," father said.

"We seem to be getting along in good shape in his absence,' mother snapped back at him. But I could see her heart wasn't in it.

When the camp was groaning into wakefulness next morning father came over to my tent. "Told your mother the whole truth about yesterday," he said. "We decided to let Stella keep on thinking like it was last night. Don't forget."

I looked over to Jones' prison when I got up. Jeff was on his way there. Hallor lay stretched out on the ground. Jeff stopped and looked at him then kicked him on the feet. While Hallor was waking up, Jeff looked in the tent.

"Jones still here?" he thundered, the best he could the way he had to talk through his mouth, same as when you pinch your nose.

"Why, Ah,—Why, ah must've gone to sleep," Hallor said in surprise. And then lamely, "He was in there."

Jeff looked up and down at Hallor for about ten seconds, then mounted his horse and headed off across the prairie. Hallor, terrified at the consequences of his act, walked away by himself and stayed until Stella brought him to the fire and made him drink some coffee and eat some breakfast.

Jeff returned in a short time and stopped at our camp.

"They sneaked in and cut Jones loose early last night. His outfit swung way around and got ahead of us." Saying that, without a glance at Joel, he left us.

Stella followed him out of earshot and asked him something I couldn't hear.

"What did you say to him, Sis?" I whispered when she came back with her face a dull red.

"Asked him not to punish Joel for going to sleep."

"What'd he say?"

"Said, 'I won't, if you promise to give him a good spanking.'"

Mother was silent and thoughtful all morning.

The various drivers expressed themselves about Hallor and how he should be punished but when Jeff said, "No," that's all there was to it.

Later, when I happened to catch Jeff by himself, I said, "How come you were so easy on Hallor for letting Jones get away?"

"Wanted him to get away," Jeff said. "Hallor's the only one'd let him, without me telling him to. Keep that to yourself."

All the time I thought it was love for Stella. But I told father and he laughed about it.

"That Jeff is sure a corker!" he said.

CHAPTER 8

Though we were on the Trail again bright and early and pushed hard all day long, we saw no sign of the Jones' caravan. They had the incentive they needed and were making the most of it. The weather was hot and dusty.

Jeff halted at a suitable place, an hour earlier than usual. Instead of giving orders to arrange the wagons for night camping he started off across the prairie on foot.

"Mother!" Stella cried. "Something's the matter with Jeff!"

"Culver! Eddie! Get to him before he falls!" mother screamed.

Father and I reached him and took him by the arms just as he began to stagger.

Mother and Stella rushed up, with others running to give help.

"What the matter, Jeff?" mother asked tenderly. "Your head hurt?"

He looked at her with staring bloodshot eyes. "What matters now, Mother Narcy? She's dead. Nothing to fight but death. Not even Cayuses to blame."

"He's dying on his feet," mother declared. "Delirious. Get him down. Put up a tent while I get busy. One of you men build a fire. Smother it for charcoal."

Beaut had come up in wild-eyed terror as the word quickly passed back to him. "God, lady! We got tuh save him!'

"His face's turned bad," mother said. "Eddie, run get a big fish hook and bend it straight. Bring me some water to wash with. Was afraid that job was too good to be true."

"It was comin' good, ma'am, till tuhday. Was watchin' him," Beaut said mournfully. "Jest like I did that time."

"Overheated," mother answered. "Take his shoes off. Loosen his clothes. Hurry up with that charcoal." She looked around anxiously. "Need clean rags to cool and put on his face, too. Stella, run see what you can find!"

Stella brought what she could, and other women brought what they had to offer.

Mother shook her head. Won't do. Dusty. Not soft and clean enough. Seems to me I ought to have something." She thought a moment. "Get our trunk out of the wagon."

As other preparations moved along, we brought mother's trunk and set it down near by. She opened it gingerly and began digging. "That's it," she said, bringing up something carefully folded and wrapped in paper. "Bright and clean and soft. We'll take what we need from it."

"What is it, Stell?" I whispered.

"Mother's great linen tablecloth," she whispered back.

Then I knew. A carefully treasured wedding present and one of the delights of her heart.

Mother set the lid of the trunk down. "Keep it covered till I need it," she said, without a look at any of us.

With Beaut and Wamsutter each holding one of Jeff's legs, father and I each an arm, and a man named Singleterry with a firm grasp in his hair to keep his head still, mother went even further. "Put a roll under his neck to tilt his head back. Stella, you sit here and hold this stick in the corner of his mouth to keep it open. Pull his tongue back if it gets down his throat or he'll smother. Keep this stick in, so he won't bite your hand off."

Deftly she hooked the splints with the fish hook and threw them to one side. "Goodness, I forgot something. One of you men, a thin twig about six inches long."

Gong to the trunk she cut two small pieces from her tablecloth. To each of these she fastened strong linen thread. A man brought the twigs she had ordered.

"Charcoal's ready, ma'am," one of the men at the fire sang out.

Mother was cool and calm. "Bring it over, please. Give me a clean knife."

She shaved off specks of dirt that clung to the charcoal and then carefully pulverized what she needed. With the twig she pushed the two line pieces up Jeff's nostrils. "Have to have something to pack the charcoal against," she said. Then she pushed in charcoal, tied a bandage under his nose to keep it there, and tossed the twig into the fire.

"Hold him sitting up, now. Better dig down a post and tie him to it. Make it a cross and tie his arms. Won't be able to hit his nose then. Charcoal'll draw off the poison. Couple of hours, we'll do it again. Tie a piece of wood in his mouth to keep it open."

"Gosh, ma'am, but you're a wonder," Beaut said admiringly.

"You're pretty good yourself, Beaut," mother replied. "Looks like his nose has set in fine shape."

"Thank yuh, ma'am. Thank yuh," Beaut replied humbly.

Then began the all night vigil. Two applications of charcoal pulled off the obstructed poison and gave Jeff relief. Removing the second application, mother swabbed in sweet oil and left his nose so he could breath through it. Stella held cool cloths to his head all night.

People milled around, unable to sleep while there was doubt.

At Jeff's usual waking time his eyes flew open while Stella was applying a fresh cloth. He looked around in amazement at his position. "What's up? He asked in the first natural voice he had used since the fight.

"You became delirious," Stella said. "Mother took you in hand."

"All right now. Untie me. Time to travel."

"Mother!" Stella called. "Jeff's awake now and wants to get loose."

He winked at me when she said his first name. "Worth it, if I get called by my front name by a pretty gal."

Stella looked at him earnestly. "Somehow, it's awfully hard to stay mad at you. You get in too many scrapes."

Mother came just then. "My, but you look a lot better, Jeff. Untie him, Eddie, since he's conscious again. You scared the life out of us. Must have been in terrible pain."

"Pretty bad yesterday," he said. "Feels good to be able to talk right again." He rose and stretched his legs. "Better hit the grit hard today and make up for yesterday."

"We didn't lose much time yesterday," mother said. She handed him six pieces of linen. "You'll need these. Don't get overheated again. Otherwise, I think you'll get along fine."

"Thank you," he said, taking the handkerchiefs.

In the dry, hot days that followed, Jeff's face and nose healed rapidly. The Trail seemed to do that to people as a recompense, I guess, for the many other trials that were constant. Even Blessing improved and began begging to be allowed to drive but Jeff wouldn't let him.

Jeff had been over the country twice before. The route was up and down as it had been most of the way, only worse. In places we had to rough-lock our wagons for brakes and in others we hitched up extra oxen to pull the steep pitches. We drove along edges and shuddered. These days he ground his words out like they were strained through sand. His face was gray and tight. His extra sharp eyes roved over the wagons and his tongue was like a whip when he saw someone slacking in care of his schooner or livestock. Hallor hated Jeff but feared him more. Jeff's tolerance of him when he went to sleep and let Jones escape seemed to increase his hatred.

We came to where the Platte divided into north and south branches. Jeff led us up the South Platte to a fiord and then we headed for Fort Laramie.

At the fiord, Jeff said, "I'll be damned. Jones is passing up Laramie. That's his tracks on up south Platte. There's going to be hell to pay in that bunch before they hit Bridger's Fort."

"Short on grub?" I asked.

"Yes. Poor devils. Didn't need to be that scared of us. Maybe Jones knows what he's doin'."

We hit Fort Laramie July 15th and spent one day there, repairing and buying a few supplies.

Our road followed up the North Platte for better than a hundred and fifty miles. Sometimes we camped far back from the river on account of the rugged country. Some of those camps were bad for lack of water. Some of them were delightful, with meadows and good water from creeks or springs.

We left the North Platte and in three days hit the Sweetwater River, filled with trout and living up to its name. Finally we began the long slope up to South Pass. Jeff kept on staying at the widow's wagon.

She wasn't playing favorites between Jeff and Hallor. Her smiles fell on each of them.

Jeff halted us at noon one day, between two low hills. "You people are now on South Pass," he said. "From here the water flows into the Pacific Ocean. Next big spot is Fort Bridger."

Men whooped and yelled while women cried in relief. They sang songs and had an interval of pathetic happiness. It looked easy from there on. Jeff let us have an hour and then gave orders to travel. That night we camped on a small stream.

"Jeff, I've long wanted to apologize for an offense I might have given you through hearsay," mother said to him, catching him near our camp in an unguarded moment. "It was the foolish nervous clacking of a weary woman; but if you don't come and eat with us this evening I'll have your scalp before we arrive in Oregon."

That from mother. Speaking of scalping like an old-timer of the plains. She was brown and weather-beaten, dried like a bean, but more virile than any of us had ever seen her.

"Thank you, Mrs. Thorne," Jeff said with a smile. "Just take you up on that. When do we eat?"

"Right away and don't you meander off and leave us in the lurch. We want your company on this happy evening. Bring Mrs. Schoolcraft with you."

When Jeff sat down with us, Susie said, "Gee willikers! Like old times again having Jeff come to see us."

Might have been my imagination but I thought I saw Jeff and Stella exchanging fleeting glances; although Jeff was in a soft, easy mood and attentive to Eleanor Schoolcraft.

Hallor was his usual mouthy self. He paid as little attention to Jeff as he could.

After supper we sat around a fire, for comfort against the chill in the high altitude, and talked. It was now the tenth of August. Due to lack of water and resting Sundays and other days, breakdowns and fights, we hadn't made much better than thirteen miles a day, but our caravan was in good shape.

"From here on to Bridger's Fort we'll be near water part of the way," Jeff said. "Our course goes to the Rendezvous on Green River, about seventy miles, where we'll cross. Shouldn't be much of a crossing. If there isn't any way to ferry, we can swim the stock and float the wagons. Ought to be enough rafts there to take the women and children over."

"Can I drive from here, Jeff?" Blessing asked hopefully. "I feel all right now."

"Yes, guess so," Jeff replied thoughtfully. "You can drive the Schoolcraft wagon and I'll scout. How about it, Eleanor? Will you cook for both of us when I'm around?"

"Certainly, Jeff. You ought to know I would without asking," she answered quickly. "But don't take too many chances wandering off by yourself. Something might happen to you."

He shrugged his shoulders. "Don't worry about me. Save it for this outfit. I can take care of myself."

Hallor didn't like that arrangement. Nothing that he said or did betrayed him, but I could tell by the look in his eye—a kind of dull-brown overcastting glint. Thought to myself, "He may be in love with my sister but he likes Eleanor pretty well."

Fires of the caravan reminded someone to talk of the Revolutionary War and how far the country had progressed since then and the great growth it had made. Then talk drifted to the *Declaration of Independence.*

"Some pretty smart men had a hand in that," Jeff said. "They got going and did a big job."

"Thomas Jefferson was chiefly responsible for the drafting of it," Stella volunteered for the enlightenment of the crowd. "He studied the *Great Charter*, drawn up in 1215."

"That's funny," Jeff said. "According to one of Dr. Whitman's books, *Aristotle's Republic* was the main card Jefferson played in that deal."

Stella flushed a blood-red and said no more.

"One of my fo'efathuhs was a signuh. If Ah remembuh well enough he mentioned the *Great Cha'tuh*," Hallor supported Stella's statement.

"Oh, well, what's the difference?" Jeff asked. "A good job anyway. Time I rolled in. Your turn to go on guard tomorrow night, Hallor. You and Burdick, in case I'm not here. Sometimes a scout gets caught out and can't get back in time. Good night. Thanks for the meal, Mrs. Thorne."

"He might be able to lead a caravan, but he hasn't any manners," Stella said to me a while later. "Imagine how I felt at being disputed that way. Before everyone, too."

"You've had him underestimated all the way, Sis, and the jar hurts. You can't tell by looking at a hen how many eggs it'll lay. If you stick your neck out and snap at flies, don't be surprised if you make a mistake and pick a bee."

"Oh, shut up, you pelican! You always side in with him."

"I'm putting my money on *Aristotle*," father observed quietly. "Jeff has a habit of being right. Don't believe he meant to offend you, Stella."

"I don't care whether he did or not."

"You're jealous," I said. "Don't see him bringing you bouquets or playing the guitar on our front door-step."

"If he did I'd set the dog on him. He's as cross as an old bear."

"If you ever have a dog that would bite a man like Jeff, shoot the brute—he's no good," father said with a smile.

Stella flounced away in a pout, after a withering look at both of us, as though Jeff were to blame for everything.

Jeff got us up at the usual hour and after breakfast gave us instructions for the day's travel.

"If I don't show up tonight, I'll see you tomorrow night," he said. "If you see Indians, circle up and look tough."

He didn't show up that evening. When it came time to go on guard duty Burdick was sick and sent word to Hallor.

"Maybe Blessing bettuh go in his place," Hallor suggested.

"Sure, I'll go," Blessing agreed. "Been missing a lot of it. I can make up now."

After standing the all-night watch, Blessing came to me next morning with a troubled look on his face saying, "Wonder when Jeff'll be back."

"Tonight, I guess, Blessing. What's the trouble?"

"Oh nothing. Just want to tell him something."

"Can't you tell me? We're pretty good friends, you and I, or at least we ought to be by now."

"Well, guess I will. Hallor skipped guard until near daylight. When he came back he said he'd kill me if I told on him."

"That's funny," I said. "Danged deucedly funny. Wonder if that skunk took a sleep. Which way did he go?"

"Was off from him about a hundred feet," Blessing said. "Just then the cattle shifted and I had to see what was up. Lost track of where he went. I'm gonna tell Jeff."

"No, don't do it, Bless. Jeff's liable to murder him. Keep quiet and next time we'll watch him. He's up to something. Today is the twelfth. His turn will come again in little over two weeks. Be fine if we could catch that lizard up to mischief of some kind. Let's try it."

"Sure. I'd like to help ketch the big sneak," Blessing agreed.

CHAPTER 9

Jeff rejoined the caravan late that afternoon. He was dog-tired and looked like he hadn't had any sleep for a week.

"Cutter Jones and his outfit came over the pass about a day ahead of us. Big band of Utes roaming around south of them. They'll jump either outfit, but if we're together we can bluff our way through. Jones hasn't any scouts out and doesn't know what he's up against. The Utes are bad. Mean as Bannacks. Big and ornery. Eat dried fruit for supper and we'll keep going until midnight, rest four hours and push on hard as we can. Might get up to them by tomorrow night. I'll make a bed in the widow's wagon and rest while we travel."

Eleanor had plenty of room in her wagon and it sounded like the best thing to do, but Stella and mother didn't like the idea.

"He could have rested in one of our wagons," Stella said. "We could make room."

"What do you care?" I blurted. "Jeff can look out for himself."

"I don't care, but it's the way it looks. Joel thinks it's positively awful and that they should be chaperoned. Bothers him because he's so used to doing the proper thing. He thinks it might reflect on us and that someone should point it out to Moorfield."

"Buffalo wool!" I snorted. "Hallor'd better keep his mouth shut or he'll get hurt. Jeff isn't in an easy mood. The widow's safe with him, besides Blessing will be driving. Even if he wasn't there, I'd trust Jeff from here to kingdom come."

"I don't know," mother said. "She never showed much grief about her husband. Hate to see a scandal start in a moving neighborhood like ours."

As we drove along in the moonlight, I thought about it. The ground was level and took no attention. The oxen followed the lead wagon like sheep. They were tired, but as long as the first wagon driven by Beaut Savage kept going the others would.

The dust was bad but the moonlight was beautiful. Stella was lonely and came back to ride with me and talk.

"The other girls bother me. Wish this trip were over and we could do something else for a change. Dirt, dust, flies, heat, food, ants, everything gets so monotonous this way."

"Love, too, maybe," I answered. "What's the matter? You and Hallor have a fight?"

"No. He's peevish tonight but I'm not going to quarrel with him. Things bother him, too. He's human even if he is so well-mannered."

"From where I sit, a fight between you two would be lovely, but there isn't much chance," I said. "You're a pretty good eyeful and you're still improving. When you get the trail dirt off you you'll be better looking than ever, which increases the threat of Hallor."

"Do you think so, Eddie, really? Do you think I'll ever be fit to look at again? Nobody pays any attention to me in this awful caravan. I haven't any of the usual ways of telling. And I am growing a little. Worries me. My clothes are getting smaller."

"Aw, don't worry about your looks or clothes. You'll always have Hallor. We can shoot a deer in the mountains and Jeff'll make you a buckskin dress—Jeff loves you."

Don't know what made me say that. Things happen that way. I braced myself and waited for the explosion.

"Eddie," she finally said, "I'm a little, spoiled fool. I like Jeff better than I did, but when I'm near him I tighten up like a fiddle string for fear he'll see it." She stopped and I held my breath for more. "But I can't think of a greater calamity than for a person like me to fall in love with a man like Jeff. Even if he does love me, which I doubt, I'd be a hindrance to him. Land isn't anything to him; he thinks in terms of thousands of miles."

"Good thing for us he does," I said. "He's a roamer, though."

"Roamer? Why, he's wild, actually wild. And we don't know a thing about him. He's had a love affair before, too. Besides that, he shot that man Brocker for calling Mrs. Schoolcraft a *floosie*. But I don't mean her. He said something about a girl drowning when he was delirious, when he called 'Mother, Mother Narcy.'"

"Don't know anything about that, but it's time you heard the truth about Brocker," I said. "You were the one he called a *floosie*. Saw you the day he was at our camp and picked you out for special favors. Brocker was the same as dead when Beaut came back and reported. Didn't realize it then, though."

"Eddie, why didn't you tell me this before?" she asked, in a small hurt voice.

"Just a few of us knew it and we didn't want you to know."

"Poor Eleanor. It was a big scandal among the women. They talked and talked. Eddie, you mustn't seek her out so much, either. You act like she's knocked you silly. Might start another scandal."

"No chance for me with Jeff and Hallor in the offing. They're both single, too," I said, getting hot under the collar.

"Slow up," Stella said. "I'll not stay and hear you talk like that."

"Yeh," I said. "I was all right until you thought I peddled all I knew. Next time I'll keep you hanging by the thumbs, you dirty little spoiled brat, with the scrawny hair and leather skin."

But she went anyway. Usually we had a good argument after I dug into her that way. Kind of had some plans regarding Eleanor, and what she said hurt my feelings.

At midnight, when we stopped, I hurried up to Eleanor's wagon to see who Jeff wanted to stand guard. He came out much refreshed and easy of mood. I looked for her but couldn't see her.

"Who stands guard, Jeff?" I asked, still looking.

"I will, and if there isn't any sign of trouble I'll pull out early." He gave me a broad smile. "Goes pretty good, sleeping like that."

I smiled back in a worried way and said, "Good thing you can stand guard. Everybody else must be pretty tired."

"Figured it was a good trick. Had it all planned out," he replied without a wrinkle on his brow.

As soon as I could, I asked Blessing a question. "Where was the widow when we stopped, Bless? Back in the wagon asleep?"

"Yes," Blessing replied innocently. "She said she was tired and could rest in the front end. Soon as it was dark she went back. About dead for sleep myself."

Our wagon was near the widow's the way we camped. I was too tired to sleep and things kept going through my mind. Hearing a noise in her direction I saw her up, making a small fire. After boiling some coffee she took it and headed out in the direction where Jeff was on watch. I went to sleep and didn't see when she came back.

Blessing stopped me for a moment while we were hitching up the oxen. "Got an idea where Hallor went the other night, Eddie. He hates Jeff worse than anything in the world. Think he was laying to shoot him, but Jeff didn't come."

"Sounds like Hallor. We'll watch him plenty from now on. All the Hallors in the world couldn't replace Jeff. If you hear or see anything more, tell me, Bless."

Jeff left before the rest of us got up. We hurried to get going as he had ordered. About noon next day we saw him on a distant rise to the east and waved to him. He waved back and motioned for us to keep going towards Green River. Before we had gone much farther he caught up to us.

"Swing way around toward the river here," he said to Blessing, who was driving the lead wagon. "Find a place to camp."

After camp was made he said, "Some of you men bring shovels and come with me. The Utes hit Jones' outfit pretty hard but they missed us. Went east."

We came to where ten wagons had been plundered and burned. The dead lay about in various positions, all scalped, men, women and children. Not a single gun lay on the battlefield and not a wounded or dead Indian.

"What about the other wagons, Jeff?" father asked him.

"Jones left these for a decoy. Pulled out with only seven. Lost three wagons getting this far. Makes twenty. Told 'em he was going to Fort Bridger for supplies. They could shortcut west and wait for him. Took their money to buy stuff for 'em."

Father looked hard at him. "Jeff, were you in Jones' camp last night?"

"Stands to reason," Jeff answered, shifting uncomfortably. "Couldn't have happened any other way."

Both of us shivered. We knew he had been by the way he evaded father's question.

"Jeff," father said, "please stay near us more. If we lose you, we're lost."

"Maybe so," he said. "But if that bunch of Utes had hit us we'd had a tough time. Have to know what's goin' on. Jones was too busy worrying about us. If he'd had a scout out he'd have seen these Utes coming south from Sublette's cut-off and tried to bunch up with us. The Utes must have been trying to raid the Bannatees and got licked. Makes 'em plenty mean when they find a small bunch of whites."

A short twelve miles took us to the Rendezvous at Green River but it was deserted so late in the season. There were several rafts that Jones had left on the far side. Jeff and Hallor swam over. Hallor was a strong swimmer but Jeff's method was unlike anything I had ever seen. He swam leisurely, half on his back, half side, and used his hands like flippers, pulling his feet forward and kicking back, with his mouth barely out of the water.

"Lazy man's way," he replied when I asked him about it. "One of Fremont's men taught me one summer on a warm lake in Oregon. Later on, it helped me with the Nez Perces."

We found a good campsite across the Green and held up the rest of the day. Mother insisted on Jeff, the widow and Blessing eating with us and we had a merry time. In little over three days we would be at Fort Bridger. We had crossed the Green and things were looking much better. Even the menace of Jones' outfit had been removed.

We were sitting around after supper talking when Susie laughed and said, "Jeff, why don't you marry Eleanor instead of an Indian woman like everybody says you will someday?"

"Susie!" father commanded, "Keep quiet. You embarrass people."

Jeff acted uncomfortable but he turned to Susie and said, "White women either fall in love with a place or hate it, Susie, and it's tough on the man if he happens to differ. An Indian woman's good enough for a rover—she's used to taking orders. Just like you won't be when you grow up, Susie."

"Oh, maybe," Susie replied meekly. "If I loved a man, I'd go where he wanted to. If I loved him enough, I'd camp and roam around with him."

Everybody laughed at the way she said it.

"Most women will do that, Susie," Eleanor Schoolcraft said, with a touch of sadness in her voice. "Sometimes it adds something to life to be in doubt—as to where one is going—and how."

"A propuh man makes a home fo' his wife and stays with huh," Hallor stated with great wisdom.

"What if a man's home is between two oceans, or between a mountain range and the sea? What if a man knows he can't stay in one place when his blood burns to roam? Might as well give up ahead of time on marriage—he's whipped before he starts," Jeff answered him sharply.

"With no more home than a buffalo or an Indian," Stella observed. "What a miserable life that would be."

"Two ways of looking at it," mother said meditatively. "I can see both of them, Jeff's and Joel's. It depends on love and what people enjoy in living."

A shout came from Beaut Savage. "Come over hyar, Jeff, and see what drug in."

They had seen an object crawling toward the river and went to examine the nature of it. It was a twelve-year-old boy, still struggling to live, even though shot and scalped. They poured some whiskey down him for a stimulant and to hear his story, if possible.

"Cutter Jones! Killed my folks and three other wagons! Took all their stuff and stock," he gasped.

"Where was it, boy?" Jeff asked softly. "Where'd he do it?"

"Back there." The boy moved his hand toward the country away from the river. "In a gully. We was goin' to Fort Bridger's for grub. Others took shortcut. Jones and two men shot us. Come to. Started for the river. Guess I'm dyin'. Hope someone gits Jones. Scalped us to make it look like Injuns. Other children too small. Didn't kill 'em. My folks had a lot of money and he knowed it." Small pause and then, "Look for little kids—starvin'."

Jeff took his small grimy hand. "Don't worry, boy. We'll find the little ones and do all we can."

"Thanks, mister. Capting of the other outfit, ain't you?"

"Yes."

"My pop figgered Jones'd git us through. Kill him, will yuh, Capting?"

"Just lie there and rest, big fellow," Jeff said, patting him on the shoulder.

"Awful cold, ain't it? Wish it was bright sunshine again—can't say I ain't game—"

The sun was still shining. Jeff glanced at us and made a sign to bring some covers for him. The boy grew quiet and soon died but his story had been told. He had lived and walked and crawled, with a wound in his breast that ordinarily would have been certain death—besides being scalped.

Jeff's face was bitter and hard. Soon as it was daylight we looked carefully for a trail and found the four wagons with their pitiful story. Five small children were hiding in the brush, terrified, hungry, and almost dead for water. Huddled together like little puppies. Stella and the girls cried their hearts out and wanted to keep all of them. They lingered for a day and died in spite of our efforts. Two were sisters of the boy who wouldn't die until he found help.

When we arrived at the fort and told Jim Bridger, he said, "Got about two days start but we kin ketch 'im if yuh kin spare the time."

Jeff shook his head. "He's done plenty but he can't do much more. Too small a gang. I'm set to get this outfit to Oregon. If he winds up there, we'll do it. If he goes to California, maybe he'll get it later. Killing him won't bring the dead back."

"Mebbe so," Jim grumbled. "Riles me tuh leave it hangin' fire. Yuh goin' tuh California when yuh git tuh Oregon?"

"Might," Jeff replied. "Might go for a look. Jones can wait."

"Ain't a gettin' soft, be yuh, Jeff?"

"Not by a damned sight, but I got a job right now."

"Wal, if yuh ever tangles with 'im, let me know and save me worryin' about it."

"Sure will, Jim. Might catch 'im if we don't lay around your place too long."

We stayed a day and a night at Ford Bridger where we kept the blacksmith shop going steady on the wagons, repairing worn rims, tightening loose felloes and hubs, fitting in new reaches, making extra ones to tie under some of the wagons for use in an emergency. No disaster loomed as big as a broken reach when the train was hurrying to get out of trouble, or trying to get to water before dark. Jeff's idea. As his sharp eyes roved over a wagon he could find more things wrong than a good housekeeper could find dirt, and half measures didn't pass inspection.

We were impressed by Jim Bridger's friendship and respect for him. Even Stella remarked about it.

"Just who is Jeff, anyway?" she asked me. "Jim Bridger treats him like he was a visiting prince of some kind."

"You're jealous because he hasn't glanced a second time at that hunk you brought along. Jim knows a man when he sees one, which is more'n I can say for some women," I growled at her.

"Does make Joel show up in a poor light, I'll admit, but it's because the setting is all in Jeff's favor. Put him in the life Joel is used to and he wouldn't shine very much."

"Now, Sis, be honest. If Jeff liked that kind of a life and wanted to live it, do you really believe he couldn't?"

She thought it over carefully. "Well, maybe not, but I don't like the way he shines around Mrs. Schoolcraft. If he's in love with me, as you say, you must be wrong about him or he wouldn't do that. He must be a double-dealer."

"I suppose you didn't see your little Joel breaking his neck for her when he was driving her wagon? And he's practically engaged to you," I said to defend Jeff.

"Not my little Joel," she objected. "And we're not engaged. Joel never had a right to even indicate it."

Just then mother called Stella. Noticing that Jim Bridger was with her, I went along to listen.

"Stella," mother said, "Mr. Bridger has a little girl going to school at Whitman's Mission. He wants to send her a letter and thought you would write it for him."

"Certainly, Mr. Bridger," Stella said graciously. "Wait till we find some paper."

"I got some, Miss," Jim said and pulled two crumpled sheets from his pocket. "Yore mother says you write right purty and thet's what I wants."

Stella wrote a beautiful hand. One look and Jim kept her busy until they ran out of paper.

"God, but thet's purty writin'! Shore glad I saved my paper fur yuh, miss. Little Chick-a-biddy shore kin read thet, which is more'n some I sent by others, I bet. Thankee, Miss."

The girls sang that night for the Fort's enjoyment and Stella sang solos. Her first solo was *The Last Rose of Summer*. Jeff, in the crowd, stayed and listened for the first time since early in the trip. She sang it even when Buffalo Pete prattled for some silly thing he wanted. Stella singing and Jeff listening was hard to forget.

Trappers with heavy beards and Indians, looking ridiculous in the white man's clothes they'd traded for, loafed about the fort. Some of the trappers were talkative fools with gleaming eyes, waiting for an easy ear in which to pour a useless mixture of sense and nonsense.

Stella with her hair caught at the back of her neck by a long-treasured ribbon, walking with careful, dainty steps within and without the fort, caused many a trapper to look with hungry eyes. Hallor strutted at her side and sounded off, taking time only to breathe.

Though thousands of Mormons had come through there a few weeks ahead of us, Black's Fork was teeming with trout and we almost foundered, as on the Sweetwater. Until then, Jeff had given us little time for fishing.

The second morning we were at the fort, Stella and I were passing Jeff and Bridger when Jeff said, "Where's Kit Carson, Jim?"

"Fightin' tuh steal land from Mexico I reckon. He wanted tuh find yuh the worst way—wanted yuh tuh come with 'im."

"They don't need me. I'm headed back to Oregon. Something else on my mind."

Jim looked at us. As we passed beyond them we heard him say, "Wouldn't be a purty gal with purty brown hair with a walk like a queen, would it, Jeff?"

"Jim, you know danged well I've got to have a woman who can lug a heavy pack and sleep in the rain," Jeff said, loud enough for us to hear.

I could feel Stella's hand tighten on my arm.

Jim Bridger laughed and said, "A purty gal kin change all thet."

"Maybe," Jeff said. "But a trapped beaver'll gnaw his foot off—if he doesn't drown first."

We could have stayed there considerable longer and enjoyed it but Jeff was in a fever to get going.

"Don't want to be in the mountains when the bad weather starts. Rain going down the Snake won't hurt so much, we'll need the water, but it's tough country to Fort Hall after winter sets in."

CHAPTER 10

Going north we feasted on antelope and venison. Wild flowers bloomed in abundance and we experienced our finest days. The road led to the fairyland of pine and spruce Jeff had promised us. It was September and lovely weather. Bees buzzed among the flowers. The oxen worked hard, but everyone enjoyed the evening campings and looked forward to the next one which took us farther into the Oregon Country.

Everyone, that is, except Eleanor Schoolcraft. She was doing poorly. Her wonderful complexion began to fade and her hair lost its luster. She didn't keep herself up in appearance as well as before and seemed to lose her spunk.

I was terribly worried. About the same time, Jeff hunted me up and said, "Eleanor cries a lot. Kind of sick, mornings. Wonder if your mother knows what's wrong? Ask her, but don't say I wanted to know."

When I finally questioned her, mother pressed her lips together in a firm line and replied, "Can't say for certain yet, Son, but it looks suspicious. Hope it isn't what I'm thinking it is."

I passed that on to Jeff, quoting mother.

"Sure hope it's something she'll get over," Jeff replied. "No time to fail now. Maybe she's sicker'n we think. Maybe we ought to ask her what's wrong?"

"I better ask mother again, first," I said.

A few days later I was glad we waited; the scandal of the train broke loose in a torrent of gossip.

Upon rushing to mother about it, she said, in a shocked, critical tone of voice, "Yes, Mrs. Schoolcraft is going to have a baby." She glanced to where Jeff was working on a wagon, trying to get it fixed before dark. "This outrage was brought on too recently, Son, to excuse; I'm terribly disappointed."

So was I when I thought more about it after that discovery.

During the whole trip the widow had kept to herself and minded her own business. Perhaps why so much criticism was heaped upon her in various conversations.

"It's a disgrace to the caravan," Mrs. Pete Wamsutter said piously. Her hair was like yellow, faded grass. "Just knew what'd happen when I saw Moorfield gittin' so thick with her 'fore we came to that massacre the other side of Green River, since then even."

"Well, I don't blame him as much as I do her. He's young and full of life—*she* turned his head," Mrs. Larry Martin added as her part. A short, muscular woman with pinched lips and pale squinty eyes, Mrs. Martin sniffed, "It's a disgrace. She ought to be tarred and feathered."

"Don't you think you're being unjustly hard on her?" mother asked them. "We're all human. Least we can do is treat her kindly. Who are we to sit in judgment? We all sin in various ways. And we practically owe our lives to Jeff."

"I kin forgive most anything but that," Mrs. Wamsutter declared. "Bad example for the children. They all know it."

"Perhaps they wouldn't have known so much if they hadn't heard you talking," mother reproached them mildly.

"Bully for you, Mother," I said to myself. "Keep it up."

"Well, you kin slick over their crime if yuh want, Mrs. Thorne, but I don't intend to," Mrs. Singleterry said, joining the conversation. "I think it's awful—positively awful."

"I'm not condoning them," mother came back at her a little heatedly, "but I don't feel any disgrace. It's their crime. Let it rest with them. 'Let him who is without sin among you cast the first stone.'"

"Mrs. Thorne, do you mean we've sinned that way?" Mrs. Wamsutter asked mother stiffly.

Mother laughed at that and said, "No. I mean its application to the forgiveness and charity we should have for our fellowman."

"That's just like the men folks look at it," Mrs. Martin snapped. "If we don't keep up the respec' of the caravan, who will? They jest laugh and say 'lucky dog' or somethin' just as silly."

Mrs. Singleterry, whose husband was close to forty, made an upset new moon of her mouth. "Do you know what my husband said when I told him? He said, 'The Lord deals an ace once in a while and we can't all have pat hands.' Now what did he mean by that? I don't play cards—it's too sinful."

That was all for that session. Jeff and father were coming and they had to carry it over to another time. Jeff had been out all day. He looked dog-tired and worried.

"Mrs. Schoolcraft is doing too poorly to cook much, Mrs. Thorne, and I'm starved. Mr. Thorne said you had some stew laying around that a man could eat."

"Why certainly, Jeff. One of you girls fix something for him while I finish this dough. Sit down, Jeff, and rest. You look tired."

"Not so tired as I'm mad. What's the matter with the women of this caravan anyway? They act like Mrs. Schoolcraft's got some catching disease. Hasn't eaten since morning. Nothing then. I should be scouting plenty these days, but if I have to stay around to see that she gets help, I will, and this outfit can take its chances."

"Goodness, Jeff, I didn't know it was serious. Keep her wagon near ours and we'll look after her. Nobody'll suffer in this caravan for want of help as long as I'm here."

"Thank you, ma'am," Jeff replied. "Makes me feel better about everything."

Stella was filling a plate for Jeff and keeping silent. I met a burning glance just then and winked at her, to which she paid no attention until she gave me a sign to lead away from the others.

"Did you wink at me on account of what mother said?" she asked belligerently.

"No. On account of what Jeff said. Taking it pretty good, isn't he?"

"You act like it's something to be proud of," she said, turning away from me.

"What do you want to do—let the widow starve? You a witch hunter, too?"

"Course not. I feel sorry for her and want to help. She isn't the only one to blame. I had begun to think better of Moorfield."

"Makes your little Joel look like a saint, doesn't it, honey?"

"Well, he's moral at least, along with some other good points."

"Yes," I agreed. "Almost too good for this earth. Wish he'd crawl into a hole and pull it in after him."

"If he does I'll go with him, after what I've endured on this trip," she said bitterly, and joined the others.

Jeff finished eating and excused himself, giving me the sign to come and talk. Eddie, the old easy-to-talk-to one.

When we were well away from the others Jeff dropped his voice and said, "Eddie, this caravan acts like a plague's hit it."

"Oh, they'll get over it and the widow'll do better," I said. "They say it's always tough on some at first. Others get by in fine shape."

"They sure don't act like they're worryin' any about her," Jeff growled.

"Naw, they just like to talk. Babies're nothing to worry about. Don't let it bother you, Jeff. They have to give somebody fits. If it wasn't the widow it'd be somebody else."

"You mean," he said slowly, "the widow's in trouble—*that* way—that she's *expecting*?"

"Yes, hurts me to say it, but the wise old dames have been reading signs and say circumstantial evidence points to some man in this caravan." I hesitated a moment, "Jeff, they think it's you."

He kind of bunched himself together, as a man does when he expects trouble. His eyes swung toward me in a slanting, penetrating look. His face grew stern and somber. His look switched to the caravan and then back to me. It made me feel like we did when we plunged into the cold Sweetwater on a hot day, during the many crossings.

He seemed to have a hard time reconciling himself to the suspicion of the caravan, that they had guessed on the guilty one so quickly. Starting to walk away, he stopped and glared at the wagons and the people moving about them. In a harsh voice he said, "Guess if I wasn't a damn fool I wouldn't be here." He began walking to where his horse was picketed.

Scared half to death I said, "Take it easy, Jeff. The men are strong for the widow. They'll step in if things get too rough. They know someone is guilty and let it go at that. Singleterry told his wife, 'The Lord deals an ace once in a while and we can't all have pat hands.' Mother said, 'Let him who is without sin among you cast the first stone and so on. It's a choice morsel of gossip. I don't even know what father thinks.'"

"Go around and tell all the men there's a big band of Indians somewhere ahead and to keep their guns handy," he said curtly. "Might mean trouble."

I passed father on the way.

"Father, Jeff said there's a band of Indians ahead and for me to tell all the men to keep their guns handy."

"While you're doing that," he answered, "tell the men to have their wives keep their mouths shut and limber up toward the widow. If anyone's going to do any crucifying around here, Jeff and I will do it."

"Don't you think he's the guilty one, Father?"

"If I did, I wouldn't say it. Be careful with your big mouth. Don't let him know the fools are talking about him."

"Guess I'd better get on with the warning," I said, feeling terribly downcast and worried.

"Lay it on as heavy as you want to; I'm disgusted with human nature tonight," he threw at me to take along.

About ten o'clock in the morning, two days later, when we had stopped to repair a broken reach, Susie, wearing a little red coat, disappeared. She had run over to a clump of trees to gather some flowers. Frantically searching, we found tracks of two horses leading into the timber. The noise of the caravan must have drowned her voice if she made a call for help.

Our family was prostrated with grief. Imagining Susie in the hands of Indians, possibly never to see her again, was beyond endurance. My heart ached as it never had before. Stella moaned and wrung her hands, catching her breath in sighs stifled with horror, the kind that aren't sighs, but some spasmodic action of a heart filled with fear. Suffering went terribly deep with her. She couldn't stand separation from those she loved. It was that quality that made her decide to come with us.

Blessing, white of face, almost grotesque-looking, was for starting out with a gun in search of her captors. Only the stern orders of the older ones kept him with us.

Hallor tried to give an appearance of feeling deeply about it but he secretly hated our little sister for her blistering frankness. The dislike had grown to be mutual.

Father, pale and terribly wrought up, took charge at once. He called Beaut Savage and others in whom he had confidence. They discussed who could best track the thieving scoundrels.

"I ain't much shakes at trackin', Thorne, but I'm a settin' out even if Jeff give strict orders fur us tuh stay in a bunch," Beaut said. "I shore wish he was here—we shore needs him."

"You lead and we'll follow, Beaut. Jeff didn't expect anything like this when he gave those orders. Catch up the horses in a hurry."

"Lord, please send us Jeff," mother was moaning to herself when we ran back to our wagons to get our guns. "Lord, I'll never do anything wrong again as long as I live if you'll send Jeff to us now—I promise faithfully."

I never thought of it at the time but did a little later. Mother wasn't praying for the Lord to bring Susie back; she was praying for Him to send Jeff to do the job. If Stella was praying she was doing it silently. She was in such misery she seemed almost in a stupor.

The widow had come to weep with mother and Stella. Deep, heartbroken sobs showing the depth of her feeling. She loved Susie and her own grief seemed to heighten her sorrow.

Suddenly Stella jumped up and screamed, "There's Jeff! Coming through the trees!"

We looked but couldn't see him and feared she was going out of her mind. He never came back so early in the day.

"I saw him. He's coming," she insisted.

In a few moments more he came into view, riding his horse at a fast trot. Then, his quick eye seeing that something was wrong, he came at a hard gallop.

"Lord, I thank Thee," mother breathed as fervently as if she had Susie in her arms.

Stella could outrun any man in the crowd and was the first to him.

"Jeff, the Indians have stolen Susie!" she cried imploringly. "Make them give her back to us. We love her so!"

"God!" he exclaimed. "Susie!" Instinctively his fine hands reached to his gun belt. "Where'd it happen? How was she dressed?" His eyes looked as though they could burn holes in a board.

"She was wearing her little red coat. Playing 'dressed up'" Stella sobbed.

"Get me the best horse in the bunch!" he ordered, looking at his rifle and revolver. "Circle up till I come back!" He ran with Stella to look at the tracks and stopped to get something out of his pack in the wagon.

I looked at father.

"Crusader!" he snapped. "Hurry up!" Keep saddles on the others."

We had Crusader there in a jiffy and were saddling him when Jeff came, wearing long shanked spurs. "What're all the others for?" he asked.

"Some of us'll go with you," father said.

"After two Banatees? You'd only be in the way," he said in a cold scornful voice. "Stay here and get busy. Drive the stock over there in that hollow in front of the timber. Build a fence. Double string the wagons in front of it. Lay in some water. Butcher an ox. Fall that spruce in back. Don't leave camp."

With that he pulled the rearing stallion down, tossed the reins over his head, caught a handful of mane and sprang lightly into the saddle as Crusader nervously charged for the open meadow. Quickly turning him, he struck him on the hips with his hand. Crusader, alive with excitement, threw his splendid body in great leaps toward the timber ahead of us. After a few seconds they disappeared from sight, with Jeff leaning forward and low to the horse.

It was remarkable how much better we felt with our problem in a master hand. We did as he told us, hoping, hardly daring to think of consequences. The Indians' trail had been almost an hour old when he took it. Could one man do what he was attempting? We were sure that if he failed, no man could have done more.

The hours ticked by, hours that seemed like years. Twelve o'clock, one o'clock, two o'clock. Our family didn't bother to try to eat. Hallor was hungry but he hid it behind his thick skin and family honor.

About three o'clock we heard a shot ahead of us in the trees. Then another one, followed by an intermittent round of them. We heard a horse heaving and pounding through the woods. Then Jeff's far-reaching bellow like a voice delivering us from prison:

"Got Susie and we're comin' in. Get ready to fight like hell."

At a hard run, on the almost spent Crusader, Jeff came in sight. Riding back of him, with arms clasped tightly around his waist, was Susie. In a few moments they were with us. Jeff jumped down and hauled Susie off with him. We ran out to meet them. Crusader's belly dripped with sweat and blood.

"Get back behind the wagons! Right on my tail. Put Crusader with the others—might get over it. Wouldn't've killed three good horses. Plugged 'em a quarter mile from main bunch. Damn near got us."

Stella ran up to greet Jeff and thank him. She stopped in horror. From the strings on his saddle dangled two grisly objects. He pulled the knot and let them fall to the ground.

"Pair of Snake flowers for you, Miss Stella," he said grimly. "More on the back trail but didn't have time to pick 'em. Only takes a second when you know how."

"Ugh," she said, backing away.

"That's squaw talk. Sounds good. How much can you pack?"

Stella gave him a quick look of horror, ran and kissed and hugged Susie as she never had been kissed and hugged before, without a ready answer for once.

"Danged scalps cheated me, I guess," Jeff said, watching her treatment of Susie.

The Indians stopped at the edge of the timber, uttering long, yelping howls that made my spine feel like it already had begun to die. The years of peace and security on our Illinois farm flashed through my mind. Disasters on the Trail up to now looked as nothing before the threat that seemed to smother hope.

Jeff's mouth tightened as he looked at them. "Got us outnumbered three to one, maybe more. The bunch that licked the Utes."

He glanced around, taking stock of our situation.

"Falling all that spruce in back was a good idea. Can't crawl through it in a bunch. Got to come head on, but we can't kill 'em fast enough."

He was silent a moment, watching the Indians. Finally he said, "Everybody lay low and quiet." His eyes searched out Hallor. "How're you at man-to-man fightin'? For your life!"

"Ah'm not a cow'ad," Hallor said, hesitantly. "What do you all want of me?"

"Don't know yet," Jeff answered. "We got to pull a trick on 'em, someway. Got an idea."

He walked out in plain view in front of the wagons and waved his hand for a talk. Quickly the Indians quieted to listen.

"Banatees!" he bellowed and then kept on in Indian language.

They uttered scornful yells and answered him. He swung his arm around toward our camp and spoke again. This time their howls sounded derisive. One big Indian stepped out in front of the others and made signs to the sky, then to the earth and swept his arms all around.

Jeff smiled grimly. "Says he can lick any man that walks on the face of the earth or ever lived. Hallor, step out in front. Paw the ground and wave your hands; you got to fight 'im."

Hallor's face paled and he gave Jeff an appealing look. But Jeff's eyes were fixed on him and there was no mistaking that he meant it. "You're a powerful man, and young," he said sternly. "Dog tired or I'd go myself. Fishin'. They might bite. End of us if we lose the fight that's comin'. I'm sayin' it straight."

Hallor was no coward but he quailed at sight of the huge Indian, apparent even from two hundred yards. 'Ah guess mah time's come. Ah'll do all Ah can. Do Ah go out now?"

"Yes. Don't take any weapon. Snort and paw the earth like he's doin'. Strip to the waist. Warm up so you can put up a good fight."

Hallor stripped, and then with a wild yell ran out, snorting and pawing the earth, waving his hands in all directions.

Jeff hurled another series of snarling gutturals at them and the big Indian began advancing.

"Let him come most of the way," Jeff called to Hallor. "He'll do it. Indian rules when they got the edge." Turning to Tom Martin he said, "Sneak back to the women. Tell 'em to load every gun we got. Keep everything handy."

As Hallor and the Indian drew together, the buck looked a third bigger. His coppery skin and rippling muscles gave the impression of great strength. I could imagine how Joel felt.

The final twenty feet, with taunts from both sides, ended in a wild rush by the Indian. But Joel didn't back down. When the buck leaped at him he stepped in and gave him a hard wallop on the chin. The buck fell and lay there a second.

"Don't jump on him," Jeff called. "Stand off and see if you can do it again. That was a corker. Watch out for tricks."

The big buck got to his feet and craftily approached. He held out his hand to Indian wrestle, foot to foot, hand to hand. Joel held out his hand to take the buck's and like a flash, laid another one on the Indian's chin. Down he went again.

But he got to his feet and came in for more. This time he dodged and got hold of Joel. They fell to the ground with one of the buck's legs twined around Joel's left one, his arms around Joel's neck and under his right shoulder.

Jeff was watching with anxious eyes. "Press your chin down so he can't bite your throat. That's what he's aimin' at. Get hold of his hair. Snap his head back. Snap hard!"

Joel pulled his chin down. At the same time he threw his right hand up to the buck's head, let it rest there for a second with a handful of hair and then thrust back hard. Dazed the buck. Joel wriggled out of his clutch and drove a left hand into the Indian's belly. The Indian jumped and got hold of Joel again, by the hair of his head, and spun him around. At the same time he struck him at the base of the neck with a hard downward blow of his forearm.

"Hold your guns on that bunch of Indians," Jeff called.

"Kill all you can when I yell fire. Get word back to the women to bring up rest of the rifles and bullets. Hallor's finished. Buck'll get 'im."

To our horror, Hallor had fallen and the Indian was pressing his arm back. Joel had put up a game fight but he'd given everything he had. In a matter of seconds the buck would kill him, in a terrible, grisly manner.

"Be ready, men!" Jeff called. "Can't stand this!"

He ran to the struggling men and got there just as Hallor's arms gave way. He pulled the Indian off. "Run back, Hallor! Grab a gun!"

The buck was furious at this denial of his right to kill. He made for Jeff, but Jeff weaved and dodged, glancing at the Indians who were crowding out towards them. Suddenly Jeff drew his revolver and shot the Indian, the heavy slug passing through his right eye. Then to our horror, Jeff fell on top of him and rolled to the near side, lying there motionless.

At this, the main body of Indians, until now intent on the fight, charged on horseback.

"Fire!" Jeff yelled. "Keep firing! Watch out for me!

Indians fell off their horses like pigeons knocked from a roost. The battle was on. Jeff leaped to his feet and ran to the wagons.

When he reached cover of the wagons he turned and began firing his revolver. Women stood behind the second row of wagons, handing rifles to us who were behind the first row. It was only a matter of turning to the opening between wagons to seize a loaded gun.

Once started, the Bannacks did not stop. At close range our slaughter of them was limited only by the speed with which we could aim and fire. The din was terrific. Indians gave their death wail as they fell. Horses screamed in agony. Others ran riderless, squealing in terror. Above it all, the ceaseless gunfire.

We numbered thirty-three men, backed up by thirty-seven women, including Stella and Eleanor Schoolcraft.

Wamsutter and Martin, near me, fell right at the beginning and lay there, groaning in agony. But there was no time to help them or the other wounded. The Bannacks, maddened with the lust to kill and plunder, seemed not to count the cost to them in dead and wounded. They jumped down from their horses when almost upon the wagons and swarmed into our midst with trappers' knives and hatchets. With clubbed rifles, knives and axes we met them. The ground ran red with blood between the rows of wagons. Whoops, screams and curses increased the uproar, added to by the poor children behind wagons to the rear of us.

We tramped on dead and wounded alike, slashing, cutting and yelling in a frenzy of despair. Several times I saw Jeff with an axe in left hand and his murderous gun in his right, and I couldn't tell which was most effective. His scalp was torn and blood streamed down his face.

A blow from behind knocked me down and an Indian fell upon me. I turned and seized his arm just as he was plunging his knife downward. He was larger and more powerful. My arm was weakening as I saw the horrible lust to kill in his eyes and felt his breath on my face, hot, fetid, shriveling breath. Just then a screaming apparition of flying reddish-brown hair, with her waist torn in shreds, plunged an axe in his head and hurried on.

I rolled clear of the Indian and lay still for a few moments regaining my strength, taking stock of the fighting around me. Eleanor's course continued. Wherever she found two men locked in a struggle she brained the Indian and looked for another. Just as I was getting to my feet I saw Blessing reach out from hiding in a wagon, strike with an axe and dart back till another came close enough.

Father's hot face loomed before me for an instant after I got to my feet, and I thought frantically of mother and the girls. The press of struggling bodies pinned me to a wagon and I hacked and fought to free myself. For an instant I saw Mrs. Wamsutter standing in a wagon. While I looked, she blazed away at a savage with a heavy buffalo gun and he fell in his tracks. From behind the canvas, an arm reached out with a loaded gun and took the empty one from her. There was only one arm and hand like it in the caravan—mother's. Jeff was high on a center wagon emptying his revolvers, Stella was standing beside him, loading.

Jeff's hawk-like eyes roamed the field as he fired with quick precision. Nothing escaped his aim or his eye. Occasionally he turned and laid out an Indian or two who had broken through the defense.

On the ground below him, side by side, stood Beaut Savage and a man named John Colman, swinging axes at Indians trying to get up into the wagon after Jeff. I ran to help.

Suddenly, the remaining savages began to run across to the timber. Jeff took another loaded gun from Stella, jumped down and ran after them. Just as he jumped, one last Indian picked up a hatchet from the ground and hurled it at him, barely missing his head. Jeff fired and killed him.

"After 'em, men. Kill all you can. Wipe 'em out," he bellowed triumphantly.

Those of us who could, seized loaded rifles, ran clear of the wagons and poured shot into them. Little more than twenty escaped into the thick woods bordering that fateful spot.

We hurried back to count the cost. Wamsutter, Blythe, Gulan, Larribee, Moser, Singleterry and five others were dead. Martin was at the point of death. Beaut Savage had a bad gash in his left side. Eleanor Schoolcraft had a bad cut on her right breast and a large scalp wound. Four other women and six children were dead. Every man had a wound of some kind ranging from bad to worse, most of them with several. Father had a scalp wound that looked ugly and several cuts on his body. Susie's right leg had been nicked by a bullet.

We found Marjorie and Mabel unhurt and looked for Stella.

"Thought I saw her jump down from the wagon when Jeff yelled to go after them," mother said. "Didn't see her after that." Presently she gave a scream and called for help. The hatchet that missed Jeff had struck Stella. She had fallen, not jumped down, and lay in the wagon unconscious, with a deep gash behind her ear.

Jeff was the first one to feel her pulse. "Still lives," he said as his face grew bleak and gray. "Poor little fighter was doing her best." He picked her up in his arms, tenderly, like she was a baby. "Run and have 'em fix a bed, while I carry her over. It's a tough life on pretty little women."

Sorrow came hard to us. The fiercest fighting hadn't lasted more than fifteen minutes but it seemed that the mourning and gloom, doubt and worry about the wounded, would never be overcome. Forlorn children weeping for their parents, the sobbing of bereft women, and tears welling out of the eyes of men who had lost their wives was too much to bear. When we had done our best for the wounded, I walked away to ease my feeling of anguish.

Dead and dying Indians lay all about in grotesque postures, some sprawling and others bent double. From among them we had separated our own dead and wounded.

Presently I heard Jeff's gun boom and saw him walking among the dying horses, mercifully killing them. His eyes were like glass and his face seemed rigid with bitter thoughts. Killing the last horse, he caught one of the Indian ponies and mounted it.

"Bannacks over there waiting for their horses," he said when he saw me. "When they get 'em they'll leave."

"Eleven Indians still alive," I said. "What'll we do with them? Some pretty bad. Some not so bad."

"We'll tie 'em on their horses and chase 'em to the timber. Give their friends something to do on the way home, like the job they shoved on us."

With foot snares, slip knot loops and ropes laid on the ground, we caught what horses we needed and tied Indians on them. Three of the least wounded Jeff held prisoner.

"Fix these up a little and tie 'em up till tomorrow," he said. "Want to make talk with 'em."

It was still several hours till dark. After hazing the Indians and the extra horses into the woods, Jeff came back and hitched up a team of oxen. Driving them to where the dead Indians were lying, he tied a rope to their feet and began dragging four at a time to a distant part of the meadow.

"Drag the rest over while I search 'em," he said when I offered to help.

Some of them wore new trousers and shirts. Others were in lighter summer garb crudely fashioned to the white man's style. He searched each one carefully and made a small pile of the findings.

"Look!" he said when he had finished. "Gold pieces, pocket knives, beads, jewelry, new pants on 'em, shirts, plenty of new guns and bullets. Must have raided Cutter Jones. Served the skunk right. Glad we kept three of these buzzards to ask a few questions."

"What if they won't talk?" I said, having learned some of their stubborn ways.

"They'll talk," he answered grimly.

I returned to the family, thinking of Stella.

Jeff came along in a short time. "How is she?" he asked, as though fearful of the answer.

"Pretty bad, Jeff," mother said, despondently, "she may not live."

"Don't give up!" he replied in a fierce voice. "Keep prayin' to God she'll live."

He went to where we had the three wounded Indians and examined them carefully. "Keep a close eye on 'em," he cautioned.

Martin died during the night but Stella was about the same when the sun came up. It promised to be a bright hot day.

Jeff had food brought to each of the Indians and sat and watched them eat it. Their hands were free but their feet were bound.

When the sun shone good and warm he cut some thongs about half-an-inch wide and three feet long from the green hide of the ox we had butchered the day before, paying no attention to some of us who had gathered around to watch him. He stooped down and said something in Indian and pointed in the direction from which they had made their attack.

"Uh huh," he said. "Kind of late to act like you don't savvy. See it by your eyes."

He tried again but with no result. Then he took the thongs and they quailed before the threat of his words, which we couldn't understand. Without further delay he tied a thong around each Indian's forehead and pulled it until it was barely tight. Putting their arms behind their backs, he tied them at the wrists and turned them face up in the sun.

"What's up, Jeff?" I asked, unable to hold my curiosity.

"Wait till the sun gets hotter. One way to make a Banatee talk."

He waved some gold pieces at them, asked a question, but they still wouldn't talk.

As the heat worked on the thongs they began to contract with a slow terrific pressure, like tight bands of iron around their heads. The weakest two fainted while we sat and watched. Jeff moved the remaining conscious one so he couldn't see his comrades. He cut the thongs on the two unconscious ones and said something more in Indian to the one still enduring the torture.

This time the Indian began to beg for the band to be removed, but Jeff shook his head, saying, "Talk first!" He repeated it in the Indian's tongue.

The Indian began speaking in low gutturals. When he was through Jeff reached out with his knife, cut the thongs and pointed to the trail. The Indian got to his feet and slowly staggered away after the blood began circulating in his legs. The other two revived when we threw water on them. Jeff motioned that they were free to leave.

"Cutter Jones gave 'em gold and trinkets," he explained to us. "Found some in their pants yesterday. He told 'em we had plenty more. Said we had a lot of food and clothes and guns and that most of the men were sick. He's only thirty-five miles ahead of us with three wagons. Gave this bunch clothes and set 'em on us. Promised more if they wiped us out. They came to murder and plunder what they thought was a defenseless caravan, but we licked 'em bad."

He was silent a moment. "Don't bury anyone till I get back. Got to make sure all the Indians vamoosed. Can't take chances on showing how many we lost."

He left on foot and returned in about an hour saying, "All cleared out."

We then had a general funeral that was heartbreaking, in a lonely spot in the wilderness, miles from anywhere. Father read from the Bible with a faltering voice and tearful eye. It was all the more touching to us because of Stella, still unconscious, lingering between life and death.

"This should have been done last night," I remarked to Jeff when it was all over.

"No," he said. "Better to take a little time for people to realize what's happened. Seems like a person can only take on so much in one day. Everybody's feeling pretty bad now, but there's a difference. Been through it myself."

Before we settled down again to other things he called us together, men, women and children.

"We're up against a tough deal," he said. "All of you still have something to live for, so don't let it bog you down. We'll stay a few days to see how the wounded come along. Going to scout around a little. Three or four of you who can hunt, bring in a few deer, the quicker the better. If you don't find enough deer, butcher some of the extra oxen. Dry the meat and melt fat over it. Want plenty of it. It's awful stuff. Put in some berries to make it taste better. You won't like it but it'll keep us alive if no game is handy. Two forts before we get to Whitman's Mission. May be short on supplies. Dried meat, packed down in good fat, will taste better'n you think."

He turned to father.

"Mr. Thorne, while they're doing that, maybe you'd better reorganize the outfit and bunch people up. Have to drop some wagons unless some of the women want to try a hand at it. Lord knows we need extra space to haul the wounded. Don't dare stay here any longer than we have to. Throw away all the stuff we can get along without and make room for beds. Make 'em as soft as you can—tough road ahead. Guess that's all I got to say."

His face was tired and weary. He showed the strain he was under and his hands kept clenching and unclenching even after he had finished. His nose still paled when he got tired but otherwise it was healed, in good shape, with only a few scars showing.

He was gone four days. The weather was clear and we worked like beavers, filling many a vessel with venison and ox meat.

He had barely left us when Hallor began holding sympathetic talks with different ones who had lost relatives. I noticed him but paid little attention, and he was clever enough to keep our family in ignorance of what he was doing.

Jeff returned, worn and weary. He went first to see how Stella was getting along, then Beaut Savage and the other wounded. When he returned to our family to have a talk with father, Mrs. Singleterry, one of those who had lost her husband, accompanied by Hallor, cornered him.

"Moorfield," she said, "we want tuh talk tuh yuh." She was one of the last ten added and other men and women of that ten, plus a large representation of the first twenty picked up at Independence, joined them.

Jeff swept them with an indifferent glance. "Hop to it. Air's free."

"We think yuh could of saved the fight if yuh'd talked an' bought 'em off, like yuh said Jones did. Mebbe if we couldn't a talked with 'em at all we could a traded better. It looks like tuh us that yuh was too danged anxious tuh carry out a grudge ag'in 'em, usin' us tuh do it. Yuh used Mr. Hallor tuh start it." She stopped to draw a breath. "Yuh shot that man Brocker, too, an' we knowed why."

I looked at father and his eyes were blazing.

Jeff looked at Hallor. "You stand with 'em on this, Hallor?"

"Ah do. Ah think you all aimed to settle mo'n one grudge at the same time."

Jeff turned to father. "Mr. Thorne, did you know anything about this?"

"First I heard of it," father gritted, appearing ready to shoot Hallor.

Jeff looked at his accusers again. "When you folks live in this country a while, things'll look different. Right now you don't know which end is up. We'll do our best to pull out in the morning, if I'm still captain by then."

"We'll give yuh one more chance, Moorfield," Mrs. Singleterry said, importantly. "But if yuh gits us in any more trouble afore Beaut Savage gits well, we'll git Mr. Hallor tuh lead us. We seen how yuh picked on 'im, an' how jealous yuh are of him. He couldn't do no worse'n git us killed, like you danged near did us!"

"Suits me," Jeff said wearily. "Glad you got Hallor to fall back on. Almost stinks at times, but hungry wolves don't care." He suddenly jumped to his feet. "Be ready to leave at daylight or you can follow him to hell and gone!"

They hurried away at sight of his wrath but the damage had been done. Even in my mind a vicious question had risen. He could at least have made a strong denial.

A little later I said to father, "Might be something to the old girl's argument—." I was going to add, "If we'd had anything to trade with and about three times as many men—" but he didn't wait to listen.

"You damned idiot," he flared and caught me on the chin with his fist. I hit the ground and lay there thinking how easily a person can get on the wrong foot. Hadn't meant anything wrong but I might as well have.

CHAPTER 11

It was clear with a heavy touch of frost in the air next morning when we hit the trail again, with our injured ones fixed the best we could. Mrs. Wamsutter, Mrs. Martin and five other women drove their own wagons. We left several wagons and a pile of things we had decided to get along without. The only way to haul the wounded and keep going. According to Jeff, the rains would start soon followed by snow.

The fourth day we came to where the trail divided, one fork going to Fort Hall, the other to California. There we found more remnants of Cutter Jones' caravan.

"Indians?" father asked Jeff, pointing to where the oxen had been driven away.

Jeff shook his head. "Part Indians, part Cutter Jones. Two wagons here—third one gone. Those two men been scalped quite a while. Bannacks scalp higher up. Looks like Jones murdered 'em and took all the money. They knew too much about him and didn't have families. He figured to lay it on the Indians. Bannacks came by later and took the oxen. Since it happened here at the fork of the trail he must have figured to go to California. Saw this mess day after it happened. Couldn't take anymore time."

Father shook his head. "Don't leave us like that, Jeff. We need you now more'n ever."

We buried the luckless ones and hurried on.

That day it began to rain in limitless drenching sheets, making up for lost time it seemed. The wounded were doing well except Stella. The jolting wagon had increased her delirium in spite of all we could do.

Father came for Jeff. "We're afraid Stella's dying," he said, his eyes misty with grief and worry. He was a bedraggled-looking figure as rain ran off his slouch hat to his water-soaked clothes in random little streams,

Jeff hurried to her and tenderly drew the covering back from her face. His hand shook and his face grew pale. "We'll go no farther while there's a chance," he said in a harsh, grating voice, causing me to remember the time when he talked with Stella and she advised him to learn how to use his hands. Seemed like years in the past.

As usual, his actions were direct and his cross words specific. "Pull out the Thorne wagons. Beaut Savage's, too. Hallor! Grab your things and move into one of the other wagons! Lead 'em to the Columbia. Captain Hallor from now on."

"Let somebody else do it," Hallor snarled. "Ah'm staying with the Thornes. If Miss Stella dies, Ah want to be heah fo' the last rites of huh pwecious existence on earth."

"Shut up! Give her something to be proud of when she pulls through, you damned fool. No time to argue."

"Come on, Mr. Hallor. We'll show 'em," Mrs. Singleterry said. "Lead us out of this hellish place."

Hallor cast a glance at the Schoolcraft wagon. He hurriedly ran to get his things and began putting them in with Eleanor's.

"Jeff!" Eleanor screamed. "You didn't mean for me to go with them, did you?"

Jeff whirled from a hurried glance about the surrounding country. "Eleanor stays with us, Hallor. Take Mrs. Singleterry's wagon and pull it up front."

Hallor sullenly obeyed. Wouldn't have given much for his life if he hadn't. Jeff was in a killing mood. Sensing this must have been what changed Hallor's mind in spite of his desire to stay with us.

Some of the others begged to stay with Jeff.

"Go on while you've got the chance," he said sternly. "We camp here until she can travel. Don't know how long."

"With that empty hide leadin' us, we'll never git nowhere," Mrs. Wamsutter said despondently.

"Jeff, keep us here!" Mrs. Martin begged. "We've got little children."

"No place for a big party, here in the high mountains. Get goin'!" he said, walking away.

Before they were gone, Jeff began swinging our wagons into a thick pine grove. It was dismal and dripping with water on every hand. The prospects never looked worse. Even father's hard grip on himself had begun to break. It seemed like the end of the world.

Jeff came and looked at Stella again. He put his hand on her forehead. He shook as though he had ague and his eyes were moist. "Got a fever. Needs a quiet, warm place," he said.

The last ray of hope faded at those words. Where could a quiet warm place be found in this terrible unfriendly forest?

"Hurry up!" he said sharply. "Get your axes and follow me." He led us to a spot. "Fall small trees until I tell you to stop." With that his axe bit into a tree and he made the chips fly.

We worked like mad, trusting Jeff to know what he was doing. I couldn't see any use in it.

As soon as he had two trees down, he cut them into poles, leaving a limb at the top end and cut off short. Two he set about ten feet apart and laid a cross piece at their tops about five feet from the ground, resting on the limbs. Then he laid poles against the frame so they would slant back to the ground. On top of those he laid boughs. On the open ends he drove short poles and wove in branches. Over the whole affair he draped canvas to make certain no water would leak through. Then he ordered me to build a fire in front of the lean-to, as he called it. Before many minutes had passed, the inside was warm and cozy with heat reflected from the fire.

We made a soft bed for Stella out of a pile of boughs on top of which we placed two feather beds and blankets. The very appearance of it had a calming, hopeful effect on me. Jeff and I went to bring Stella and mother.

When mother saw it she could hardly believe her eyes. "What a warm, lovely place," she sobbed as we placed Stella upon the bed.

"Now, ma'am," Jeff said, "you tend the fire and keep it warm while we finish some more lean-tos. Mr. Thorne, you split wood until you drop. Need lots of it. Need to work to keep your mind off the way things look. Eddie and Blessing, you come with me. We'll make this camp into something to be proud of."

Before dark we had another lean-to for Beaut, opposite Stella's, and three more near them. Close at hand we had a square roof of boughs on poles under which we could cook and eat. Warm fires, where needed, made the world look fit to live in again. An hour before dark, Jeff seized his rifle and brought down a buck.

For supper that evening we had fresh venison, cornmeal cakes, dried fruit and coffee with cream from the morning's milk.

Before we sat down to eat, Jeff went and looked at Stella. "She's better already. Cheer up. Could have it a lot tougher."

By morning she had passed the crisis and we owed it to Jeff for saving her life. We stayed there a week to give her a little more time in a pleasant camp, living like kings in contrast to the dismal outlook that had been ours.

Crusader had recovered and was lording it over the herd in great style. The oxen had a needed rest on good feed and we made better time from there to Fort Hall. Stella kept improving slowly and we were happy again. She had enough vitality by then to hold her own in spite of the raw dampness.

I hated to leave that camp and was ready to stay there forever rather than hit the trail again. I had learned, that if one knew how, the forest could be made friendly.

A man from the British Isles, named Henty, was resting at Fort Hall when we pulled in there. Jeff knew him and they shook hands.

"How far ahead's the rest of our schooners?" Jeff asked.

Henty threw up his hands. "Gor blime! Hi hin't seen such a bloody mess in Hall me bloody life! Prawb'ly in the Snike, by now."

We hurried on and caught them a few miles before coming to the Snake River. Fifty Indians had them surrounded in a small valley. We broke into view of them all of a sudden and Jeff halted us at once. Mrs. Singleterry and Hallor were waving their hands, trying to make the Indians understand that they wanted to trade, Lord knows what, while the savages sat their horses with grave faces, saying and doing nothing.

"Damn fools'll give the wagons away and set out on foot if we don't get down there pretty quick," Jeff said dryly, after a long searching look. "I know those Indians."

He halted us about five hundred yards from them and gave a long, piercing yell, ending up with a few Indian words, at the same time jumping down from his wagon and walking out in front of it.

The Indians heeled their horses and headed for us at top speed. They surrounded Jeff and jumped off before their horses had time to stop. All tried to talk at once. Jeff laughed and poked some of them in the ribs, while every one of them insisted on shaking hands, white man fashion. It was clear that they knew him and liked him. He pointed to us and told what appeared to be a story of our experiences. I heard the name "Banatees" several times. At which the Indians pointed to twenty or thirty scalps hanging to their various saddles.

The discussion finally ended and the Indians had to shake hands with each one of us. They looked at Stella, lying in her bed in the wagon, pale and wan. Their leader came back for a second look. He touched her on the breast over her heart and then touched Jeff over the heart, saying something in Indian. Jeff looked sheepish and said something that sounded like a denial.

"What'd he say, Jeff?" I blurted at him.

"Aw shut up! You ask too danged many questions."

Then the Indians laughed and grunted. They sensed his answer even if they couldn't understand his words to me.

One of them took a keen look at Eleanor and made a movement of rocking a baby in his arms, asking Jeff a question. Jeff laughed at that and gave him a shove. They all laughed again.

After a while they jumped on their horses and left us with a few parting yells to Jeff.

He stood and watched them go while we stood near him.

"Those danged Nez Perces sure know how to get under a fellow's hide." He laughed deeply. "Watch 'em stop and give their windfall back to Hallor and his gang. They'll laugh all winter about that trading spree. Said they hadn't asked for anything, but the two 'with mouths that worked like beavers' began shoving it at 'em. The scalps belonged to the last of our Banatee friends. These boys ran into them, with all the extra horses, and made a clean sweep." He paused a moment. "Guess we better drive up and say hello."

"Jeff, what's the difference between Bannacks and Banatees?" I asked while I thought of it.

"Bannacks is the white man's name for Banatees."

"Didn't know Indians ever laughed that much," I said.

"Do sometimes when there's a big joke. Have a lot of fun by themselves. Nez Perces are pretty good Indians. They figure me same as one of 'em."

The caravan welcomed us with open arms. All except Mrs. Singleterry and Hallor, who were standing off to one side.

"We wants yuh tuh lead us again, Jeff," John Colman shouted. "Danged well got our bellies full of them two."

Others supported him with loud cries.

"Suits me," Jeff said. "Might as well finish the job, if that's what you want."

"Thank the Lord yuh came before we hit Snake River!" Mrs. Wamsutter declared. "We'd never a made it."

If Jeff's sins had been a hundred times greater it would have made no difference. By contrast, his ability to lead had assumed great proportions. They threw their hats in the air and yelled when they knew he would be captain again.

"Don't get to celebratin'," Jeff growled. "Snake's right ahead and mighty tricky. Wait till we get across."

When we came to it I shuddered, as did many of the others. Solid earth never looked better to me and I felt that, if we could only keep going on land, I wouldn't begrudge the moments spent in tallowing axels, even using pitch at times, binding wheels with ox hide and changing reaches. Wouldn't even minded going on and enduring the thirst that came to us on the high land; on the edge of the canyon where there was no water while millions of gallons poured below us, out of reach of stock and men.

Different times we had camped without a speck of water. At other times we let a man down with a rope to bring up enough for the human beings, while the stock bellowed and whinnied all night long in complaint at a thirst that gnawed at their bones. No matter how much it rained, soil and rocks drained it off, or licked up most of it and we might as well have been on a desert.

My eyes betrayed me at Snake river. Jeff came along and gave me a sharp look, saying, "Scared? So was I, first time, but now it's just hard work. Don't look sick! Act like it's a lark. When you're on the other side you'll be glad you didn't show the white feather. Maybe you'll learn how to be a man, yet."

He gave me a hefty kick on the rump. He hadn't been very kind to me for several weeks.

He led with the stock that had showed they were the least afraid. Then we prodded the more timid ones into following. Pretty soon we had all of them in the water swimming for dear life and they made it, except eight of the weakest that gave up and were carried away.

In the meantime, we had calked the seams of the wagon boxes with rags and tallow and pitch. Jeff had long ago fashioned several sets of paddles to use in guiding the various "arks" on their way.

"All right," Jeff commanded. "Eddie, you and I go with the first one and I'll bring it back. One of your father's wagons, made the way it should be. No trick at all."

With the tongue in place and tied back to equalize the weight, bearing a long rope with which to snub a large rock on the other side, we took our seats.

"Shove 'er off!" Jeff cried. "Beats a raft any day." And away we went, quartering to the opposite shore.

Water rippled at the edges of the wagon box and the sensation was pleasant after the endless jolting of the rocky plateaus. After the first shock, seeing that I was still above water, my emotion changed from insane fear to one of delight.

We emptied and stripped that wagon and Jeff took it back to the other shore to give directions and see that they were obeyed; to paddle along with the fearful ones to give them strength. On the last trip he brought mother and Stella over in safety. He worked like a demon and his word was law, instantly obeyed.

When they beached, and mother stepped out on dry land, she ran up and gave Jeff a hug and a kiss, saying "Jeff, you're the most capable person I ever knew—you're like the shadow of a great rock."

Jeff was terribly embarrassed. "Now, ma'am," he managed to say, "don't let excitement make you do anything you might be ashamed of."

Others came up and wrung his hand until he said, "Let's go. Tough road ahead."

That crossing gave new spirit to the crowd of weary overlanders. The cry was now, "On to Boise and we'll get to Walla Walla by and by."

Going to Boise was just plain, hard, wearisome, bull-headed maneuvering up hill and down dale.

Fort Boise, with its run-down state of affairs, on the heels of the great decision which gave this territory to the United States, wasn't anything to make us want to stay longer than we had to for a few repairs and then we were on the Trail again. Hudson's Bay company had nineteen years to go before they had to move out, but you'd have thought they were getting ready then.

The second crossing of the Snake was a repetition of the first, which when completed gave us the relief of better ground to travel over on our way to Whitman's Mission.

We had rain, snow and good weather alternately, but we pushed steadily on through beautiful valleys and stately groves of pine. Venison was on every table daily, and trout when we crossed the streams.

Stella was then in a wan state of recovery, quiet and thoughtful, smiling occasionally as though pleased about something. She was very grave and courteous to Hallor, while her eyes sought Jeff, when she knew he wasn't looking.

Jeff, poor burdened humanity herder, was a sorry sight. His clothes were ragged and he had let his beard grow for want of time to shave. First up and last to go to bed, he spent little time with our family—driving, pounding the caravan to get it over the ground, on to the Willamette and off his hands. He never said it in words, but I was certain he felt it.

Eleanor Schoolcraft now was like one of the family, inducted by the force of sterling qualities under trying conditions.

As mother put it one day, "My idea of sinners has changed on this trip. Look at Eleanor and Jeff. Jeff has led us like a beloved tyrant until he's worn to the bone, and many a night Eleanor has snuggled down beside me when your father was standing guard and calmed and soothed me against the terrible trials ahead. Never again will I think in terms of who is a sinner. I'll look to see who's being crucified and who is doing the crucifying, then I'll judge righteous judgment."

And that from mother was something to hear.

CHAPTER 12

Jeff didn't tell us how close we were to the Whitmans on November 15, 1847. He was in the lead and let us drive up to their mission without announcing our nearness. A tall fair-haired woman came out and waved a welcome, followed in a few moments by a tall man, slightly stooped, as though carrying a great burden of thought against uncountable odds. Coming behind him were children of all sizes and grades.

Jeff pulled up with his wagon and stopped. "Hello, Mother Narcy," he yelled as he jumped down.

"Jeff!" she cried, running to meet him. She took his head in her hands, she was almost as tall as he, and kissed him on the forehead while he put his arms around her with great affection. "Oh, Jeff, it's so good to see you. We didn't know where you were. Marcus, here's our boy again—he's come home!"

Doctor Whitman seized Jeff's hand and threw a fatherly arm about him. Tears were in his eyes and he had a kind face, seamed and burdened with solicitude. "Jeff!' he boomed. "Our pride and sorrow. We're happier to see you than words can tell. Have your friends come in and share our poor place."

He waved to us with a kindly gesture and we warmed to him and his wife. We were like forlorn travelers, led to a cozy fire and food.

Then all became a hubbub of confusion and greetings. Little Mary Ann Bridger inquired for a letter from her father. We met a boy named John Sager, about sixteen, his brother Francis, Catherine and several sisters. A bright-eyed little girl, Helen Meek, was in the forefront of welcomers, smiling and happy. There were other adults and children. The number was surprisingly large.

But those two wonderful Whitmans! It was a few moments before the doctor could place father, and then he remembered full well. From then on it was like a homecoming.

Narcissa Whitman and the doctor were everywhere. They fed us and looked after bruises and chill blaine until we glowed with warmth and hospitality.

"Come on, you pemmican eaters!" Jeff called to his weary band. "Rest up for the next siege."

"Jeff," Mrs. Whitman said with a look of worry, "you aren't going to leave us again so soon, are you?"

"Now, Mother Narcy, I've got to get these people to the Willamette and then I'll be back for a while. "They're land hungry and nervous. Can't have that, can we?"

Mrs. Whitman smiled. "There's plenty of rich land for all and you'll love it, Mrs. Thorne. You'll have a farm out here that will warm your heart with joy."

"If I ever develop a tenth part of your generous nature, Mrs. Whitman, I'll be rich beyond complaint," mother earnestly replied.

"We love the weary travelers who come our way," Mrs. Whitman said. "The spirit of it will come to you as you live out here. We love them all." Her eyes swept the surrounding country, meaning Indians, I took it. "But we love our own kind best in spite of ourselves." She laughed gently at her confession, as though it were a sin to say it.

Jeff roamed around outside and came back in a couple of hours not so easy as when he arrived.

"What's the matter, Jeff?" I asked. "Itching to get us on the way?"

In a low voice he said, "I hadn't ought to leave here again. Something's brewin'. Can't tell what, but it's in the air. These damned, lousy Cayuses! The only two people in the world who'll ever love 'em are living here, year after year, taking their abuse. I'd like to move the Whitmans away for a while and show the ugly brutes a thing or two. Don't answer! Mother Narcy's too close."

"Don't let Jeff prejudice you against our converts, Mr. Thorne." Mrs. Whitman said as she passed us. "He mistrusts them at every turn and they fear him." She glanced fondly at him. "The Doctor and I wish you would settle down here, Jeff. We need you. The crops and everything make a great trial for the Doctor and our charges never worked so well as when you were with us. Most of them have the measles now, but the white people seem to be rather immune to it. Probably their food and rigorous living."

"I'll be back before spring, Mother Narcy, and help, even if a lot of the crop goes to feed ornery Cayuses."

Mrs. Whitman glanced behind us. A fleeting look of anxiety showed on her face. "There come Delaware Tom and Dory; be sure to treat them kindly, Jeff. Their people are in sore straits, many of them dying."

"Half-breeds," Jeff replied with a grimace. "They choose Indians when they should stick by the whites. Like to shoot both of 'em. But I'll be good, Mother Narcy."

"Thank you, Jeff. I must be about my duties now."

Delaware Tom and the one they called Dory were walking in an arrogant and insolent manner, looking at the new arrivals at the Mission with hateful faces. They came within fifty feet without a hint that they saw us.

"Hi there, Delaware, and you, Dory!" Jeff called to them sharply. "You didn't expect to see me here, did you?"

Both of them dropped some of their insolence. They answered him in the Cayuse tongue.

"Speak English. You two wolves know it as well as I know Cayuse."

"We do not like English," one of them replied.

"You'll like it less if I ever work you over again. What mischief you dirty crow-eaters up to now?"

"No mischief," the other replied. "Come as friends."

Jeff scowled and began speaking in the Cayuse tongue. His eyes blazed and his manner was a threat of physical violence.

The one called Delaware Tom sneered. "You do not look like you have done well. You are like the rest of the ragged travelers who eat this country like the grasshoppers."

I gathered that this was said for my benefit since he chose to say it in a tongue that I knew, but Jeff kept on in Cayuse.

"They have brought us sickness and they will not cure us," the other said. "We will do as we please."

"You'll pack tales and breed trouble for your best friends," Jeff replied. "Stand by the Whitmans and they'll stand by you, even though many years bring many people."

"It is because of them that the strangers come. They give them food and we have sickness and die," Delaware Tom replied with his lips drawn above yellow teeth.

"Many strangers will come and you cannot stop them. Make the Cayuse a strong nation by obeying the great white Doctor. Do as he says and work. The measles'll leave you. The Doctor is a great man in the land where the sun rises. Many people will listen to him." Then Jeff's jaw stuck out a little farther. "But if harm comes to them the Cayuse will be a hunted nation—you'll die as murderers who have no God."

"We hate the white man's God; He is not for the Cayuse." Dory replied and spat on the ground.

"Then you'll despise the white men's guns to your sorrow, fools. The crows will pick your bones from the trees where they hang you. I have spoken. Tell it to the chiefs of the Cayuse. I have heard tales and I believe them and I will kill if they are true. The great doctor and his wife are your friends and they will stand for you when you need a friend. I spent many years here and I know your whims and fancies; they are foolish."

The two of them exchanged guilty glances and walked away.

"You heard an earful, Eddie, and so did they. Don't think they'll have the nerve to bother too much until I pour another dose in their ears next spring. They hated to hear me say it and things look bad. Ornery lot. Bullets are the medicine I'd give 'em if I had my way. Don't let on you heard us. It would only worry the doctor and Mother Narcy. Love them as if they were my own parents. Soon as I can, I'm comin' back and stay a while. Even stomach these miserable Cayuses just to be with 'em."

He was deeply moved. His stern face, hardened by self-discipline, softened as he spoke of them and talked of returning.

We spent two grateful days there and I saw many pretty young women in the throng that the Whitmans had drawn to them by their kind courage and high ideals. The school seemed like a mountain peak in a barren land, beautiful with their personalities and work to abolish ignorance.

Mrs. Whitman clung gently to Jeff as we were leaving. "You will come and see us again soon, Jeff? The latch string is always out to you." She kissed him with much affection.

The doctor put his arm about Jeff's shoulders and said, "You people were fortunate in having our young fire-eater for a guide. The mountains and the valleys have no mysteries for him nor the Indians. He speaks Cayuse, Snake, Nez Perces and Willamette with the best of them." He gave Jeff a pat on the shoulder. "Come back to us, Son. Don't wander all your life away from those who love you. Marry and settle down like a good rancher."

"I'll be back soon, sir," Jeff said in a low voice. "Missed this home more than you'd believe."

I wondered if anyone had told the Whitmans of the caravan scandal and if that was the way Doctor Whitman had of conveying the fact that he was welcome regardless.

In a short time we had our first view of the mighty Columbia.

"To me that river proves what Jeff said of this country," mother remarked. "Now I'll look for big trees and all else that he told us. I'm ashamed of myself for doubting him."

"Wonder what Stella thinks of it, Mother? She thought Jeff was a blowhard at one time."

"She doesn't say much these days. Really believe if it weren't for that disgraceful scandal she could be won away from Joel, if Jeff were so minded. As it is, there's no choice in that direction. I think it's Jeff's intention to do the right thing by Eleanor. It'll be almost like having him for a son-in-law. I've grown to have a deep affection for her. Wish men weren't so impulsive and generous in their love affairs. They surely spoil better plans. I've thought, as we plodded along, how sweet it would be to see a budding romance grow between two people like Stella and Jeff. Be a great love match when they finally quit their coltishness." She sighed deeply. "How I'd have enjoyed seeing it."

"You aren't by any chance a booster for Jeff, are you, Mother?" I said, cinching the deal while she was in a confessing mood.

"After what he's done for us I'll be a booster of Jeff's as long as I live, Son."

This part of the journey was not hard in the sense of hardness as we had known it. Jeff regarded the Indians with contempt and we had no fear of them. The road was better and almost always we were in sight of the Columbia to remind us that we were on the last lap of the trail, where we would turn down the famous Willamette.

It was wintertime and there was little fuel to be had away from the river, but with driftwood cast up on the river bank we made a comfortable camp most nights. The thrill of being so near the end of our journey minimized the discomfort of snow and cold.

On December 7, 1847, when we had halted to camp, a day's journey below the Dalles, a trapper hurrying down the river hailed us and rode up. Jeff was making a rawhide boot for one of the oxen while the rest of us were busy gathering wood and helping to speed up suppertime.

"Howdy, folks," the trapper said. "did ye hear the bad news? Guess ye hain't had a chance, mebbe. The others went down by boat."

Jeff stopped his work and listened.

Like many people who live a great deal by themselves, the trapper hesitated in order to give the affair its full drama.

"Hurry up, man! Out with it!" Jeff cried impatiently, as though he guessed what was about to be said.

"The Cayuses raided the Whitmans and killed 'em, along with a lot of others. McBean at Fort Walla Walla sent word by boat to Vancouver. Cayuses took a lot of prisoners."

"God forgive me!" Jeff groaned and walked away to be alone with his sudden grief. None of us ventured to follow him, feeling that such grief had no room for words with a man like Jeff.

"Who's he?" the trapper asked.

"Jeff Moorfield," father replied with tears in his eyes. "He was like a son to the Whitmans."

The trapper's eyes lighted up. "So thet's Jeff Moorfield. I ain't ever seen him but I heerd about him. The Whitmans brung him up. Bannacks killed his folks in 1837. Borned on the plains. Father was a trader. Whitman an him was friends. Moorfield won't go no further. He'll go back an' fight Cayuses till they kills 'im. Guess I better get along now." Then he added as an afterthought, "Heered it dang near killed Moorfield when Whitman's little girl drownded in a ditch. She was two years old. Broke him all tuh hell. Ain't had no patience with anythin' sence then. Well, see yuh ag'in, mebbe."

Stella went to Jeff and consoled him while he sat on a rock looking down at the Columbia. It was one time I couldn't eavesdrop even if I had felt like it and I never knew what she said. Later she took him a cup of coffee and made him drink it. We still had some and it came in handy that night.

Jeff stayed there until the next morning when he ate a good breakfast and no one could have told that he was mourning, except by looking at his eyes. They seemed set on scenes back in his head, away from the rest of us. It made me think of what he had promised the two half-breeds.

After breakfast he called father and me to one side. There was a piece of paper in his hand.

"If I know Oregon, they'll be organizing to chase down the Cayuses. I'll be going with 'em. May have time to get to the Willamette. Anyway, here's a map leading to a fine place to build and settle on. Little farther out than you might want, but this whole country's going to settle up pretty fast and you'll need plenty of ground to pre-empt if Congress passes a helping act. Lot of farm land and grazing. Fine stream runs through it. Woods farther back. Got a claim in the center of it. I'm selling it to you for a twenty-dollar gold piece. Don't want any doubt about the ownership of that claim hanging over me while I'm traveling. Pick of the country. You won't regret having it, sir."

"But, Jeff," father objected, "you'll want it yourself later, perhaps, and it wouldn't be right for us to take it this way. Your grief will soften in time and you'll need a place to center on. We'd like to have you near us. Let me buy it from you and hold it. We'll take up more of the surrounding land. That's the only fair way."

"Won't be needing it. Plenty more good places—will be for a long time. Know how you feel about it, but this is the way I feel. Take it at my price or no deal. I may be busy for a long time. Don't want any strings anywhere."

The widow's plight flashed through my mind and the fate of her unborn child. My loyalty for Jeff and my sense of the fitness of things, involving the hero of the caravan, confused me. I had nothing to say and my sense of loss was overwhelming.

"All right, Jeff," father said sorrowfully. "If that's the way you want it, then that's the way it'll be. But boy, don't take needless chances. The Cayuses should be punished but I'd hate to have you lose your life doing it. The West needs men like you. It's wild and has few masters—few who know it as you do and have the same ability. For our sakes, Jeff, be careful. There's hardly a person in this caravan but what will grieve when you leave us. Here's the twenty dollars." Father choked up and the deal was completed in silence.

"Hallor won't grieve when Jeff leaves," I thought to myself as they completed the transaction. "And what will become of the widow?"

Jeff crowded us hard. We were almost to where the Willamette joins the Columbia when Peter Skene Ogden, Hudson's Bay Company's factor and a number of men in a long canoe paddling up the river, hailed us and stopped to rest.

"How-do-you-do, Jeff," Ogden said in a high, thin voice. "Trapper Lang met us and said you were in the country."

Simple statement. No foolish question as to what Jeff intended doing. I liked Ogden instantly. His steady eyes alone betrayed that he was glad to see Jeff.

"Howdy, Mr. Ogden. More coming behind you?"

"No, Jeff. We go to negotiate the release of captives."

"Anybody comin' to smoke 'em up? Wipe 'em out?"

"None, Jeff. May be none. We're on a mission of peace. What the Americans choose to do will be decided in due time."

Scowling, Jeff said, "Well, here's one American that won't be waiting."

"You wouldn't go far alone, Jeff," Ogden said and ordered his men to begin paddling. "Wait and see what the others do."

"I'm heading back to the Dalles," Jeff declared when Ogden was out of hearing. And no argument could change his mind.

"Crusader's your horse, Jeff," father said. "Take him!"

"No," Jeff refused. "Too good for where I'm goin'." He tied a bundle on one of his pack horses and turned to us as he mounted. "Good luck! Hang tough! You're in a great country."

With a wave of his hand he left us, riding alone up the river. No flourishes. No jiggering around. He chose vengeance on the slayers of his foster parents and death alone would stop him.

Mother wept and father cursed like a Mississippi bargeman, with tears rolling down his cheeks. Marjorie, Mabel and Susie cried as though they had lost their big brother. Stella's face was gray and tightly drawn. The blood had gone from her lips, leaving them ashen-hued. Her shoulders drew together as though with a deep pain in her bosom, and her eyes were dull with suffering.

Hallor, alone, enjoyed his going. The widow tried her best to keep the tears back but failed. It was a bad day for the caravan. In glancing around I saw men with drawn faces and several women crying.

Beaut Savage's wounds were about well. Under his and father's leadership we drove our thin, terribly exhausted oxen on to Oregon City. Soon after Jeff left us I cut my foot with an axe but managed to keep on driving.

Going by Jeff's map, we found the place he had owned and there we camped with the four wagons, in the timber, under lean-tos that we remembered how to build. Deer abounded and the stream was loaded with trout. Other supplies were purchased in Oregon City.

Father hired several men to build the house we had planned and events moved quickly. Everybody was busy. We kept Eleanor with us, for she was now in full flesh and going strong.

About the campfire at night, when the hard toilsome day was over, we lived the Trail again while we waited for word from the avenging Jeff. In January the captives were returned and there was bitter news. Little Mary Ann Bridger and Helen Meek had died. The pretty bright-eyed young women I had admired were taken prisoner and abused ceaselessly by their savage captors. Doctor and Mrs. Whitman had been among the first killed. It was a long, sad list of heroisms, futile death and terrible privations for the captives, many of whom were children.

But Jeff did not return and our heart sank. The last word of him was from the Dalles where, after taking what ammunition they could spare, he headed off into the wilds, alone.

"Yuh can't do anything with Jeff when he gets goin' on things like this." Joe Meek, Helen Meek's father, told father and me when we went to inquire. "Don't set yore mind on him comin' back. He'll kill Cayuses until they kill him or he wears out his hot spell. An' when I think of my little girl and Bridger's, aw, hell, no use talkin' about it! Just gits a man riled up all over again. Colonel Gilliam's organizing tuh raise hell with the dirty dogs."

We returned to our homestead and broke the news to all the family. Our hearts ached for Jeff's safe return, though the odds were against him. We didn't give up hope entirely but it seemed foolish to ever expect to see him again. We couldn't forget Joe Meek's words. When we heard that Jeff was not with Colonel Gilliam's volunteers, our hope all but ended.

Mrs. Schoolcraft was in a continual state of sadness these days and Hallor's disgust, when his sensitive eyes fell upon her extended condition, did not help her any. His "holier than thou" expression pained me especially. Stella was very kind to her and Hallor's bugged eyes didn't further her regard for him, if there ever had been any, really. More and more she reproached him for his manner until one evening I overheard her taking him to task.

"Joel, you act as though Mrs. Schoolcraft should be put out of sight somewhere or burned at the stake. I detest your attitude."

"Ah love purity in womankind, Miss Stella. Ah can't become accustomed to what goes against mah idea of honuh in a woman. She is almost brazen in huh mannuh. It doesn't set well with me. Ah wish Moo'field would come back and do right by huh."

"But you should be considerate of her in her trouble. This affair isn't for you to judge hourly."

"You have changed, Miss Stella. You almost condone huh waywa'dness. The pose is most becoming and adds to yo' gentle beauty, even if Ah can't unde'stand it. Yo' purity is like a lily of the valley, a beacon to the eyes of—" His "purity" sounded like pewity.

"Oh, shut up!" Stella snapped. "I'm sick of your sweetly dripping honeyed words. You pick me for a subject, saying one thing to me and being openly hateful to Elean'or who should have your sympathy. Why cut the heart out of her? She isn't the first woman who ever did wrong."

Hallor was silent a few moments. Something new for him. "Ah may join the volunteahs and fight Indians."

"Eddie would have joined long ago if his foot had healed in time," she said. "You could buy a rifle in Oregon City."

"Ah'll bid yuh all good evening, Miss Stella, hoping yo' mood will be bettuh tomorruh."

CHAPTER 13

One evening the last of March, when the weather was busily mixing snow and rain in fitful absent-minded quantities, Jeff rode in dripping wet. He was shaved and his hair was trimmed, but his clothes were ragged. Above the starved hardness of his chin his eyes burned in the lamplight. The condition of his clothes hinted that his money was low. He was like a man returned from a long fast with nothing in his hands to live on but tightly clutched ideals.

"Thought I'd come by and let you know the Cayuses didn't get me," he said with a weary grin when the commotion of welcome died down. "Big gold strike in California and I'm headed for it. Cayuses are done for. Main fight's about over."

While we were glad to see him, our expectations fell. He had not come back to honor the widow with his name. It made a difference and he sensed it, for he glanced at Eleanor and looked away again, quickly.

"Take me with you, Jeff," Blessing said instantly. "I want to dig some gold, too."

"Suits me, Bless, if you can travel till you drop and work like a fiend. What do you say, Mr. Thorne?"

"If Blessing wants to go, Jeff, I don't see how he could find safer company to travel with," father replied, happy over the fact that he knew Jeff still lived, ending one phase of our uncertainty.

Jeff's glance was danger-hunting. I saw him look at Stella and saw her return the look. It seemed that the weight of his conscience pulled his eyes away. We sat and talked before the huge fire until he nodded with weariness and we urged him to get some sleep and rest. Mother led the way to a hastily prepared spare bed, robbing the others of a quilt here and a blanket there.

"No, ma'am," he objected. "After the way I've been living I couldn't sleep in a rig like that. I'll throw my pack down in the barn where there's plenty of hay. Thank you just the same."

So much the better for us to rake him over the coals now that he was a living, breathing person among us again.

"You look tired, Eleanor. You mustn't overdo yourself and stay up late. Take one of the quilts from the bed I made up for Jeff when you go," mother said.

Eleanor took the hint and quickly retired. Before she left the room, she looked around self-consciously and was about to say something. Her glance collided with Hallor's and she kept silent. I could have beat him to death, then, with an ox yoke.

Hallor sensed the Thorne clan's desire to make the fur fly without others present. He retired with many stale words and phrases.

The girls and Blessing hurried to follow suit, leaving the stage set for the battle scene.

We were sitting around the large table; mother at one corner and Stella diagonally across from her; father at mother's side, opposite Stella and me on the corner, opposite mother. Our one-time benefactor was in the barn. Ours was a close-unit family about to go into action on an outsider.

"Well," mother began, "it looks like Jeff is unconscious of his duty toward Eleanor. What shall we do about it?"

"Think one of us should have a heart-to-heart talk with him," I said. "Maybe we can right things, keep Jeff with us and have a happy family again."

Father was silent. Stella looked at me with burning eyes but said nothing.

"Think I'll talk to him," mother declared. "This thing has to be righted. Looks like a job for a third party."

Father walked over and kicked the logs together in the fireplace, then cleared his throat. "Was afraid of something like this cropping up," he said disgustedly. "There'll be no inquisition. Jeff's problem is his, and Eleanor's is hers and it's up to them to work it out. When he leaves, I want you to send him away with a smile. Grace! It's bedtime."

And that was that. I think we all felt relieved. We were braced for unwilling slaughter and had the props kicked out from under us. A stern father's a handy rig sometimes.

Stella puttered around and signaled me to tarry until our parents had gone to bed. I waited with expanded ears. It wasn't going to be a fruitless evening after all.

"Eddie," she said with downcast eyes. "If Jeff loved me, would it mean anything to you?"

"Suspected it for a long time and don't like it. Why bring it up now?"

"Don't you know?" she said, emphasizing 'you.'

"I'm not his guardian angel but I am yours, partly. Say some more and I'll give you the answers. Has he said so?"

"No. But I'm sure he does. What would you say if I said I loved him?"

"Lord," I groaned as I pictured the pride of my life getting in a mess like that. "You're making it bad for me, Stell. Don't give in. There's a mortgage on him."

She looked me in the eye—a deep, searching look. "I do love him. Doesn't that make a difference?"

"No," I said, ready to fight. Be darned if it does. Jeff's got a job to do."

She began to cry, softly and bitterly. "Can't you think of anything to help us?"

"No," I said harshly. "There isn't any 'us.' Jeff'll weaken and marry Eleanor. If you don't love Joel, hold your fire for someone else."

"Jeff will never weaken," she said quietly. Then she flared, "You're a fool to think it. What kind of a brother are you? I'm in trouble—."

"Trouble!" I snorted and looked at her wild-eyed. "You, too?"

"No," she said coldly. "You're insultingly quick to jump to conclusions. Meant that I don't want to hurt Joel too much and I don't want to lose Jeff"

"I'm going to bed," I said angrily. "The devil himself couldn't straighten this mess out."

She didn't answer me but sat hunched by the table, her shoulders rounded as she held her head in her hands.

I lay awake thinking, wrathy one moment, heartsick the next. Eleanor's folly had finally engulfed the high mark in my thoughts—Stella. I hated Eleanor and Jeff by turns. I shook my fist in the dark and even paced back and forth outside in the cold hours of the morning. Gradually I calmed down and really began thinking. Her stating her problem, and asking me if it made a difference, kept weaving through my mind. About daylight the solution came. What she meant was clear. No wonder she hadn't put it in words. Her code of honor wasn't the same as mine. I'd never be happy again, but if she, in her selfishness, wanted it that way I'd do it—I'd tell them I was the guilty man and she could have Jeff. At least it would take Hallor out of the picture. I could and would do it for Stella.

At first I felt like a martyr and pictured myself a hero—known only to three people, Stella, Eleanor and Jeff. Satisfied, I slept until called for breakfast. After I got up and ate and walked in the sunshine, a black unreasoning anger came over me. I would do it, eventually, but first I'd give Jeff plenty of time to declare himself to me. I'd follow him to California—let them wait and think it over. If Jeff loved Stella, and I know it for a fact, then I'd bring him back on some excuse, make a false confession and stand the consequences.

Blessing was packing his things when I entered. Jeff was talking with father. Hallor was preening around outside. Stella was sitting in a corner mending some clothes. She hadn't looked at me during breakfast and paid no attention when I entered the big main room.

"I'm going to California with Jeff and Blessing," I said as an opener.

Stella whirled around. "No!" she cried. "You can't!"

"Oh, can't I? We'll see about that."

"Don't take him, Jeff!" she commanded. "He shouldn't go."

"He's free and almost twenty-one," Jeff answered, looking at me coldly. "Maybe he shouldn't, but he's his own boss as far as I'm concerned. Have to stand on your feet in a gold rush."

"The devil!" I flared up. "Maybe you think I can't stand on my own feet?"

"Maybe," Jeff answered indifferently. "I can pick horses but I've given up on people."

I felt hot and chewed up inside. Things were leading to an open break and I didn't want that.

"Here, here!" mother objected. "Calm down, everybody. Why do you want to go, Eddie? Don't you know we need you here? Your father must have help on the place."

I looked appealingly at her. "Father can hire help. Have personal reasons. Thought bout it all night."

"Will you look after him and Blessing, Jeff, for my sake?" mother asked.

"I'd do most anything for you, Mrs. Thorne," Jeff answered.

Stella's eyes were dark with resentment.

"Well," mother said, "I don't like to lose all my boys but I have to go by conscience. Thought during the night that Eddie would be attracted by the prospects. It'll influence his whole life. Since he wants to go so bad, perhaps he should."

"Same here," father said. "For the same reasons."

"I've been thinking," Susie declared solemnly. "We've got plenty of land here and some money, I guess, so we don't really need any more—" she hesitated and looked around—"but father's been spending money right and left, so I guess I'll have to say for Eddie to go with Jeff and Blessing and all of them bring back a sackful of gold apiece. Bless, you work hard and bring back your share."

"Hurray for you, Susie!" I yelled. "How soon do we leave, Jeff?" Hallor entered just then and sat down to listen.

"Two hours," Jeff said without enthusiasm, give me little time to get ready.

"Where are my things, Mother? I begged. "We got to hurry."

Stella wouldn't talk to me or let me talk to her. The hurt look on her face stayed with me. Not that she was on the right track; I knew she wasn't. I was the one who would pay for it. But I hated to part with her, deeply at cross purposes for the first time in our lives. The shoddy streak I had seen in her hurt me the most.

"Jeff," father said quietly, "Crusader's your horse; take him on the trip."

A glad light leaped into Jeff's eyes for an instant, then as quickly died. "Can't take him, Mr. Thorne. Keep him for a breeder." His enthusiasm rose as he thought of the stallion. "Me take a horse like that? He's worth ten thousand dollars here in Oregon."

"Nothing, Jeff, compared with what you did for us," father declared. "We want you to have him."

"No," Jeff said, with the same firmness we had seen many times before. Thanks just the same. Appreciate it."

"He's still your horse," father said, as quietly as before but kindly determined. "Just been holding him for you."

"Then I accept him," Jeff said, smiling with pleasure. "But I'll leave him here at stud in your charge, sir. They'd steal 'im where we're going."

Hallor's face flashed a look of jealousy and resentment.

We left inside of two hours, riding ordinary saddle horses, leading two packed with our outfit, food, one large tent and cooking utensils.

We hadn't gone far when Jeff said to me, "Maybe your sister was right. Why don't you do like she wanted?"

"No sir!" I said. "Me for the goldfields. No fun here."

He might not have heard me. His look was dark and far away. He made no answer.

Blessing and I were crowded to the limit. From daylight till dark Jeff never slackened the pace. Rain or sunshine, it was all the same, until we reached the vicinity of Sutter's Mill and began digging until we dropped in our tracks.

We knew little about placer mining but soon learned that even if you had gold in the gravel, water governed the situation. And California dried up its streams in large areas during the summer. It took water to carry the gold-bearing gravel over the sluice boxes and separate, in varying degrees, the precious metal from its burden. Finding gold, and water with enough fall to it, was the problem.

At Sutter's Mill all the first rich ground had been taken but we managed to get in on some that paid us good wages. Prices were high for everything. It was a guess any day where we stood financially. Jeff chafed constantly at the poor showing and finally quit, to wander about and observe others.

When he came back to camp that night he said, "Count up what we've got. This country's lousy with gold, more places than one. Met four other fellows today ready to head out of here. Looks all right to me. Need to gang up against Indians and holdups. You fellows can go along if you want to, or stay here, or go back to Oregon; I'm through at Sutter's Mill."

I was just as determined he wouldn't shake me that easy. "Suits us," I said. "Blessing and I hate this madhouse. Take the money and lead off; we'll follow."

"All right," he said, still holding his mad spell toward my family, with me as a living reminder. "Makes seven in our party. We'll buy plenty of grub. Maybe catch a stream before the water drops. We'll find gold or my name's mud. Deer and trout if we get back far enough."

We pulled stakes and Jeff took us to the other four men, all about his own age, some a trifle older.

"You two are lookin' at Bandy Hackett, Gillis Shores, Hank and Bill Freedman. Get acquainted while I head for a store. Our pile's three hundred dollars, Bandy; where's yours and how much?"

"Five hundred," Bandy Hackett said. "Hyar she is, Moorfield. Take 'er and git all yuh kin an' let's git out of this danged place. We'll round up the pack hosses an' meet yuh in about a hour."

"Fine," Jeff said, and he thawed out more than I had seen him in a long time.

Blessing had us all beat for excitement and enthusiasm. He was after his share, following Susie's orders.

Jeff was buying like a good fellow when we arrived with the horses. It wasn't long until we were on our way to any place that looked promising.

I liked our four new companions. Bandy Hackett and Hank Freedman were the talkers for them. Bill Freedman and Gillis Shores were quiet, Gillis to the point of painfulness. He just didn't have anything to say. Never in my life have I seen a man who despised to use his own tongue in speech more than he, though he listened keenly to everything that was said by others. Bandy did the talking for him when he was around and when he wasn't, the other party soon gave up, the problem was too much.

Hank and Bill were both giants in stature. They had been roaming around over the West since they were fifteen and sixteen, respectively. Reminded me of two bluff young grizzly bears, good-natured and surprisingly quick with their bodies.

Bandy had been the leader of the four and was canny of judgment and tactics but soon gave way to Jeff after the parties threw in together. It wasn't long until we were a closely knit group ready for anything, while over us all Jeff exercised a hard indifferent leadership and I might as well have been a boil on somebody's chin.

We roamed through mesquite, manzanita, sagebrush and cactus, miles upon miles, finding water but little gold. Occasionally the two were in agreement and we tried the ground until satisfied it wasn't going to yield the bonanza we were seeking. It kept us in money for food and travel but little else. Fish and game helped make up shortages.

Gradually we worked back into the mountains to higher ground. Jeff and Bandy had a theory and we were giving it a trial.

"Stands to reason," Jeff argued, "that, gold being heavy, there's a pile of it somewhere, where the vein's been worked on for ages, cracked and broken and ground, with the gold settling down in holes and cracks; we got to find a place like that. When we find it we'll have something."

"That's my idea exactly," Bandy said. "We gotta hunt until we find her and then she'll be thar."

Simple logic, I thought. If we didn't wear out, first.

By October, 1848, we hadn't found what we wanted and we were worn pretty thin, like a piece of the gold we were looking for, after it had been coined and kicked around in countless tills and pockets, tossed on many bars and dropped on a million counters. But we kept going.

Those days were among the toughest I ever experienced. Jeff kept on with his guilty conscience. He grew more hostile toward me if anything. My theories on mining had been exhausted long ago. One thing or another didn't check out and I learned to keep silent except in general arguments. But one day, in the Sierra

Nevada mountains, I looked to the south of us and observed one small canyon we had not prospected.

"Might be gold over there and water to wash it," I said timidly.

"Worth a try," the others surprised me by agreeing.

We finally arrived about dark, on a nameless little stream of good proportions and made camp in a grove of pine trees. Grouse and deer were plentiful. I went down in the deepening twilight and caught enough trout for breakfast, baiting with grasshoppers.

Gillis was up first when daylight began to break. It was his turn to water and picket the horses. Hank Freedman was cooking breakfast and the rest of us were attending to various chores; hanging food in trees, and anything else that hungry bears and their able confederates, squirrels, mice, rats, and so on, dig into and spoil.

We heard a yelp from the direction of the creek. Gillis was running in our direction waving, clutching a handful of sand and gravel. Without a word he tossed it into a plate for us to see. He was wet from head to foot.

Peeking at us from the gravel were some pieces of coarse gold, hammered and beaten by pressure of floods and bottom drift until the quartz have been knocked off.

Gillis swung his arm in the direction of the river. "Joolry store!" he forced himself to say as a big concession to his excitement.

We dropped everything and ran to see. Satisfied that we had found what we were hunting we ran back to eat and get busy. Taking lunches, we spread out to prospect our find, drawing lots for the nearest distances.

My lot was farthest away and I found gold in wonderful quantities in numerous gravel bars. That night we knew that we had stumbled on to our bonanza.

Life then became a succession of days of feverish hard work to get to bed rock in many places, hewing out riffles and washing tons of gravel. Our gold pile grew by leaps and bounds. We kept it in camp for a while but later took to burying it at night for fear of visitors, working with dread in our hearts that someone might come along and spread the news.

Jeff worked hardest and had little to say. I studied his moods and came to the conclusion that the widow preyed on his conscience but, having fallen in love with Stella, he couldn't bring himself to the point of righting his wrong. He must have considered me his silent accuser, the way he treated me.

We stayed through the winter. Several times we sent Hank and Bill to Sacramento with gold, to return with food and clothes. By April, 1849, the yield was still good and we were worth in the neighborhood of fifty thousand dollars apiece.

In all that time I had been sending short letters home but had received no word in reply. The craving to return became greater than the urge to stay and dig for gold. Blessing was content to have his pile grow, but Jeff gave no indication of how he felt about returning, until one bright, sunshiny morning.

When breakfast was over he said to me, without warning, "Through here. Got gold enough to do me for a while. You and Bless better go home. Promised your mother I'd see you back safe and sound."

"Cripes a'mighty, Jeff, yuh wouldn't leave this here spread now, would yuh?" Bandy complained.

"Nothing to stay for but more gold. Got other things on my mind. You fellows stay if you want to. How many want to stay?"

Bandy, Gillis, Hank, Bill and Blessing were for keeping at it.

"Would you be going back with us, Jeff?" I asked.

"Yes. I'll see you for a trip home."

"Me for it then," I gladly agreed.

"Blessing that means you, too," Jeff said grimly. "Contract's a contract. Remember what I told Mrs. Thorne."

"Got to make a stake while I can, Jeff," Blessing groaned. "Wish you'd settle down and be comfortable for a while."

"No deal. The three of us get out of here today. Pack your things."

"Well, I guess I got enough to see me through what I hope to do," Blessing complained. "How big a sackful is fifty thousand dollars worth of gold?"

Jeff looked at him long and hard. Finally he said, "Plenty. Must be nice to be able to look at things that way."

In four hours we were on the road home and I could hardly wait, glad that Jeff was returning and wondering how he would work things out regarding Eleanor.

We kept off the main trails and took shortcuts to Sacramento where our money was held for us, with the exception of the considerable amount that we were carrying in our belts.

"What do we do with the gold?" I asked Jeff. "Take it home or leave it in Sacramento?"

"You and Bless take yours. Think I'll leave mine there for a spell."

One thing cheered me. It was good to see Jeff so impatient to return. As the distance lessened I could hardly restrain myself and neither could Blessing. But Jeff was short-spoken and preoccupied.

"Never did see anything that looked like Cutter Jones, did we?" he said to Blessing when about thirty miles from home. "Wonder where that pirate's hangin' out? Wonder if he's in California?"

"Might have made his stake and gone back East," I said.

"You steer clear of him unless I'm around," Jeff said shortly. "Not much chance, though. Wouldn't dare come to Oregon."

We made twenty miles more to where the trail forked and the west one led to our homestead. There Jeff halted us.

"You two can make it from here before dark. Know the trail as well as I do."

"Jeff," I said in a strained, cracked voice, "aren't you going home with us?"

"You two fellows're goin' home. Mine went with the Whitmans. Give all your people and the widow my best regards. Split the outfit. Need a few things to camp with."

We took down the packs and gave him what he needed. Repacking it on one of his horses, Jeff mounted and so did we.

He looked grimly at me, reining up but not offering to shake hands. "Wish you luck. Here, give this to the widow," he said, holding out a rawhide sack weighing about fifty pounds, filled with gold dust. "Take her over some of the rough spots, maybe. So long!"

His "So long!" echoed in my ears for the rest of the day, beating at my mixed mood of anger and failure.

The effect on Blessing was pitiful, torn as he was between two loyalties and desires. "I want to go home with you but, gee! I don't see why Jeff has to go away alone all the time," he said, more downcast and forlorn than I had ever seen him.

"Looks like he didn't want company, Bless. His business. Guess we can get along if he can. Seems to hold a grudge." Out of consideration for all his help on our trip to Oregon I said no more.

CHAPTER 14

It was dark when we got off our horses and ran up to the house. The family was gathered around the fire. All too quickly came the question "Where's Jeff? Didn't he come home, too?"

"Jeff wouldn't come," I said regretfully. "Don't know just where he was headed. Oregon City, maybe."

Their faces fell.

"We brought back plenty of gold," I hastily added. "Come on, Bless, and we'll show 'em something."

Unpacking the horses we lugged the sacks of gold into the house and laid them on a table.

"Where's Eleanor? Here's a bag Jeff sent her." I held up one of the sacks.

"She's gone," Susie said. "How much gold is there? One of those sacks yours, Bless?"

"Betcher life," Bless proudly answered. "Eddie and I got fifty thousand apiece. Ten thousand in that sack for Eleanor."

"Hurray!" Susie squealed. "Good boy, Bless. You did like I told you to. Now you can buy stock and build a house"—she hesitated when she saw us listening—"and put the rest in a bank," she added, blushing.

"We could a got a lot more if Jeff hadn't been in such an all-fired hurry to make us come home," Blessing grumbled.

"Oh, that's enough," Susie said airily. "You're just a boy yet."

"Tell us more about Jeff," Stella said impatiently.

"There isn't anything much to tell, Sis," I said sorrowfully. "He wouldn't come any closer'n ten miles. Guess he's still shy of Eleanor. Where is she anyway? And where's Hallor?"

"You tell him Culver. It's your story, most of it," mother said.

"You're convinced Jeff was the guilty party, Eddie?" father asked me.

"Sure. Who else could it have been?"

"Hallor. Stella got so she wouldn't even speak to him and he decided to leave. He came to tell me good-by. I was in a bad mood. Just finished shooting a horse that broke its leg. Pointed the gun at him and said, "You'll do right by Eleanor or I'll shoot you down like a mad dog.""

"'Why, suh, what do yo' mean?' he said, like he was surprised.

"'Marry her,' I said, 'You're the guilty one. Happened the night you stood guard with Blessing, about the middle of August. Saw you leaving her wagon in the morning.' Hadn't actually seen him get out of the wagon but it looked that way. 'Own up or I'll organize a lynching party and tell all I know.' That got him. He begged me not to do it. He'd marry Eleanor and be glad to. He'd been foolish and would do well by her if given a chance—just one more chance. Susie came rambling by just then and I sent her for Eleanor.

"When Eleanor came, I said 'This man has promised to do right by you, Eleanor. Thought I'd let you know and take the worry off your mind.'

"She looked at him disgustedly and said, 'I'd as soon marry a magpie, but—the quicker the better, I guess. I'm not a bad woman, Mr. Thorne. Must have been out of my head.'"

"'I'll send for the preacher and we can get the job done tomorrow,' I said. 'How about it, Hallor? You agree?'"

'Ah agree, suh. Ah'm glad to right mah wrongs, so fah as possible.'

"'Eleanor,' I said, 'did you know that Jeff was blamed for this?'"

"Her eyes opened wide and then she began crying. She pointed at Hallor. 'He threatened to kill me if I told on him. Threatened to kill the whole family and himself. Didn't know what to do. If I'd known soon enough and told Jeff before he left he'd have straightened things out plenty fast. But he was gone and I was afraid this hyena would do something. Was afraid no one would believe me. Except Jeff, he would have. He was so kind to me. What a fool I've been.'

"'No use crying over spilt milk, Eleanor,'" I said. "'The best you can do now is marry the critter—tomorrow. Do you hear, Hallor?'"

'Yes, suh,' he said meekly.

"The session ended there. Was afraid he'd run away. I stood guard over him half the night and then was spelled off by the hired man we had then. Hallor was gone next morning. We trailed him south for a ways but lost track and had to come home. The hired man skinned out for the gold rush. Hallor must have bought him off."

"Eleanor felt disgraced more than ever. When she was strong enough—after the big event—cute little twin girls—she decided to leave. Let her have what money we could spare and she went south, too. She didn't find Hallor. She's working in San Francisco, trying to save up money and buy a rooming house. That's my story, son. Felt bad the way it turned out. Eleanor was heartbroken for her little girls—that they didn't have their rightful name."

"Gosh," I said, glancing at Stella. 'Wait till I find Jeff and tell him that.'

"That's just what you don't want to do," father objected. "Jeff isn't the kind. You can't say, 'Well, we've found the right one. You can come back now.' Get it over to him in some round about way. He's sensitive and knows that we shouldn't have suspicioned him in the first place. Can't blame him much. I'd feel the same way. Time we thought of his side instead of how it suits us. When you find him, Eddie, your job's cut out. Be careful how you talk to him."

"Yes," mother agreed, glancing at Stella. "Don't drive him away again."

The talk continued a long time. Blessing and I covered the ground to California and back and all our trials and tribulations. Jeff was still the center of our little world, as he had been on the Trail.

"Those partners you had must have been fine men," mother said, after my account of how true blue they were and how we had depended on each other.

Stella lingered to have a few words with me, alone. "You will find him, won't you, Eddie? It worries me sick. He seemed to think so much of our family life and enjoyed it so."

"Never showed much love for you," I reminded her. "Might be in love with Eleanor. Sent her a present, don't forget."

"I know it," she replied miserably. "It seemed so easy once I'd made up my mind, and then everything fell to pieces, all on account of that despicable Hallor. Why wasn't he man enough to confess instead of deliberately trying to throw the blame on Jeff?"

"Because, my darling sister, you didn't pick good stuff to start with. Always knew he was a spoiled egg. Riled me every time I saw you throwing yourself at him. Someone should have shot him at the start."

"Didn't either throw myself at him. Nobody else paid me compliments. I was beautiful to him, no matter how ragged and dirty. I knew it. Women have ways of telling. At the start, all my thoughts were in Virginia, where he came from. The Trail was terrible but, now it's back of me, I wouldn't have missed it for anything. Jeff brooded over us night and day. I can see his hot eyes now, driving us, looking for enemies, standing between us and destruction. Everything he told us was true and we didn't believe him. And then at the very first chance they blamed Eleanor's affair on him. Something he would never stoop to do."

"Just a minute, Sis," I interrupted. "Where were you when all the blaming was going on? You think he was such a saint, why didn't you speak up and defend him? Who did you think did it?"

And then the tears that had been near all evening came in a flood.

"I won't answer that," she sobbed. "but I had faith and confidence in him after I got to know him, even if he did treat me—like I treated him."

My sympathy went out to her in her loneliness and disappointment. She deserved better treatment.

"Never mind, honey," I said, giving her a friendly squeeze, "I'll find Jeff and square everything. I'll bring him in, roped and tied, ready for the harness. Cheer up. Watch your old brother help things out."

"Don't, Eddie! Don't do that! Don't tell him anything. For goodness sake don't give me away. If you find him and he wants to keep on with Eleanor, don't try to stop him. If he won't come to me of his own free will, don't try to influence him. Promise, Eddie!"

"Lord help me if I take on any more contracts after I get through with this thing," I bellyached. "All the dad-blamed advice! You and father. You act like I haven't got a brain in my head."

"Don't be cross, Eddie," she begged. "I just wanted another chance. He must be terribly lonely and hurt."

"You'll have it," I growled. "if I have to hunt all of North America I'll find him and bring him back, some way. Then I'll sit and watch the wise ones do it. Maybe we'd better get some sleep. Leaving first thing in the morning."

"Eddie," she said hesitatingly. "If Jeff comes back, do you think—do you think he'll find me—will he see anything in me to attract him? Have I changed? There isn't any way of telling. No usual way that girls have when there are plenty of boys to go with—and other girls. Like at a dance—in Virginia—or back where we came from. Tell me, Eddie, just what you think."

"Well," I said studiously, "You've grown. Look like a real woman now. Still carry yourself well and your waist is still thin and waspy. Hair's soft and beseeching. Complexion good. Little darker from the trip but makes it even better. Yes, I guess, Sis, you'll pass. If Jeff can't see you when he comes, I don't know what he'd want. Be blind, I reckon."

"Or have somebody else's picture in mind. Eleanor was more beautiful than ever when she left," she countered. "Glad I don't know. If I did, I'd worry about it."

"You're almost brazen about this fancy for Jeff," I said. "It don't do yuh jestice, gal."

"Oh, I can say anything to you. It's just like talking to myself. Nobody else ever knows how far it goes."

Sounded like a threat to me to keep quiet about the conversation before I left for California. "You don't need to worry about me," I said meaningly.

"Goodnight," she said, with a far away look in her eyes. "Do your duty tomorrow, be sure."

I rose early in the morning and helped feed the stock. Something seemed missing. "Where's Crusader?" I finally asked when it dawned on me.

Father kicked a clod. Tears came to his eyes as he looked away at the trees in the distance. "We couldn't tell you last night, Son. Hallor rode him away."

My heart felt heavy. "Might have been in California," I said bitterly. "Wish I'd looked around some."

"Hallor wasn't a true southerner, Son," father said gently. "A spoiled fool. All he had was their way of speaking. He rode Crusader south. We followed hard for almost two hundred miles. We found Crusader—dead. Been dead about two days—where he dropped after running his heart out." He choked up with rage and sorrow.

I stood there unable to put my emotion in words, not wanting to.

"Eddie," he said, "you know all about it now. Let's not mention it anymore. Hurts everybody too much. Bred some good mares and have some fine colts. We'll build from them."

None but Joel Hallor could have done such a thing. It was as if we'd lost part of the family. His revenge was complete.

As soon as I had breakfast I was off on the trail of Jeff, with the family's advice and best wishes for success ringing in my ears.

Didn't see anyone I wanted to question until I got to Oregon City. Beaut Savage was standing in front of a store.

"Hi, thar, Eddie," he called.

I got off my horse and hurried to him. "Hello, Beaut. Good to see you again. Looking for Jeff Moorfield. See anything of him?"

"Nary a sign. Jest pulled in a while ago. Like tuh see him myself. Town sure looks good after yuh come in from the brush. Been he'pin' 'em put the kibosh tuh the Cayuses. Jeff's got quite a repatation, ain't he?"

"Guess so. Been away myself. So has he. What'd you hear?"

"Wal, he's the one they blame fur keepin' the Nez Perces friendly whiles we was wallopin' the Cayuses. He's heap big Tillicum with 'em. Swum the Columbia once an' saved a wife an' kid of one of the chiefs. Made him a blood brother or somethin'. When he left us jest after the Massacre he headed back tuh the Dalles, burnin' like a rag. Didn't stop thar but kept on a goin'. Right tuh the Nez Perces. Shot some Cayuses on the way. They aimed tuh ketch 'im. Ten was chasin' him, but only five was left after he picked some off. When he got to the Nez Perces he claimed his rights and the Nez Perces knocked off the five what was left fur tryin' tuh kill a blood brother. That didn't do the Cayuses no good. After Jeff got in a few more licks, the Nezes wouldn't turn a hand tuh wipe out the whites but stayed friendly.

"Boy, that was like getting' in out of the rain. Kept us from a full-fledged war. If the Nezes had a gone wrong, all the other gol dang tribes would a ganged up. Des Chutes, Walla Wallas, Palouses, Willamettes, Clatsops an' the whole mess was a achin' tuh go. Some of 'em did but it kinda damped their powder when the Nezes wouldn't. We licked hell outa the Cayuses. No more Cayuse tribe. Jeff kept makin' visits on 'em an' the Nezes would pertect him. When they makes a blood brother out of a feller they means it. Too bad about the widow scandal, warn't it?"

"How's that?" I asked.

"All us danged busybodies laid the blame on 'im an' then it got around that he pulled out an' wouldn't marry her. It warn't Jeff."

"How did you know, Beaut?"

"I axed him jest afore he headed fur the gold rush. He said it warn't him. Axed him who he thought it was an' he said he wouldn't say fur a million dollars. Who did yuh think it was, Eddie? Ever find the skunk?"

"Yes. Hallor. He confessed and pulled out."

"Shoulda hung 'im. Ever'body musta been asleep."

"Distant relative. I wasn't here or we might have managed, someway."

An old fellow who had been standing near, poked his head into the conversation then. "I seed Moorfield a ridin' South this mornin'. Goin' hell-bent. He waved tuh me an' I waved back tuh him."

"Funny I didn't pass him. Came that way myself."

"Heh, heh, heh," the old fellow cackled. "Jeff watches his hosse's ears. If he don't want tuh meet people, he don't." Then he walked away, still cackling.

"What did that old buffalo chip mean by that, Beaut?"

"Guess Jeff still found the poison ag'in 'im an' didn't like it. Whar's the widow now?"

"California."

"Wal, mebbe he's on her trail. Liked her purty well, looked tuh me. Told me she'd make someone a good wife, but he'd be danged if he was goin' tuh take the blame an' hide the coyote what did, if the coyote didn't have gumption enough tuh own up on his own hook."

"Sounds like Jeff. Better be on my way. Got big news when I find him."

Thought maybe Jeff might have gone to the ranch and would be waiting when I got back. He might have taken a different road and not seen me coming to town. The story of Hallor's guilt hadn't circulated, but Jeff might have heard the truth anyway, else why had he gone south again toward our place? It cheered me and I hurried back, ready for good news instead of bringing it.

Stella was down the road a ways when I came along. Her face fell when she saw me coming alone. None of the Thornes could hide their feelings beyond a certain point, which was about skin deep.

"Didn't Jeff come?" I asked, knowing very well he hadn't after one look at her.

"Haven't seen him," she answered dully.

"Heard he headed South this morning. Some old rancher told me. Said he recognized him."

"South?" She studied it with a caved-in expression. "Would that mean— California—again?"

"Guess so. Looks like it, now. Saw Beaut Savage in Oregon City. Said to tell everybody hello for him."

"Thank you."

"Do you know what he told me, Stell?"

"No idea."

"Said he asked Jeff if he was the guilty one and Jeff told him he wasn't. Beaut asked him who he thought it was. Jeff said he wouldn't say for a million dollars. Told Beaut the widow would make someone a fine wife but he'd be danged if he was going to take the blame and hide the coyote who did, if the coyote didn't have gumption enough to own up to it."

"When did he say that? Did Beaut see him?"

"Naw. That was when Jeff pulled out for the gold rush. Beaut missed him this trip."

"Wonder what that means?" she asked, tensely. There was a hardening look in her eyes.

"Did you folks tell anyone about Hallor?"

"No. We let it be known that Eleanor left for California but we just couldn't tell the rest of it. Family pride, I guess. So far as any outsider knows, Hallor is coming back—later."

"Of all the fool moves! You let people go on thinking it was Jeff when you knew different? This family must be locoed."

"I wanted to but father wouldn't have it. Made us promise. Said it was bad enough and that we could straighten it out when Jeff came back. But I think it's been gossiped around."

"Well, it's out now for sure," I said angrily. "Told Beaut Savage. After the harm's done. Too bad someone around here hasn't got some sense."

"Well, don't quarrel with father about it. If Jeff wants to follow Eleanor to California, let him. It's his business," she flared at me. "He must have heard and decided."

"Now listen, Sis," I argued, "you're going at this wrong. For once, Jeff's on the wrong trail without knowing it. You're hanging him without any evidence."

"Let him hang then. I can get over how I feel. It'll wear off in time. Let me have enough money to go back East and finish going to school. I've stagnated here long enough."

"I will not. That's just peevishness. You'll stay here until I find Jeff and tell him the whole story."

"I'll run away then. If he had any feeling for me he'd have come home with you—"

"Listen, you hot-headed little brat, can't you see how it is? Jeff thinks—"

"I don't care what he thinks. I want to go East and teach school—"

"You've got enough education to teach school here. Wait till I find Jeff—"

"You'll not follow him. I'd be disgraced after you got through. He'd think I was running after him. I'll not run after any man, Jeff Moorfield or anyone else." She stamped her foot. "You stay home where you belong and help out. Father needs you."

"Not by a darned sight."

Mother called from the house, "Any news, Eddie?"

"Be there in a minute, Mother," I answered. "Buck up, Stell, and listen to reason. Give him a chance."

"He's had chances enough. If he loved me he would have figured things out. He never even liked me."

I grabbed her and spun her around. "Did you see him after the Indian fight, this side of Green River? Did you see him when he made us stop in the blinding rain and camp until you were better? No, of course you didn't. But I did—"

"He would have done as much and more for Eleanor. She's the one he really likes. If he doesn't care for the Thorne family he doesn't have to."

"You're so mule-headed no one can argue with you," I bellowed.

"Go on to the house, then! Shut up and leave me alone!" she threw at me. "You're no help anyway. You never were."

It was a bad evening at home but not dull by a long shot. Stella was determined I'd look no farther for Jeff. Mother was referee and didn't commit herself. Susie was definitely with me. Marjorie and Mabel were quiet for once. They were terribly disappointed and took that way of showing it.

Toward the closing scene, when the battle was going against me, Susie said, "Did Jeff ever shoot Cutter Jones like he promised? Did he, Bless?"

"Never found him or he would of," Bless answered somberly.

"Looks to me then, like Jeff fell down on his job. But we have to give him time," she added quickly.

"Probably forgotten about Cutter Jones, too," Marjorie chirped up.

"Hate to be in Jones' boots if Jeff ever meets him," Blessing said grimly. "That's all I got to say."

"I hope he shoots him," Susie added, "and leaves him lying in a pool of blood a foot deep—"

"Susie!" mother scolded. "Such terrible talk. Stop it!"

When we finally turned in to get some sleep we all were on edge.

I got up in the morning, moping mad and showed it. After breakfast I went out to the sunny side of the house and sat down. Sat there most of the morning.

About noon Stella came out and sat down beside me. "What are you thinking about, Eddie?"

"None of your business. How do you like that?"

"Are you going to California?"

"You going to pull out of here?" I snarled back.

"I couldn't. Mother's had enough trouble the last couple of years. Her health might fail again. You hadn't better leave, either."

"I'd die here, now. Don't you people like Jeff anymore?"

"Yes, we do," she said, taking her time about it. "But things have changed. You talk to mother and see if you should go."

I went in the house and mother motioned me to one side. "You going to California again, Eddie?"

"All depends," I said cautiously. "Why?"

"Been thinking of what you told us about it. Must be a beautiful country. The climate, I mean, must be so different. So much sunshine. Captain Sutter's ranch—did he really have orange trees there? Joking, weren't you?"

"No, Mother. Only saw parts that the gold hunters hadn't wrecked, but what I did see made me wish, almost, that gold hadn't been found. Shame to spoil it. Sun was pretty hot at times but with water—irrigation, I mean—there isn't any limit to what one could do." I looked at her suspiciously. "Where's all this leading to, Mother?"

She blushed in confusion of trying to gather information and not betray her thoughts. A struggle went on in her face before she decided to take the leap.

"Eddie, I don't know what's got into me; I'm not satisfied. We could have a farm here that would be a wonder to behold, but I keep yearning to go on and see some more. Can't understand it. I'll never be happy until I see California, and I wouldn't have your father know it for anything. Seems like as soon as I got comfortable again I ached to be leaving. Been that way ever since."

I looked at her with mock seriousness. "Mother, you've got the same disease father had. First symptoms are when a person climbs a ridge to see what's on the other side. Have you done that?"

"Yes, I believe I have—" then she glanced sharply at me and gave me a little poke—"oh, you're just making a fool of me."

"It starts out like a joke, mother, but after a while you get so you'd give your eyeteeth to see the other side of the ridge. Most people in the West have it. Guess you'll just have to fight it out alone since father's got the ranch he's been after."

"He has so much land now, and plans to go with it; there'll never be any going any more," she said wistfully. "You know, it wouldn't be hard to move to California. Not near like our trip here. It'd seem like a picnic. Just a few hundred miles would put us way into that country. We could get land near the ocean and have sunshine and orange trees, too." She shook herself loose from her thoughts. "What am I talking about? Must be getting dotty."

"Confidentially, Mother, it's got me, too," I whispered. "Can't see Oregon any more. Thinking about using Jeff as an excuse to roam around in California again. What do you think?"

"You must find him, Eddie. We simply can't let him go on believing the way he does, whatever it is. If he learns the whole story and then chooses to keep away from us, why we've done our duty by him. Don't back down on that. Haven't said much but I've been thinking."

"That makes me feel like an Indian with a lot of fresh scalps, Mother. Do you know what Stella said? Said you couldn't stand it if I left again. Thought your health was failing. Had me worried."

"Health!" she scoffed. "If I felt any better I'd complain. Nothing to do with health. It's this country. Too dense for me. Seem hemmed in all the time. Feel like I want to climb to a point that's higher than the whole country, fill my lungs and squall like a panther. Isn't that an awful way to say it?"

"Same old ridge fever, Mother. Bad case. Have it myself right now. Let's climb up on the barn and squall together."

"Would, but it isn't high enough," she said, smiling. "Squalling doesn't count without distance. What are you going to do with all your money, Son?"

The answer came to me on the spur of the moment, brought on by our common desire. "Going to take some with me for expenses, but the rest I'll leave with you. If a chance ever comes to jar father loose and head south, feel free to use the whole pile. Be worth it. Will you?"

"Not a chance in the world, Son, of ever getting your father in the notion now. But it's nice to think about. Now, if Jeff had come home and married Stella and we all thought the same way—goodness, there I go again. Shoo along. Next meal's looking me in the eye. Dreams don't fill a stomach."

"No, but they help an appetite, Mother. Keep dreaming. I'm standing on what I said—Jeff, California, the whole shebang."

"That's good, son. Do what you think best in carrying it out," she replied staunchly.

With Jeff's head start I knew I couldn't catch him unless I rode night and day. But I was tired out and waited a while before beginning my hunt for him. Put the time to good use complaining about the Oregon weather and praising California, winking at mother when I knew no one was looking. We had quite a game of it.

Nothing jarred father out of his glumness. He moped around like he had lost his last friend. Went about his work listlessly and took little interest in the conversation. Finally one day, catching me away from the house, he said, "Stop bragging so much about California. Doesn't help us any. Wish things had turned out better."

"All right, father," I meekly agreed, stroking the stubble on my chin for assurance that I was man enough to speak up to him. "You might as well know I've decided to chase him down and clear up a few things. What's the matter? Don't act like yourself these days."

"Different things. One's Jeff. Thought a lot of him. Depended on having him around somewhere. Kind of like to go along for the trip but it's out of the question. Can't leave the family. Your mother wouldn't stand for it."

"No, I don't think she would. Might want to go, too." I hoped to say more if he gave me a chance.

"Don't start harping on it," he said moodily. "We're all set here. Place would go to rack and ruin. Started out to have a home in Oregon and we'll have it. How does your mother feel about you pulling out again?"

"Want's me to find Jeff. Can't quite understand Stella objecting so hard. Says we mustn't leave things this way."

A quick anger swept his face. "Stella's another Thorne fool like me. Can't stand disappointment. If your mother feels that way about it, go ahead. But don't give Stella away. Was hoping she'd change toward Jeff and she did. When you find him tell him about Hallor. Let him find out anything else for himself. Affairs like that usually swing around. If they don't, they didn't amount to anything in the first place. Remember. Don't rattle too much. When you leaving?"

"Tomorrow. No use waiting any longer. Nobody saw Jeff around here except that one old man. Must have gone south. If I don't pick up his trail I'll come home. He may join Bandy Hackett and the bunch."

"Don't take Blessing. Needs some home life for a change. Too young to keep on roaming around."

Blessing didn't put up much of a struggle but he did say, "I'll stick around here. If you give up, Eddie, you can figure on me headin' after him. Nothing'll stop me."

"It's a bargain. If we have to, we'll work it in relays."

Before leaving, I said, "Get in some dirty work while I'm gone, Mother. I'll spot a good place if you make a deal."

"How do you think your father would take it?" she whispered.

"Couldn't tell for sure. Might need to be bluffed. Damp climate here part of the time. Blame it."

"Oh, I wouldn't do that to your father. Wouldn't be right."

Stella walked a ways with me after I told the others good-by.

"How about it, Stell? You going to wait until I bring Jeff back?"

"That, my dear brother, is for Jeff to find out," she said. "Wish I could go, too, for the trip."

"That's what mother and dad both say. Funny family. Never satisfied. But you shouldn't give up until you've seen California. Down where they pull water out of rivers and put it on the ground. And then grow trees. Different here. Trees pull the clouds. No gold here."

"Wish I were a man." Her eyes seemed hungry with thoughts of roads and trails. Rebellion. "You go everywhere, free as the wind. Women are prisoners. Kiss me good-by and get out of sight. You act like a prophet from the sun, selling land."

I kissed her tenderly. Her mood was like an open book.

"Eddie, be careful." Her voice had the quality of a bell, tuned for sorrow. "Come back soon. J. McQ. Tilden sent word his family was moving to Oregon. You remember Patricia Tilden."

"Do I? That case of puppy love grew up to be a big dog. Still whines when the moon gets right—" I looked at her. "Say, if I remember correctly J. McQ. kind of hoed a row with you, too, as a kid. How about it? You plotting something?"

"Jealous for Jeff?" she said with eyebrows lifted. "I told you I was through. J. wouldn't have come so near without seeing me just once. He isn't any Joel Hallor, either." She paused and looked at me at an angle. "Pioneer women have to be careful or they die old maids. J. wrote me a letter months ago. Just got it. He asked me—to wait for him."

"What'd you tell him? Did you answer him?"

"Yes. Right away. Told him about the wonderful opportunities out here. About the fine land near us. Hunting. Fishing. And everything else."

"What else?" I took her arm and shook her excitedly. "Did you promise him? Did you tell the folks about it?"

"Not yet. Saving it until you leave on your wild goose chase. And what I told J. McQ. Is my own business."

"Well," I said savagely. "It's a tough trail out here. Be months before they come. I'll be back with Jeff before then, you miserable little flirt."

Her laugh was aimed to dig me down. "Try to be back for my wedding, Eddie, dear. Bring some nuggets for a present. Good-by."

No use. I jumped on my horse and wheeled him around. "If I don't find Jeff I won't be back. This family makes me sick," I hurled as a parting shot. Above the clatter the horse made galloping away, I heard Stella call, "Eddie, wait a minute!" but acted like I didn't hear her.

J. McQ. had me worried. He was a regular fellow. Smooth and likeable. Plenty of money and he meant business. With Stella doubting Jeff, feeling like she was in prison, she might marry him when he came. She liked him pretty well before we left Illinois. If we'd stayed, it might have grown into something.

CHAPTER 15

I was traveling light. All I had was a blanket roll, a gun and a few supplies. In five or six months I could cover a lot of ground in California, find Jeff and get him to come home with me. I'd figure out some excuse.

Taking the gold Jeff sent to Eleanor I headed for San Francisco and located her. She was working from early morning to late at night in a restaurant as waitress.

"Howdy, Eleanor," I said, easy like, when she came to take my order.

"Eddie," she cried, dropping a pitcher of water, looking at me wide-eyed. "Did your folks come with you?"

The proprietor rushed over. "What's goin' on here?" he said, glowering at her and gnawing at his long plow handles. "Clean up that mess and git busy."

Eleanor flushed and stooped over to pick up the pieces in a hurry.

"You look sick, mister. Something wrong?" I said.

"Who's this big mouth?" he asked Eleanor.

"None of your business, uncle. The girl's quitting her job."

"Eddie, don't," she implored. "I need this work for my babies—"

"Yuh mope too much," old Plow Handles said. "You're fired."

"Get your coat and hat, Eleanor. Got a present for you. You won't have to work anymore."

She still had a doubtful look on her face when I met her at the door.

"Jeff sent you ten thousand dollars. Got it locked up for you. Here's the receipt."

She stared at me in surprise. "Where's Jeff now?"

"Somewhere in California. I'm on his trail."

"I can't take all that money, Eddie. It wouldn't be right."

"You'll have to. Jeff sent it. Don't know where he is."

"Tell me all about everything. Been so lonesome I could die."

"Well, first off, give me a kiss and say you're glad to see me."

"Don't, Eddie. Be serious. Where's the family? How is everyone? Tell me."

I proceeded to tell her all that had happened since she left. She was disappointed to hear that the family hadn't come, too.

146

"I could take the money as a loan. There's a rooming house I could buy and make enough to pay it back," she said, kind of dazed. "Good of Jeff to think of me. He's a fine man."

"How about the man who brought it all the way here? Risking his life, fighting robbers?"

"You're a fine man, too, Eddie. I'll hurry and dress and we'll have a long talk. Can you spare the time?"

"Can I, Eleanor? Would an Indian scalp? Does a wolf like buffalo meat?"

"Let's hurry! I'll stop for my babies on the way. You can take care of them while I get ready."

"Oh, yes, babies," I said cautiously. "You're looking mighty fine, Eleanor."

"Thank you, Eddie. So are you. Your moustache is very becoming."

"Just a starter, gal. Got real whiskers ordered. These are my hope hairs."

"Does Jeff wear one, too?"

"Full beard sometimes," I answered grudgingly. Didn't like the way she kept dragging Jeff into the conversation.

"How does that suit Stella?"

"Don't know. He hasn't been back."

"He hasn't? Why, I thought they'd be married long ago."

"He—uh—Jeff is—he never heard the particulars."

She blushed a dull red. "Thought the whole world knew about it by now. My babies are awfully cute. You'll like them."

"Yes, I like babies," I said, feeling like a dog that had been kicked across the street. "Great things—babies. Like to hear 'em cry and everything."

"That's just lovely, Eddie. So many men haven't time for them, you know."

"Yes, and they wouldn't if they could. Funny animals, men."

She looked at me and laughed. Same teeth. Same hair. Same eyes. Only better. My memory hadn't done justice to her. More potent now. Some little change since I last saw her. Kind of got me. Had a hard time concentrating on Jeff and keeping her from it.

The babies were cute. We left them with a friend. I took her to supper and we talked for hours. Great night. When it was too late to undo the damage and boost my own stock, I wondered why I hadn't thought to bring her the money as a present from me. I swore to myself I'd keep Jeff away from her if it was the last act of my life. Gold was where you found it. So was a good-looking gal like Eleanor.

I hung around for a week and helped her buy a rooming house out of the ten thousand. When I set out again on the trail of Jeff, my eyes were bulging from looking at her and my heart was beat to a pulp. I wanted to stay and I wanted to get away. I'd herd Jeff into Stella's influence first, or die trying. Toward the last, when I was leaving, she said she thought Hallor was in San Francisco, or had been.

"Thought I saw him leave the restaurant one day when I was coming on shift," she said. "Looking kind of prosperous, like a gambler. Don't forget, Eddie. When you find Jeff, tell him to come and see me."

I had that to ring in my ears from then on. A sensitive nature like mine. I'd see them in Halifax before I brought them together. Just as I was leaving, I grabbed her and kissed her smack on the lips.

"Wages," I said. "Worked for nothing long enough." Knew I was blushing like a girl and flustered like a fool.

She let those eyes rest on me kind of startled like for about a minute, seemed to me, and then her face broke into a smile and her voice was even and steady. "Eddie, I didn't know you felt that way about me. Here. I'll give you one for luck. Put your arms around me and don't ever think I'm not grateful for what you've done."

Well, a starving dog snatches at anything in sight. I kissed her hard and plenty. Staggered away with a feeble wave of my hand, half blind. Looked back after I was about a hundred feet away and she had gone into the house. I was convinced, down in my heart, that Jeff had the inside road there.

Went to Placerville and searched the diggings. A new saloon was opening. Waited to see if Jeff was in the crowd. Ran smack into Cutter Jones, the proprietor, but he didn't recognize me although he looked kind of puzzled. Then I stuck around a while longer to see if Jeff had wind of Jones and was going to look him up. He had four or five tough mugs hanging around like bodyguards—of the same stripe and bloodthirstiness, it seemed.

Went to Hangtown and any other place I thought of. Even made a trip into the old diggings where we made our stake, but found none of the bunch there. Was held up and robbed three times and had to go to work each time to make money to travel with. Months passed by and it looked pretty black. All the time the thought gnawed at me that Jeff might have found Eleanor and was with her. That I was a fool not to go back to Frisco and look in on her again.

Then I overheard a remark about Major Fremont making a killing farther south and I headed for him. He and Jeff had been friends. He might know where to find him.

The major was far to the south on forty thousand acres, different ones told me. Thought that was a little fishy but found it true when I got there. Not only that but he had some good gold mines on the property and was making money hand over fist. Making up for his bad luck in having to resign from the army after a military court decided against him.

He was a quiet, short-spoken man, sitting behind a big desk figuring up mine reports when one of his men finally let me in to speak to him.

"Howdy, Major," I said. "I'm looking for a man named Jeff Moorfield. Seen anything of him? Heard he was a friend of yours."

"Who are you?" he shot back at me.

"A friend of his."

"Sorry. Don't give out information here." He looked at me all the time, hostile as an old bear. His face was deep-tanned from sunshine and rain. "Don't call me *Major*."

"See here, Mr. Fremont," I said, "I'm a friend of Jeff's and got to find him. Means a lot to him. We crossed the plains with him. He captained the caravan. The only family train he'd ever look at."

"Your name Thorne?"

"Yes. My father is Culver Thorne. Lives in Oregon."

He looked at me with new interest. "You come to do justice by Jeff?"

"Yes," I replied hopefully. "You must have heard the story."

"Some. Pretty good friend of mine. Too bad he isn't here. Left yesterday."

"Where'd he go? I'll go after him."

The major took his time about answering, then it was blunt and to the point. "He went to shoot Cutter Jones in Placerville."

"The devil he did!" I said excitedly. "I got to stop him."

"Why?"

"Jones' got a bunch of outlaws like himself hanging around his place. Jeff wouldn't have a chance."

"Hmph!" he snorted. "Thought you knew Jeff. Didn't go alone. Took some help along."

"Bandy Hackett? And the others? Did he find them again?"

The major nodded. "Partners in a mine next to my property. Steered him on to it. Doing well."

I thought that over. If the major would answer my next question I had a strong indication of how the land lay with Jeff.

"One more question, Mr. Fremont. If Jeff had property here and was tying into trouble, did he say anything about the mine if he didn't come back?"

The sizing up the major had given me before was easy to the cold hard glance he gave me then. "Yes. Said to cut the widow in as a partner with whatever ones come back. Give her the whole thing if they got in too tough a jack pot. Said your folks would know where to find her."

"Thank you, sir," I said in a daze at what the words meant. Nothing could be plainer. "Guess I'd better be going. How many in Jeff's gang?"

"Six, with Jeff."

"I know Hackett and Shores and the Freedman brothers. Who's the other one? Can he hold up his end with a gun?"

Fremont smiled kind of funny. "Name's John Scanlon. Deputy U.S. Marshall on a vacation."

I walked to the door and then turned back to the major. Want you to know this much, Mr. Fremont. Jeff laid himself open to suspicion and he isn't treating my family right by not giving them a chance to square themselves. Don't know all he told you but—"

"Jeff told me very little. Figured the rest out," he interrupted. "Wanted me to understand how it was with the widow. Haven't got time to fool with you today. Better leave before I have you run off the place."

"I'll find Jeff and make him listen if I never do another damned thing in my life. You sit here like a little Caesar on a throne, passing judgment—"

"I'm Jeff's friend. Clear out!" he said, biting the words off at the heels."

He meant it and I knew when I was well off. Left him with my feathers all turned the wrong way and my wattles red. Beat the world how one small incident on a lonely caravan could reach so far and split up so many people who ought to be friends.

Jeff, as usual, didn't waste time on the trail to Placerville. I couldn't cut down the day's lead they had on me no matter how hard I tried.

My thoughts were scrambled. Planning to herd Jeff Stella's direction was one thing, him heading for trouble was another. I could help some in a pinch. Even had visions of being a hero by adding one more gun to the fracas. I'd stick out my chest and say, "Well, Jeff, guess I got here in the nick of time."

Arrived in Placerville late at night and peeked in at Cutter Jones' saloon. He was playing cards. No sign of Jeff and his gang. I hung around until early in the morning. Nothing happened. I put my horse in a stable and managed to find a room. That was all I remember until about four in the afternoon.

Hurried to look in on Jones and could see that no big upheaval had taken place yet. After getting something to eat I began scouting around town hoping to run into them. Remembering my experience with the bartender in Independence I picked out a likely looking one and asked him if he knew anyone of Jeff's description.

"Nope. Ten thousand men around these diggin's. How kin I keep track uh all of 'em? What's his name?"

"Jeff Moorfield," I said.

"Nope. Never heard of him. Maybe dead. Did yuh look in thuh graveyard?"

That set me back and I started to leave when a tall man, about thirty-five years old, slightly stooped, wearing long moustaches, with a cold, space-guessing eye, stepped in stride with me. "Jest keep goin', young feller, ontil yuh're outside. I wants tuh talk tuh yuh." His hard flat voice almost threw me into a stampede, but I hid it the best I could.

He stopped me at a spot where we couldn't be overheard. "Heerd yuh mention names back thar. It ain't good bizness," he said as his eyes bored into mine.

"Was only inquiring to find a friend. Been hunting him for a long time," I answered.

"What proof yuh got at bein' a friend?"

"Mister," I said, "you got the drop on me. I'm not fancy with a gun. But I'll be damned if I tell you any more until I know who you are." Scared but had to play the same game.

The hard, piercing eyes weighed me plenty. Kind of bleak eyes as though they had looked in on a lot of trouble. He lit a cigar. "Ain't passin' my name around. What yuh know about the man yuh was askin' fur?"

"That's my business."

"Will yuh tell if I sez my name?"

"Right, if it means anything to me."

"John Scanlon. What's your'n?"

I jumped as though shot at and broke into a broad grin. "You're his partner near Fremont's. My name's Eddie Thorne."

"Heerd Bandy Hackett mention yuh. Yuh're from Oregon whar yor fam'ly lives. Yuh come in a caravan led by Jeff."

"The same and glad to see you," I answered.

"Let's git down tuh bizness. What's yore all-fired hurry tuh find Jeff?"

"You fellows are up here to get Cutter Jones and I want to talk Jeff out of taking a chance. Too much depends on him. Want to tell him something first."

"Cutter Jones?" Scanlon was puzzled. "Danged if I ever heerd of him. Who is the varmint?"

Surprised at that, I told him the whole story. John shook his head and said, "Thet accounts fur it. I knowed Jeff war up tuh mischief. Ain't seen any of the buzzards sence about noon. Makes me purty danged sore."

Pulling out a huge silver-cased watch, he looked at it and studied. "Wal, it ain't more'n six. Skippin' out an' hidin' from me means it's goin' tuh bust tuhnight. Whar's yore outfit?"

"Pretty close. I can get it in a hurry."

"Got tuh do some scoutin' around. Take yore outfit out tuh our camp by thet old cottingwood tree five miles south uh town. Might see the gang thar. Ef yuh does, don't let on yuh told me. Ef yuh don't, meet me hyar in two hours. Tell thet bozo watchin' camp yuh knows me. Savvy?"

"You bet. I'll be here."

The old man watching camp didn't pay much attention to me so long as I wasn't taking anything away. I met John at the time he set and we headed for Cutter Jones' place. A fire and a fight delayed us. We didn't arrive at Jones' layout until nearly nine.

"Thar's them danged galoots," John whispered after we took a careful look inside. "All spread fur trouble. Who's thet Jeff's playin' cards with?"

"The man I told you about," I answered cautiously.

"Uh huh," Scanlon said speculatively. "Jest as I thought. Pullin' a deal withouten me. What's yore move?"

"Going in and call Jeff out for a talk. Think it's all right?"

"No use," Scanlon said, shaking his head. "It'll just postpone thuh fireworks. Yuh cain't talk Jeff outa deals like this. Set tuh keep thet promise tuh the kid yuh tol' me about. Looks like a rattlesnake's nest, don't it? Life don't mean nothin' in thar. Go on in ef yuh want. Stayin' by the door fur a while till I sees more. Head fur the hosses ef we git separated. Plenty hell cookin' up. Shore yuh got the nerve?"

The way he said that didn't sound good to me—like he thought I didn't have. "Well, if I haven't, I won't yell for my mother," I said and ploughed on in.

Hackett, Shores and the Freedman boys all saw me but didn't give a flicker of showing it. Jeff was watching me out the corner of his eye. No look or sign that he knew me. His eyes went over me and found Scanlon. He looked back at Jones.

"Pass," he said.

Jones tossed in the cards for a new deal on the jackpot.

Jeff wore a full beard. I was smooth shaven.

"Howdy, Jeff," I said.

"Get to hell out of here!" Jeff growled, looking at his cards.

Jones eyed me suspiciously, and then a knowing look came over his face. He glanced meaningly at his four bodyguards. I recognized them from the time before. They were lined up by the bar about five feet apart. Bandy and the boys were on the opposite side of the room apparently paying no attention. Jeff and Jones' table was toward the end of the room from them.

"Set down, kid, an' play a hand," Jones said.

"No," I said. "Just wanted to have a few words with my friend here."

"He don't sound friendly tuh me," Jones said, dealing the cards. "Not like he was once."

He picked up his hand and looked at it. The air seemed hot and heavy.

Jeff suddenly got to his feet. "Thorne, get out of here! See you later." He stepped back a few feet and watched things in general.

"Set down Capting Moorfield! Yuh'll live longer," Jones said, shoving his chair back.

"Guess you know why I'm here, Jones," Jeff said, paying no more attention to me.

"Figured it out when I see yore friend's mug. An' heard him call yuh Jeff. But it won't do yuh no good. Yore whiskers had me fooled."

"That's the way I figured it, Jones."

Jones sat still. His eyes darted back to his men. "Yuh're the same as dead. Set down. Only chance is tuh make a deal."

"Make a deal with you? For the schooners you wiped out? For that little shaver that crawled into our camp on the Green?" Jeff said in a loud voice.

The place came to a standstill. No cards moved and no chips clinked on the tables. My knees shook as I backed out of the way.

"You're packin' a gun. Stand up!" Jeff's voice was cold and biting.

Jones jumped to his feet and stepped away from the table. At that instant Scanlon roared, "I'm the law hyar, takin' charge!"

He pulled his gun and shot at the light, missing it. Bandy and the bunch fired from across the room. The four Jones men near the bar crumpled like the floor flew up at them. So many shots I couldn't tell where they came from. Just before the lights went out with Scanlon's second shot, an instant after his first one, a booming roar came from near me and I saw Jones wilt, with his hand on his gun.

The place was like a madhouse with men fighting to get to the door, cursing, swearing and shoving each other. I felt a hand from Jeff's direction grab me and practically throw me over toward the end of the building, only the hand didn't let go. I was shoved and bumped through a hallway to the outside. I ran to meet Scanlon.

"Head fur the camp, pronto," he said.

When we arrived at the cottonwood tree I looked in surprise. The watchman was nowhere around.

"Musta stole ever'thing loose," John grunted. "Now they gotta git outa town."

In a few minutes Jeff and the others rode in.

He struck a light and looked around. "Where in hell's all our stuff?" he roared.

"The old plug stoled the works," John said.

Jeff looked at me. "You still here? You danged near spoiled our game tonight. You and your big mouth."

"Wanted to tell you Hallor confessed—" The other fellows pushed around us, and I didn't get to finish what I was going to say.

"Le's go tuh Frisco," Bandy said. "I craves excitement. Howdy, Eddie. What yuh doin' runnin' aroun' with old Legal Eyes hyar? He ain't no good. Cain't even shoot straight."

"Listen, you hyenas!" Scanlon said. "Yuh started tuh pull a deal withouten me tuhnight. Of all the damn fool stunts, you buzzards take the cake. Why warn't I in on it?"

"Yuh was in on it, Shurruff," Bandy laughed. "'I'm the law hyar, takin' charge!'" he mimicked. "Then he shoots fur the house an' hits the light. Second shot. The light moved over an' waited fur him."

"Wal, it didn't do yuh no harm. Yuh didn't answer my question," John snarled.

"Thet's why we done it, John," Bandy said, still laughing. "We reckoned yuh'd fergit yuh was on a vacation, an' Jeff had a contrac' fur us what liked a little fun."

"Ain't no law right now!" John snapped back at him. "Jest a stall tuh give yuh a signal tuh git goin'. I'm sore at not gittin' a invite."

"We goin' tuh talk all night or go tuh Frisco?" Hank Freedman asked. "I'm fur celebratin'. Cleanin' out a bunch uh skunks ain't no good reason but better'n none."

Jeff turned to Scanlon. "You goin' to Frisco with us, John?"

"Naw. Wouldn't go across the road with you dudes. Yuh're a bunch of Utes."

"My idea, John. Didn't want to get you messed up with the law. Rest of the bunch wanted to cut you in. Turned out better'n I figured." Jeff chuckled mirthlessly. "Missing that light first time was all right. Started things. Gave us the jump on 'em. You danged old fake, makin' out like you missed it. We'd a got 'em, but this way worked fine. How'd you figure it all out so fast?" He looked at me. "Somebody tell on us?"

"Aw, I ain't talkin', Jeff. Not now. Got a two-day mad spell on. Don't know jest why I'm mad but I am. Git over it in time. Pullin' back tuh Placerville so's they won't hang any innercent men fur your crimes. You birds can git along withouten me."

John spurred his horse and headed back to town.

"You reckon he'll get in trouble by himself?" I asked.

Jeff didn't bother to answer me.

"Thet ol' maverick?" Bandy laughed. "Ef they don't know him now they'll danged soon git acquainted. He's a roamin' U.S. Marshall takin' a year off. He don't like nothin' else. He ain't so mad. Jest got his ways uh doin' things. Pro'bly got our stuff swiped so's we'd have tuh leave fur a spell."

"Let's go," Jeff said, paying no attention to me. "Nobody'll miss that Jones bunch. Anybody don't like Frisco, say so."

We stopped and ate at a ranch house about daylight. Made arrangements to sleep in the barn and rest up. Jeff came over before we hit the hay. He didn't look sociable and what he said wasn't any better.

"Met Hallor in Frisco six months back. Said he and your sister got married and she was with him on a trip to Virginia. Jibes with the way things looked when I cleared out. Don't try any more funny stuff on me. Where's Eleanor?"

It had never occurred to me that Jeff wouldn't believe my story when I found him. After all the trouble I had. "If you're going to believe Hallor instead of me, no use in me saying anymore," I bellyached. "The folks at home would know where Eleanor is. They kind of adopted her, after her trouble."

"Should think they would," he said, frowning. He walked away without another word.

CHAPTER 16

The new angle on things almost kept me awake, but I was too tired. When I awoke and thought back on what was said it had me bluffed. Jeff evidently didn't want anything to do with the family. He believed Stella had married Hallor and he was plenty interested in Eleanor. Bringing them together now in Frisco would defeat everything. Felt pretty blue at the prospects.

Bandy and the boys joked as they traveled. Jeff seemed to be thinking and turning things over in his mind. The boys were friendly toward me but he paid no attention. I decided to settle it regardless of who got hurt—I'd take Jeff to Eleanor's rooming house. She could tell him. He could marry her if he felt like it, bad as I hated the idea. She was a a year or two older than I but the gal for me, if I could have worked it. Women like her were pretty scarce.

I waited until we arrived in Frisco and they were about to settle on a place to stay. "I know a better place, where everything's spic and span. Not a bedbug in it. Quiet and off from the center of things," I said.

"Hell, we don't want a place like that!" Bandy objected. "Too tame. Me fur whar we kin raise a racket an' ever'body likes it. Better come along, Eddie!"

"No. Money's low. Got something else on my mind. Don't feel like celebrating." I'd sneak away and ask Eleanor to marry me before Jeff found her.

Jeff looked at me suspiciously. "You go through that fifty thousand this quick?"

"Left most of it home. Been robbed three times in the last year traveling around alone," I answered. "Looking for you," I felt like adding.

He still eyed me. "You're staying with us," he said flatly.

"Yeh, yuh been in on the shootin', yuh might as well be in on the shoutin'," Bandy declared. "How much yuh want tuh borry?"

"Could use five hundred till I get home, Bandy? You got that much extra?"

"Hell, yes. So gol danged loaded with money I itch, an' they's plenty more whar it come from. Wait'll we git a room an' I git this danged money belt off. Come on."

I went. If Jeff got drunk he might be easier to talk to. Then I could sneak away to Eleanor. He looked pleased when I decided to throw in with them. Bandy made me take a thousand dollars. We went out and bought new clothes, spent a wad in a barber shop and then cut loose.

Jeff's face after losing all the whiskers was lean and firm, wearing a look of disinterest, almost to the point of sadness. The old ideals still burned in the setting about his eyes, the way I remembered him. To see him this way brought back such a feeling of regret for the scramble that had been made of our relations with him, I decided to take on a little elixir of life and cheer up. A little whiskey and plenty of water and I could stay with them all night. No drunk for me. Not with the plans I'd just made.

Every place we went Jeff had a little talk with the bartender and slipped him some money.

"What you so danged good tuh the bartenders fur, Jeff?" Hank asked.

"So we can get better stuff to drink," he replied. "I'm particular."

I warmed up after a while and even felt better towards Jeff. Early in the morning I gave a speech. Don't remember what it was about but they all laughed. Figured I was doing pretty good and increased my whiskey a little. We took in all the sights and ate every so often.

Two days later I woke up in the haymow of a livery stable. My head hurt when light first began to bore holes through my eyes. Looking around I saw Jeff waiting for me.

"Gee," I said. "Took a lot to put the others out, didn't it? You and I stayed pretty sober but they had me worried for a while. What makes this place shake so?"

"Lie still," he said, looking down his nose. "I'll bring some stuff to stop the barn from jumpin' around."

"Been poisoned," I groaned, holding my head in my hands.

Whatever he brought, I drank, but it was late afternoon before I could get out of my crouch of dumb misery. He went to round up the rest of the gang. Seemed to be feeling plenty spry.

"Suppose you'd be going north now, if you had a horse," he said when he returned.

"Got a horse," I answered dully.

"You mean you had one before you and Bandy got to playin' poker. Managed to save most of your money for you. Regular wild man when you get going. "Did you know that?"

"No. What happened?"

"And you threw a baked potato and ruined a big clock in one place. Upset a couple of tables in people's laps. When we got thrown out of there you stuck your knife in both sides of a bass drum and bent a trombone over the player's head, after you tore it out of his hands. Party cost us nearly four thousand dollars in damages to calm 'em down."

"Wasn't my idea," I groaned. "How much am I stuck for?"

"Nothing. Our party. Only next time try and behave yourself. You insulted a woman and we couldn't square that. Her husband's lookin' for you with blood in his eyes. Better get out of town."

"Sure. I'll get out," I said wrathfully. "You've been trying to get rid of me ever since I located you. Don't know what I'm sticking around here for, anyway."

"Wrong there. After we look in on John at Placerville we'll go north with you, along the coast. The boys want a trip. Feel like a little salt air'll do 'em good."

"You going to Placerville again?" I said in horror. "Not me. I got enough."

"That's the way a fellow always feels after a big time. You'll come out of it when your head clears up."

I went with them to Placerville but I wasn't happy about it. They rode right up the center of main street and stopped at Cutter Jones' place. It was early and no crowd had collected yet.

"Whar's Cutter?" Bandy asked the new bartender. Everything seemed to have changed hands.

"Gosh! You fellers strangers here?" the bartender said. "Jones got plugged between the eyes an' died with his boots on four-five days ago. A bunch came in here an' shot the daylights out of things. Got him an' four of his cronies."

"Gee," Bandy said innocently. "Thet's too bad. Warn't a bad ol' buzzard last time I seen 'im. Kind of harmless like."

"Who'd they hang for the shootin'?" Jeff asked belligerently. "Ought to do something about that."

"Naw, they didn't hang no one. Ever'body figgered was Jones' hard luck. Maybe you gents didn't know him but he wasn't no angel by a long shot. Have a drink on the house, boys. Treatin' today tuh rustle trade."

"Don't care if I do,' Bandy said. "Make mine straight." When the drinks were poured he added, "Here's tuh pore old Cutter, boys," with a sad face and lips drawn down.

"Amen," Hank and Bill said reverently.

"Here's hopin' law and order hits this town, so crimes like that won't happen again," Jeff said, looking stern and virtuous.

They gulped their drinks.

"Let's git out of hyar afore I starts bawlin'," Bill Freedman put in with a mournful face. "The danged rats et my hankercheef."

"Aw, don't take it so hard, fellers," the bartender said. "Tough tuh lose a friend but you'll git over it."

"Shore hopes so," Bandy said. "'Twar a sad, sad thing."

We filed out like a procession of mourners.

When we reached our horses John Scanlon stepped from a doorway. Carefully looking around he whispered, "You outlaws air all under arrest fur murder. Whar yuh headed fur?"

"North," Jeff answered.

"Git outa town afore someone rec'nizes yuh. I'm gonna play around hyar fur a spell an' clean things up. Gonna stop roamin' an' go tuh lawin'. Need some excitement fur my health. See yuh on the way back."

"So long, yuh ol' female hen," Bandy said. "Shore hope yuh have a good time findin' the dirty skunks what got pore old Cutter."

"Shore hopes so, too," John answered. "I'd shore make it tough fur 'em. Mebbe you boys'd stay an' help me?"

"Yuh air too pure fur us, John," Hank said. "Bet yuh got perfoom on them hair handles danglin' off yore lip, so's every'thing'll smell good."

John scowled ferociously. "Git outa town afore I arrests yuh on suspicion." He deliberated a moment. "Look me up on the way back, yuh wicked hyenas."

Jeff called John off to one side but I heard snatches of the conversation. John objected to his proposition and I heard Jeff say, "You're the best one I know of to do the job, John. Personal favor I'll never forget." They talked some more in a low voice. Jeff won John over it looked like. Heard Jeff say, "If you find him, you know what to do, John?" "Sure do, Jeff. I got ways uh taking keer uh guys like him." Later Jeff said, "You ought to be able to find her easy. But don't give me away. I'll write to you at the hotel or you hang tough till I come back."

"Shore, shore," John replied. And the talk ended.

Was glad I heard that much. Jeff thought Hallor was still in 'Frisco and had set John on his trail. Also on Eleanor's. Looked like John was to get rid of Hallor and keep an eye on Eleanor until Jeff got back. I must have given him a clue during the big party. About the time I lost my horse. Didn't mind the Hallor part, but it looked bad for me with Eleanor. But sister Stella had plenty of come-hither in her eyes, if she wasn't married to J. McQ. Tilden. If I could get Jeff under her influence again. If they hit it off like they ought to.

Jeff was in a fever for speed as usual, but the boys wouldn't hurry. Soon after we crossed into Oregon we swung towards the home place.

As we approached the ranch, I said to Jeff, "Better come and take a look in on the folks, Jeff. You and the boys."

"Guess we will," he said. "Kind of like to see 'em again."

We rode up to the place. Jeff and I got down and walked in.

"What you want?" a strange woman asked me, her eyes wide and lips trembling.

"I'm Eddie Thorne," I said in amazement. "Where're my folks?"

"Land sakes, but you had me scared. That's the family we bought the place from. They all went to California. Bag an' baggage. Said if they miss yuh, yuh was to go to Bush Green or Beaut Savage at Oregon City. They'd tell yuh the whys and wherefores."

Bad luck still dogged me. I looked at Jeff.

"Still an orphan." Jeff said. "Had your trip for nothing. Let's pull for Oregon City."

"When we went back out to the boys Bandy said, "How long we goin' tuh stay in this danged country, Jeff? Had our trip. Le's go back."

"Maybe we will. Want to look in on some things in Oregon City. Eddie's folks sold out. He's ready to head back right now."

Bush Green had bought a store in Oregon City and knew all the news as usual. Beaut Savage was his partner. We found them together.

"How long have my folks been gone?" I asked as soon as we shook hands.

"Soon as they could travel this spring," Bush answered me. "The Tildens came out last fall and stayed all winter with 'em, then they all headed for California. Seems like yore mother couldn't stand the climate, an' when yore dad found it out he said he'd been ready tuh travel ag'in fur a long time. Yore mother was tickled tuh death. So was all the girls. Stella 'specially. Thought they'd meet yuh down there."

"Yeh, at the widow's place," Beaut said. "She's got a roomin' house in San Francisco. The one yuh helped her buy. Doin' right well, too, they say. Said tuh tell yuh tuh go see her an' she'd know whar tuh find 'em."

Jeff raised his eyebrows and looked at me.

"Did J. McQ. come with his family, Bush?" I asked, though I dreaded to hear the answer.

"Sure. He an' yore sister hit it off in jig time. Stella said she promised yuh she wouldn't git married till yuh come home."

I cut loose and cussed a blue streak. Jeff hid behind a poker face, laughing at me probably.

"Tell this dude how things turned out, Beaut," I said, pointing to Jeff. "He wouldn't believe me."

"Only one I heerd the story from was you, Eddie," Beaut replied. "Never spread it, 'cept tuh say it warn't Jeff. Had Jeff's word fur it. Yore father never did mention it."

I wheeled desperately to Jeff. "Come on, let's go back. I'll prove it yet."

"Glad to know right where to find Eleanor," he said. "Want to see her pretty bad."

On the way to California again I got Jeff by himself, determined to make a clean breast of things. "Set out on your trail, Jeff, to bring you back to Stella. Thought maybe you two could hit it off. I knew Eleanor lived in Frisco. That was the place I wanted to take you fellows when we hit there. But you wanted a trip after the big spree, so I figured that was just as well."

"Right nice of you, Eddie," he said.

"Went through hell and high water to find you," I added.

"Certainly appreciate it, boy."

"That all you're going to say?"

"Gosh, what can I say? What you want me to say?" He looked at me long and hard and was silent for a while. "Got something to tell Eleanor if everything turns out all right. Always liked her pretty well and thought she got a raw deal all around."

That was that. I let the matter drop. It wasn't cheering.

"Did you ever see prettier hair than Eleanor's" he said one day when we were riding apart from the others.

"Stella's is prettier," I said. "Never saw hair to beat hers. Eleanor runs a close second, though."

"But your sister's just a kid, and kind of frail. Now take Eleanor—I bet she could pack fifty pounds all day long if she had to. Maybe seventy-five. You know, if a fellow wanted to roam around and take a wife with him—a long-haired pardner—"

"Why don't you marry a pack horse?" I asked disgustedly. "Never find a woman to fit the deal you got in mind. Stella's stronger and has better health than any of the women in my family. Seemed to like the pioneer life after she got used to it. Changed a lot."

"Always was a peach but maybe she belongs in a museum with all that beauty and hope. Ordinary fellow'd be crazy to think of marrying her. Head full of Virginia and a lot of frills. Don't figure me wrong, Eddie. I mean she's the cream off the top in a lot of ways but she'd be a hobble to a plug like me. Take Eleanor now, she's been through the mill and ground pretty fine. Follow a guy till she dropped in her tracks. Had a lot of trouble and knows the good side from the bad. Stuff like that counts plenty. Got to settle down some day. She might of stepped off the path once, but a fellow can't be too proud."

"Yeh," I said derisively, "Eleanor's got a pretty strong mind herself. Running that rooming house'd bring out the bossy side of a woman. She made up Schoolcraft's mind to turn back and come with us. You got a lot to learn about women. You flare up too fast."

"Maybe so," he said. "We'll see. A fellow takes a lot of chances. Marriage can't be so tough—not any tougher'n some other things he bumps into. I'll tame down, maybe."

Next day I saw a roan horse coming our way and it looked familiar. Then I recognized the rider. It was Blessing, about a foot taller and filled out. When he recognized us, he let out a whoop and galloped up.

"Golly! You fellows been to Oregon? Gee, I'm glad to see everybody."

"What you doing up this way, Bless?" I said, after the meeting cleared up and he had said hello all around.

"Your father sent me to see if I could find you. Heard you'd been in Frisco and left again. Some old codger came around to see Eleanor. She got suspicious and made him tell what was on his mind. Heard his name but can't remember it."

"Wasn't John Scanlon, was it, Bless?" Jeff asked.

"That's it. John Scanlon. Said you fellows'd been in, painted the town red and headed north."

"The danged ol' skunk," Bandy grumbled. "Jest like 'im. 'Spose he told her he went tuh church, himself. How in hell'd he find her when Jeff didn't know?"

"Had a hunch she was in Frisco and gave him a little job to do," Jeff said easylike. "Shows he did it. Don't you fellows jump on him for it."

"Where's home now, Bless?" I asked. "Where's the Thorne patch?"

"Fifty miles north of Frisco on a little bay with a long beach. Your folks're crazy about it."

"We might as well stop on the way," I suggested to Jeff, playing a long shot.

"Sure. Might as well for a while. I'm in a hurry to see Eleanor, though."

Bless led us by the shortest route. Susie saw us coming a mile away and the family was waiting for us.

Mother wept and father never looked so well pleased before. Never saw either of them looking better. Also saw, almost in the same glance, where a healthy part of my fifty thousand was going.

"So you're the boys Eddie had as partners?" mother said after introductions. "My, but I'm glad to see you. Jeff, you haven't changed a bit. Same old caravan leader—the Plains, South Pass, Green River, Fort Bridger, Snake River—you haven't changed a bit."

"Thanks, ma'am," Jeff said uncomfortably. "The one and only family train for me. Never again."

"More's the pity, Jeff." She looked at him fondly. "When I think of the poor people coming later, I think of how you took care of us." She turned to the others. "All our happiness here is due to Jeff."

"Yes, ma'am," Bandy put in. "He's jest a little curly-haired angel, ain't he? Look at them cute little fingers—ain't got a wart on 'em."

Mother looked shocked for an instant at such disrespect for her hero and then we all laughed.

"He kin shore suck aigs, ma'am; watch yore henhouse," Hank added."

"You reptiles," Jeff protested. "When Mrs. Thorne knows you better, she won't let you on the place."

"Where's Stella?" I finally asked, wondering at her absence, fearing the worst had happened.

"Stella would be gone on a day like this," mother complained. "She went to visit with the Tildens in San Francisco. She goes to Eleanor's everyday to see if there's any word from you."

"It's been a long time since we saw you, Jeff," Susie butted in. "What you been doing with yourself?"

"Just wandering around, Susie, tryin' to keep out of trouble."

"Then you didn't pay Cutter Jones back for what he did to that little boy on Green River, did you? You're my hero but I'm almost ashamed of you."

My quick glance around showed that none of the boys flicked an eyelid.

"Last time we came through Placerville, Susie, we heard Cutter Jones got in a gun battle in a saloon he was running and died with his boots on," Jeff replied evenly. "Just a few days before. The new ones running the place took us for his friends and tried to cheer us up with a drink. But we didn't weep—much."

"Then if he'd been there when you came along you would have tended to him?" she cross-examined.

"Well, Susie, we'd a made a good try. Looked for him in Placerville a long time ago, right after Eddie came home, but I guess he was layin' low."

"Your intentions were good, so I think I'll let it count on your side," Susie said brightly. "The murderous reptile, the low-down varmint—"

"Susie!" mother exclaimed. "You're talking like a prairie waif. Remember we have company. They might form a bad opinion of you."

"Aw, I bet they wouldn't," she scoffed. "Bet they'd even teach me to shoot a revolver."

"We shore would, Susie," Bandy agreed. "We likes yore style. Say when."

Mother gave Bandy an exasperated glance but saw that he was full of the dickens all the time, with Hank and Bill right behind him. Silent Gillis almost said something but changed his mind as usual.

First chance, I got father by himself and told him all about Cutter Jones and Placerville. Made him promise not to tell the others until Jeff had gone.

"Figured Jeff might have been in that first bunch. Great fellow. Hard to beat. What'd he say about Stella?"

"Brace your legs for bad news, Dad. Jeff's in love with Eleanor."

"Doggone!" father groaned. Had my heart set on him and Stella. Stella's had me worried about J. McQ. Had us all on pins and needles. Dad gum the luck! What makes you so sure? Stella's got Eleanor beat four ways from the start."

The old Thorne loyalty to the front again.

"Well, Dad, that's open to argument, looking at it from a man like Jeff's standpoint. Told me all about it on the way down. Better break the news when we leave."

We didn't stay more than two hours. Jeff was burning to travel. And I intended to stay in the game until the last dog was hung. Heavy-hearted but game.

Once in Frisco, Jeff headed for the Bella Union Hotel and left word for John that he'd be in the barber shop. When John showed up, and Jeff was all slicked up, they went apart where I couldn't hear and talked a while. Jeff was pleased as all get out when they finished. Slapped John on the back and said, "You're a dinger, John. I'll do something for you sometime."

"Eddie, you know where Eleanor is located. Take me there quick as you can. The rest of you fellows make yourselves at home for a while. Got big business on. See you later."

On the way he said, "Don't pick dusty streets, Eddie. We don't want to get all dirty again."

"Too danged bad about you," I snarled. "I like plenty of dust, myself. Ought to shot you when your back was turned. Wanted the widow myself. Guess you didn't know that?"

"Gosh, that's too bad, Eddie. But you're slow. Shoulda hopped in when you had a chance."

"Spent too much time lookin' for you. I'd never do it again."

"Cripes, Eddie, don't feel that way. Didn't mean any harm. Just the way things happen. Can't have everything, you know."

"That's for me," I mourned. "You seem to get along all right."

"You don't know how I feel or you wouldn't talk that way," he said.

Jeff carefully avoided the dust my horse was kicking up. "You know, Eddie, I feel kind of ornery about you—"

"Ought to know it by now," I bellyached.

"Aw, shut up. You're as bad as Hallor used to be. Wait'll I get through. Was goin' to apologize for something."

"Don't want any damned apology. Can't smooth things that way with me. Like a lot of people. Don't mind apologizing as long as you get your own way."

"Just wanted to say I'm sorry I thought Hallor was innocent."

"Huh? Hallor? Innocent?" I cackled. "don't tell me it was you after all."

"No," he said disgustedly. "Thought it was you, the way you hung around her. Didn't say anything on account of your family."

"Me?" I exploded. "Gosh! Never thought of it. You did treat me pretty mean after that."

"Think your sister had you picked as the guilty man, too."

That even shook my horse, it hit me so hard.

"So that's what she meant," I said, after a minute or two.

"Meant what?"

"Nothing. Thinking out loud." Funny I hadn't figured what Stella meant, that time at home, when she told me she loved Jeff.

"Well, here we are," I said. "Your rooming house. Go in and kiss her."

"Sure'll try if she's there," he said, batting nervously at flecks of dust on his pants.

Stella was playing with the twins when I led Jeff in.

"Jeff! Eddie!" she screamed when she saw us.

"Kiss him first—while he's still single," I said for spite, just to embarrass Jeff and warn the extra glad look in her eyes.

"Guess her brother comes first," Jeff said, kind of bashfully.

Stella just simply kept shining with happiness. Could see J. McQ. wasn't the man. Never had been. Never could be. Felt terrible sorry for her. She didn't realize.

"Maybe you'd better bite an apple. Big bite wins," she said mischievously. The light in her eyes, and her hair puffed so prettily—couldn't see why Jeff was after Eleanor.

"Nope!" Jeff said. "His mouth is bigger'n mine. I'd lose, sure."

Stella blushed a sunset pink—high in the mountains, on a tall peak kind—and dropped her eyes.

Eleanor stepped in the doorway just then and took a quick look. "Eddie! Get out of there and leave 'em alone for a while! Hello, Jeff."

"But—" I started to protest.

"Come!" she commanded, grabbing my arm and giving me a jerk.

I went. Even though they had forgotten we existed, or the twins tugging at Jeff's legs, yelling "Candy! Candy! Candy!"

"Jeff—darling!" I heard Stella murmur and I looked back in confusion. Jeff reminded me of a water spaniel, walking on his hind legs, holding out his paws.

Shook my head. "Can't figure it out, Eleanor. Heap big medicine gone wrong, somewhere."

"That's love. What else did you expect, honey?" she said softly, with a film over her eyes. "I'm free again, too."

"Didn't know you weren't," I said, sure of myself now.

"Hallor died two weeks ago. Married him on his death bed. John Scanallon came and got me."

"John Scanlon," I repeated in a daze, correcting her.

"Jeff told him to." Then all of a sudden I came to life. I grabbed her, kissed her, and squeezed her before she could say scat.

Then I got mad. "Jeff!" I bellowed. "Gol dang that big dish breaker! He's been making a fool out of me ever since we hit Frisco that time! Honey, I've sure been suffering over you."

THE END

VALLECITO

The Second Novel by Lester Fulford Kramer

Vallecito means "Little Valley" in Spanish. It is the lush and beautiful area near the mining town of Silverton, Colorado. Not quite a sequel to Pioneer Lady but Bandy Hackett and his friends, along with Exxon Moorfield, the son of Jeff Moorfield, show up in this compelling story of the young mining engineer running from his past in New York City. Here is a portion of Chapter One.

CHAPTER 1

His face was grave and studious, yet a look of relief was on it. He had turned from reading the sheriff's dodger board at Montezuma Stables and was watching the horseshoer ply his trade, the people moving about, the scattered barns and corrals. His eyes were scanning the scene deliberately, as though holding at arm's length for closer scrutiny all that his eyes beheld. While his clothes followed the careless manner of Westerners, there the comparison ended. He was not a part of it and a close observer could see it.

His glance roved about, over the huge draft horses with tug marks ground deep on hindquarters and collar scores high on their withers; mules with saddle sores; saddle horses limping in separate pens; until finally it switched to the human beings gathered there. Some were cursing carelessly, others professionally passing on the remaining value in horses, wondering how long it would take for sores to heal. Then his glance came to rest on a comely Indian girl and he studied her, until she saw that he was watching her and moved out of his range of vision.

A large swarthy man walking from the hitching post where he had left his horse gave a start of surprise when he saw the stranger and turned quickly to his companion, a small old man with white eyebrows and white drooping mustaches, spry and alert-looking.

"Sam," Jort McQuain rumbled in a low voice, "if that ain't our man I'm a two-year old. Over thar by the board."

Sam Sarjent looked and nodded. "Ain't had time tuh git this fur from Noo York."

"Shore has," Jort replied. "Stand off a ways where he cain't see us, so we kin watch him."

They stepped over to a less obvious place and Jort pulled a letter from his pocket, saying, "Yuh ain't read this letter yet."

The older man took it, put a cheap pair of spectacles and pored over the writing, pointing each word with a scrawny forefinger.

"Dear Jort: Sorry to bother you but I've lost an engineer. Checked out of his hotel ten days ago and didn't leave a forwarding address. Judge Kindonnel's son.

The judge visited out there years ago and had some favorite spots and I think maybe Bill might have gone in that direction.

"If you remember what the judge looked like you'll know Bill. Strong resemblance. Blond hair. Beard comes out reddish. Big and strong. Natural born mining engineer. Twenty-eight years old. High sense of justice. Hot-tempered when he sees weaker things getting the worst of it. Terrific fighter.

"I've spent six years and thousands of dollars training him. Had him in Europe, South America and Africa. Smart as a whip on technical affairs. Highly executive. Had big plans for him.

"Now, if you happened to see him write me. He might be in trouble of some kind. Planning to move into that great Silverton district and could use him there, now that the railroad is in. May put a smelter in Durango, where you are located. Anyway, Jort, I need him badly—"

The letter ended with best wishes for Jort's personal welfare and a caution to behave himself.

When Sam finished reading, he looked up at the other. "Think he's in trouble? On the run?"

"My guess," Jort said. "Graydon don't tell it all." He chuckled. "Got a lot of nerve, writin' tuh me." He folded the letter and put it in his pocket. "Got any ideas, Sam?"

"Hell," Sam exploded, "we kin use a man like him. You owe this here Graydon anything?"

"Not a damn thing," Jort replied. "He's got plenty money anyway. Ef that's young Kindonnel we'll make friends with him an' move in on some of the jackpots in minin'. Glad Graydon wrote, even if it don't do him no good."

"I better stay in town a spell," Sam said. "Mebbe help yuh."

"Shore," Jort agreed.

Sam beckoned to the Indian girl standing at a distance. When she came to him he said, "Young Fawn, go catch this newfangled train tuh Needleton. Tell White Owl I won't be back fur a few days. Got business." He fished in his pocket. "Here's money fur a ticket."

The girl's eyes gleamed at prospect of riding on the train.

"Savvy," she said and took the money. "Tell White Owl. Vamoose?"

"Vamoose," Sam said easily. "Git goin'. Catch train. I'll fetch horses."

"Some gal," Jort remarked as Young Fawn started across the grounds toward the depot. "Purty as hell. Funny some young buck don't steal her."

"Don't look crosswise at 'em," Sam replied. "Ain't the marryin' kind, yit. No trouble a-tall."

"Thar's Jatelin an' young Cal Allan ridin' in, hell bent." Jort observed. "Look's like Allan's team behind 'em, with Willabelle drivin'. Bet they don't know it."

"Git a shoe on this hoss," Jatelin snarled at a stable helper. "Hurry up, or I'll kick the pants off'n yuh."

The helper let everything else go and moved over the Jatelin's horse with his shoeing outfit. The stranger heard Jatelin and watched him, apparently lost in study of the scene, as though it were new to him and of great interest.

Willabelle Allan tied her team and carefully picked her way towards her brother, biting her lip in vexation, plainly disdainful of her surroundings.

Just then Jatelin spied Young Fawn walking through the grounds. She had paused to admire a particularly beautiful horse. With a hasty stride and jump he caught her as she turned and saw him.

"Purty breed," he yelled as she silently struck back at him to free herself. "Com on Cal, let's steal her."

"No, no," she protested, never once looking to where Sam and Jort were standing. "Must ketch train."

"Yuh caught me, honey," Jatelin mocked her. "Gimme a kiss."

"He can't do that tuh Young Fawn," Sam growled. "Forgot my gun. Gimme your'n, Jort. We got tah kill him sometime."

"Wait," Jort said with his eyes on the stranger. "Ain't hurt her yit. Our man don't like it either."

Sam swung his angry eyes to the stranger who was looking around, wondering if someone would intercede. Willabelle Allan had come to the edge of the small crowd. His look included the disgust on her face. What men he could see appeared interested but afraid to protest.

The stranger fidgeted nervously from one foot to another.

"Whoee!" Jatelin crowed. "I likes a spitfire tuh tame. Gimme my hoss. Shoe him tuhmorrer."

"Gimme that gun," Sam said again.

"Comin' in, too," Jort replied. "Good time as any tuh start things."

He and Sam stepped out a pace but stopped as the tall stranger gave his had and coat a toss and sprang in front of Jatelin, his face showing a cold fury.

"Leave her be," they heard him say.

Jatelin clutched Young Fawn in one hand and turned, surprised that anyone should challenge him.

"Yeah?" he sneered, sizing up the man. "Mebbe yuh'd like tuh try makin' me? Here, Cal, hold 'er a second."

Cal dutifully seized Young Fawn by an arm, though she stopped struggling to look in wonder at a man who would stand up to the fearful Jatelin.

The instant he loosed Young Fawn, Jatelin squared himself and lunged at the stranger, one of his fists swinging for the head.

The stranger side-stepped, shifted his feet and drove a terrific right-hand blow to Jatelin's chin.

Jatelin fell, tried to get up, and then settled back to the ground, unable to rise from his stupor.

Cal, thick headed with the mixture he had been drinking, didn't think to turn loose of Young Fawn.

The stranger moved fast. He struck Cal's hand from the Indian girl's arm, but suddenly pulled the punch aimed at Cal's chin. "Just a stripling," he said disgustedly.

But the young fellow was game. He flailed a fist at the stranger and struck him on the side of the head. Whereupon the stranger seized a handful of shoulder and shirt, straightened him up and snapped him a quick sharp blow on the chin. Holding him as his knees sagged he laid him gently alongside of Jatelin.

"You can go in peace now," he said, turning to where Young Fawn had been standing. But she was hurrying on across the grounds.

Willabelle Allan had come nearer and was looking at his two prostrate opponents. Their eyes met. The stranger looked hard at her, wondering what business had brought her to a place like this.

"That last one was my brother," she said regretfully. "In bad company."

"Didn't hit him hard," he protested, rather embarrassed. "Come to pretty soon."

"What he deserved," she replied. "I saw it all. When I bring my team over will you put him in it?"

Stooping down he placed an arm under Cal's knees, another under his shoulders and lifted him from the ground. "Where's your carriage?"

She led the way, glancing apprehensively to where someone was tossing a bucket of cold water on Jatelin.

When they reached the team she said, "Lay him in the back seat. Couldn't have worked out better. I'll have him on the way home before he comes to. Away from that bully, I can handle him."

He stepped up and draped the unconscious brother along the back seat.

"You'll have time to get out and away before Jatelin sobers up," she said gravely.

"When I leave town it won't be because he's in it," the stranger quickly replied.

"You should. No one else interfered. They all know him. He's a terrible fighter when he isn't so drunk."

Suddenly a thought seemed to strike him. He glanced about apprehensively. "Maybe that's good advice."

He held a hand to help her into the rig. "Been a pleasure seeing you."

She looked at him earnestly. "Oh, I do hope we meet again. You were a gentleman. Good-bye."

As she gathered the reins in her small hands he turned and walked from the Montezuma grounds. No one accosted him and no one praised him. Jatelin still lay where he had fallen.

Jort and Sam looked at each other.

"Linin' up on the right side fur us," Jort said. "We'll trail him."

When the stranger stopped at a hotel they waited a few minutes and entered. Their man was in the lobby glancing at a newspaper.

Sam and Jort spoke to the clerk and sat down.

When the stranger rose and asked for his key the clerk said, "We'll have a better room for you tomorrow, Mr. Tuttle."

"Never mind," was the answer. "I'm leaving tonight."

He pocketed the key and walked upstairs to his room.

Sam followed quickly enough to see him enter his room. Jort waited a few moments, asked the clerk and question and left the hotel.

Sam knocked boldly on the door. It flew open with a jerk. They looked each other in the eye. The stranger critically, Sam the spirit of meekness.

"Howdy," Sam said quietly. "Seen the fracas at the Montezuma an' wanted tuh talk to yuh."

"Friend of his?" the stranger snapped belligerently.

Sam smiled dryly. "Do I look that ornery?"

The other carefully surveyed the hall. "Come in," he said.

"Thet ain't exactly why I come," Sam explained, entering and taking a chair. "Look at me. Old man. Years ago I had a friend what was the spittin' image of yuh. Yuh're goin' by the name of Tuttle, here, but if yore name ain't Kindonnel my name ain't Sam Sarjent. Own up or not, jest as yuh like."

A look of relief swept the other's face. "Sam Sarjent! You were one of my father's best friends, the one he went into Vallecito valley with."

"The same, son," old Sam said softly. "We was like brothers. What yuh doin' way out here? Minin' scout fur some big company? Yore dad said yuh was goin' tuh be a minin' engineer."

"Not connected with any company," Kindonnel said cautiously, wondering how much he dared confide in this inquisitive old man. His father had praised Sam highly but that was years ago. A man with a charge of murder against him couldn't take chances.

"Goin' tuh settle out here?" Sam persisted.

"On a vacation," Kindonnel replied. "Dad said so much about Vallecito valley thought I'd spend some time there. Intend to prospect and study the geology of it, live on trout and wild game and enjoy life for a change."

"Don't know a better place. Haven't changed none in all those years. Wild. Jest like when yore dad was there with me that time. He liked it purty well."

Kindonnel drew a paper from his pocket. "Brought a map dad made after he got back but it's kind of hazy."

Sam scratched his head. "Worst way in is over the mountains from my place at Needleton. Forty miles tuh where yuh'd want tuh camp. No trail. Take better'n two days tuh make it if yuh hurry, more if yuh don't.

"'Bout sixty from here, swingin' around south. Easier goin'. Don't cross no mountains. Ain't many people knows about the place. Yuh picked a good spot tuh rest up in. They's a hot spring if yuh kin find it. Heat makes the grass stay green all winter. Could build a cabin an' make things purty homey."

"Sounds good," Kindonnel said.

"Kind of tough tuh be in there by yoreself."

"Suits me."

"Get purty tiresome," Sam persisted. "When yuh want tuh go?"

"Soon as I get an outfit."

"That's the hitch," Sam said flatly. "Yuh don't dare show up aroun' town; yuh got tuh git an outfit an' horses."

"Nothing to it," the other objected. "Got money to buy all I need."

"Jatelin," Sam said. "Yuh're on his list now. Won't be safe. He's a terror tuh hell. Caught him plenty drunk. Be layin' fur yuh from now on."

BIOGRAPHY

Lester Fulford Kramer was born on May 2, 1895 in Twin Falls, Idaho as Lester Fulford. His father and brother were killed in a snow avalanche when he was a babe in arms. When Les was six, his mother remarried. Her new husband, Alvin Kramer, was the sheriff of San Juan County, Colorado at the turn of the Twentieth Century. Les, adopted and adored by his stepfather, lived with his family on the ground floor of the jail in the high mining town of Silverton, nestled among the Needle and Red mountains of Colorado. His bedroom faced Mount Kendall for which his son, Valen Kendall Kramer was named.

Les graduated high school in Silverton and later was chosen to escort fellow army recruits to Denver for service in World War I. After the war he returned to Silverton. But his beloved stepfather soon died at the early age of 54 years, crushing the plans they had to run the Congress Silver Mine together. Les struck out for the West and made his way to California and then up through the Pacific Northwest. He had hoped to go on to Alaska but he fell in love, married and settled down in Washington state.

BVG